W9-CDK-583

"I don't know anything about you, Jack Smith, so how could I think you stole anything!" Denney said, pouring out the tea. She pushed a cup half-way down the table. "Come and get it."

She turned to reach for matches, and she heard him edge over to the table. When she turned back, Jack Smith was backing into the chair, the tea in one hand and the gun in the other.

"Oh, for God's sake put that gun down!" She was tired of being frightened one minute, indifferent the next. "We might as well have our tea in peace. . . ."

L M

NOBODY READS JUST *ONE* LUCY WALKER!

Available in Beagle editions

If not available at your dealer, they may be ordered by mail. Send 80¢ for each book (includes postage and handling charges) to Beagle Books, Dept. CS, 36 West 20 Street, New York, N.Y. 10011. Please note that not all books may be available at all times.

Peggy Clark

MONDAY IN SUMMER

Lucy Walker

BEAGLE BOOKS • NEW YORK

The characters in this book are entirely imaginary
and bear no relation to any living person

Copyright © 1961 by Dorothy Lucie Sanders

All Rights Reserved

Published by arrangement with the author and
the author's agent, Paul R. Reynolds, Inc.

First printing: June 1973
Second printing: December 1973

Printed in the United States of America

BEAGLE BOOKS/A division of Ballantine Books
201 East 50 Street, New York, NY 10022

CHAPTER ONE

When Fate produces a pink rabbit from a hat there seems to be no direction from Providence as to the doorstep upon which that rabbit should be dropped. There is no discrimination about visitations from God, in the form of lightning, floods, or even a snake in the backyard.

Not that Jack Smith was a pink rabbit, though he might conceivably have been a visitation from God. Not angels in Heaven, let alone the members of Denney's family, placidly resident by the glorious limpid waters of Pepper Tree Bay, could read God's mind.

Of one thing they were certain.

Denney was not a fit subject to be visited by the problem of Jack Smith.

God, if we must bring Him, reverently but with a touch of reproach, into this, had not previously arranged to equip Denney with a calm, logical, law-abiding mind. She couldn't be counted upon to act with the normalcy of the everyday right-abiding citizen.

Denney Montgomery was gay, happy-go-lucky, impetuous, occasionally courageous, sometimes incorrigible, invariably kind and altogether lovable. She thought the Law was an ass and didn't have very much to do with her . . . until Jack Smith came.

It happened on a Monday in summer and thereafter, for three days, Denney found out what it was like to live in the shadow of the Law.

It began this way.

Denney lived on a small farm in the Hills twenty miles from the city of Perth and twenty-three miles from the green and blue rolling waters of the Indian Ocean. When coming down from the Hills on market day in her second-hand station wagon she had, of necessity, to cross the waters of the Swan River at the Causeway. Around the bends and bays of the Swan River Denney's married sisters lived, in houses here and there, not too near one another and yet not too far. They were near enough to have a finger in one another's pies but distant enough to escape when teacups rattled if storms

5

were brewing within them.

Mama, at that time being abroad in foreign parts, namely the Eastern States, was not at home to lend her guiding hand to the affairs of her original, if slightly and charmingly eccentric, brood. This terrible adventure befell Denney in the early years following the war, and had Mama been around there is no doubt the end of the story would have been quite different. Mama would have seen to that.

Denney was the only renegade. She had gone twenty-three miles away from the family. The wisdom or otherwise of this move is still debated in the drawing-rooms round the Bay.

Had any one of the Montgomerys been unkind she would have said of the Jack Smith incident . . . 'Well, that's what you get for moving away so we can't keep an eye on you, our fingers on the pulse of your activities, our ears to the ground on which you tread.' Not one of them was unkind. They laughed, quarrelled, agreed or disagreed with one another; talked about one another behind backs.

In spite of these normal family reactions they each and all guarded one another, watched with loving and anxious eyes the rise and fall of any other's fortunes, and they wove an intangible yet indestructible barrier around themselves as a unit and, in a sense, set themselves apart as one unique family with a unique destiny . . . as yet undefined, even by themselves.

The long and short of it was that though Denney had set herself up on a farm twenty-three miles away, no one believed she would stay there long. This was a temporary aberration on Denney's part. The family waited patiently, but with an implacable certitude, for the return of the wanderer, the homecoming of the prodigal.

The fact that Denney saw them all at least once a week, when she came down to the markets, was neither here nor there. She had technically gone away from the Bay. One day she would come back. It was as simple as that. The family, metaphorically speaking, folded hands in laps and waited.

Yet over the Jack Smith incident no one uttered a reproachful word.

They made huge pots of thick soup, they offered Denney a home and security for life. Vicky and her husband bought her a new car. But not an unkind word was said.

But why Denney? was the only question they asked, and they asked it of God, not one another.

Denney was tall and slim with violet-blue eyes. Her skin was meant by God to be a beautiful Irish skin, but a childhood swimming and boating in the Bay and a girlhood suntanning on the ocean beaches four miles to the west of the Bay had given her a permanent tan and taken away the peach bloom. Denney did not mind, or even notice this, because it was the lot of all her countrywomen past the age of twelve. She had thick dark brown hair that swept away in two excellent widow's peaks from a square forehead. Her nose was good and so was her mouth and chin. If she had been a man she would have been undeniably handsome. As it was she was striking and the lines of humour round her mouth and the little wrinkles forming on her forehead and at the corners of her eyes dismissed the descriptive word 'handsome'. There wasn't any word to describe Denney because she was too strong featured to be called pretty and there were too many lines of character in her face and too much expression in those blue eyes to call her beautiful.

Whatever she was, everyone looked twice. When she talked everyone laughed, and when she asked, everyone came to her aid.

This was not a one-way business.

Let any of her market friends, Italians, Yugo-Slavs, small-time Australian 'cocky' farmers, have a worry in their lives and Denney hear of it, Denney was to their aid. She knew Members of Parliament, members of the City Council, members of the police force. Doctors, lawyers, and even dentists. She was forever on someone's doorstep fixing something up for someone. Denney fought their battles to victory through sheer persistence by alternate use of the art of denunciation and blarney.

Nobody that Denney befriended was ever wrong. If anyone was oppressed, then Denney was their friend.

Once her father said of her . . . 'Denney is always on the side of the underdog.'

During a short career of journalism Denney had become acquainted with all the classic rules for pulling ropes. With her reporter's pad and pencil she had penetrated every public and private office that had news for sale. This career was short-lived and she had given it up in favour of the land, but she kept all her old friends on the city beat . . . and she never forgot to make use of them if she had a 'Galahad' in woe.

There was many a dark-haired dark-eyed vegetable vendor

7

who blessed the sound of her indignant voice.

Denney entering the market at the crack of dawn each Monday and Friday was a master craftsman in the art of being with but not of the business of trading in vegetables.

She drove her station wagon into the narrow roadway between the auction floors and the Treaty floors. With the greatest aplomb, and innocent of the claims of any other car or truck driver, she managed to manœuvre her wagon into a place that was neither safe nor useful as far as the destiny of her produce was concerned.

She would get out of her wagon, dressed not for the auction floor but rather for a morning's shopping in town, coffee at Luigi's, then afternoon tea with one or other of her sisters round the Bay. She rarely presented herself at the Wednesday market. Prices were always dull on Wednesdays and she couldn't afford that much time away from her farm. She had only McMullens and his wife to help her, and it was a busy, sometimes hectic, way of moving from point to point along her life's span.

Everyone knew Denney round the precincts of the Metropolitan Markets, and Denney knew everyone. Someone always extricated her station wagon for her, unloaded her small . . . for it was a small . . . contribution, then drove the wagon into the parking lot.

This was an imposition on friendship and Denney knew it, and so did the obliging help. That was why Denney always spoke of her friends in that locality as the Market Galahads and why, in her absence, these same Galahads debated the theme . . . was she slightly mad or merely very shrewdly sane?

Whichever it was, they brightened under the beneficent beam of her smile and chuckled in reply to her gay 'Hiya!'

She was, they thought, quite a character.

The long and the short of it was Denney didn't deal in vegetables, fruit, flowers and eggs in the market herself. Someone else did it for her. When she had ceased growing and transporting she wiped her hands of the low-class business of selling.

Generosity and hard work was very much a two-way business down there amidst the carrots, apples, cabbages and flowers of the Metropolitan Markets.

On that Monday in summer when Jack Smith came into

8

Denney's life she had been to the market as usual, and as usual she had had coffee at Luigi's with Ben Darcy.

This latter was a ritual, and if Denney was in love with Ben Darcy she was not prepared to admit it to herself. Her farm was her salvation in life, and a spur of the range divided her farm from Ben's property. It was unthinkable that she should abandon her farm for Ben's farm and there was no question whatsoever of Ben abandoning anything for anybody. They drank coffee together on market day and spent an occasional Sunday together, shooting on the range or riding into hitherto untraversed gullies on the northern spurs. In summer they did a little swimming in the deep pool of the creek. And that, said Denney, explaining the situation to her dubious family, was that.

This business of drinking coffee on this particular Monday might have been no different from usual, if it hadn't been for Ben's attitude about a gun. Five hours later, as Denney was nearing her own boundary fence twenty-odd miles away in the hills, she heard that gun rattle in the back seat, and she remembered it.

She had just swung her station wagon sharply right to cross the old railway line that once had run up the Zigzag through Gooseberry Hill to Kalamunda and the timber town of Karragullen farther along the range. The railway line was a clay bank now with nothing to remind anybody that once adventure had ridden high, if very slowly, along that way. Never once did Denney cross it without feeling nostalgia for those days of flower hunting and picnicking along a line that wound here and there and round about towards the plain through the loveliest vistas of bush, granite cliff and blue gully. A children's paradise, that busy way had been.

She was thinking of this as she swung her station wagon across the old line and the rattle of the gun in the back brought her thoughts sharply back to the present.

'Dear God!' said Denney, always a little dramatic even in her conversations with herself. 'Fancy forgetting the gun, not to mention the murderer. And I told Ben I was more afraid of the gun than the murderer.' Denney in her ignorance of lethal weapons called any kind of firearm a 'gun'. On their occasional Sunday outings Ben let it go at that. He didn't expect women to know anything about firearms or mechanics. Moreover, he didn't expect Denney to manage alone on that farm while McMullens and his wife . . . the married couple

9

. . . were away on their annual holiday. He had said so, as had Denney's family, but she had ignored all comments. She would as soon have parted with life as leave her farm during McMullens's absence.

Denney did not tell anyone what went on in her mind about a great many things. For instance, she would have been incapable of explaining why her farm was her salvation and the reason for existence. And she certainly wouldn't have told anyone that last night before going to bed she had left out on the verandah an old suit of McMullens's clothes, a parcel of food and ten shillings in silver in case Jack Smith, wanted man, did come that way.

Her reasoning was quite logical.

She had bought her block of land and started farming because it gave her something hard, almost insurmountable, to do that would acquit herself in her own eyes. As a young girl, ten years earlier, she had made a runaway marriage and had meant, in this defiance, to prove to the family she could do what she wanted to do and make a success of it.

Unfortunately Providence outwitted her, for she had only been married a few months when her young husband, who by this time the family had forgiven and come to love themselves, had died suddenly of an unsuspected illness.

Denney had had to come home.

Journalism and an erratic social life had stopgapped the years of aftermath. But it wasn't enough. Denney had to do something real, and hard, and big. Or die. So she did the zaniest thing of all, she went farming on her own. It was like calling on Diana to shoulder Atlas's load. She shouldered it, and nothing but death would make her drop her world . . . forty acres of orchard farm in the Darling Ranges.

Nobody, not Ben nor the family, quite understood what it was all about. Denney had done one more zany thing, but they loved her for it and prayed, for her sake, it would not end in tragedy.

At this period in time, this summer Monday, it looked as if, far from tragedy, it might just turn out to be a success. That is, until eight thirty p.m. on Monday night.

Denney had had her own ideas about how to deal with a wanted man if he transgressed the way of a young woman living alone on a farm six miles from her nearest neighbours. Again her thinking was devastatingly logical to Denney.

A woman had been found killed in a beach cottage out on

the West Coast three days earlier and the newspapers and radio had announced the description of a man wanted for questioning in the matter. This 'wanted for questioning' formula didn't pull the wool over anybody's eyes. It was merely a way of avoiding a libel action until Justice had pronounced guilt. Even in the farthermost corners of the British Commonwealth a man was innocent until he was proved guilty. Western Australia, bar Antarctica and possibly Cape Howe, was indeed a farthermost corner, but British Common Law prevailed there as it did in the heart of London. In short, the police and Press went no further than describing Jack Smith as a man 'wanted for questioning'.

The detailed description of this man made it clear to the simplest citizen that Jack Smith would not wander about paved streets. He had a scar on his chin. He wouldn't pass a quizzical eye anywhere. He would have to take to the bush.

Twenty-four hours after the first official announcement it had been announced that the police had strong indications that Jack Smith had headed for the Hills district. A strange man in clothes of the colour described by the police had been seen on a little-used track near Gooseberry Hill. Unfortunately the one orchardist who had used that track on the Saturday morning, and had seen the man, had not put two and two together for quite four hours. By that time the man had vanished again into the limitless grey bush.

Denney had heard the radio news on Saturday night. She only had the time or the inclination to listen-in on Saturday and Sunday nights.

She thought, quite sensibly, that Jack Smith would be desperate for food, and money for further food. He would want different clothes from those that were so publicly described. He couldn't be seen in a town because of that scar on his chin, so he would have to break in somewhere to get these things. But, Denney reasoned, if these articles . . . food, money, clothes . . . were provided for the taking he wouldn't have to break in, would he? In fact it would be crazy for him to break in. It would be leaving a marked trail, wouldn't it?

What's more, if he broke in while she was home, he might murder her too. Even Jack Smith would reason that you can only hang for one woman. All the others that came after just didn't matter, there wasn't anyone left alive to hang for them.

So Denney, because she was alone and not so very far distant from that bush track where the strange man had been seen, put out the clothes and food and money in case Jack Smith came her way. Then he wouldn't have to break in and she wouldn't be murdered in her bed. He could just take them and go.

She went to bed on Saturday night, well locked in but feeling secure, all on account of the fact that Jack Smith would have no reason to molest her.

On Sunday Ben Darcy had ridden through the gully, up over the eastern flank of the range and down through the shallow cross-wise valley to Denney's homestead.

Over a late tea, eaten in the long shadows of sundown on the verandah, he had tried in his quiet authoritative voice to persuade Denney temporarily to vacate her farm. Her nearest neighbours were six miles away, she must go to them in the evenings. Because he was a farmer who also loved his acres, as a man prefers life to death, Ben understood the necessity for Denney to remain near her property. Near it, not on it, was Ben's idea.

On his own farm Ben had forty horses, a hundred head of dairy cattle and two thousand sheep reared for their fleeces. Like Denney, he worked his farm with a married couple living in and casual labour that came in seasonally. Like Denney, he had to let his married couple go off for their annual holiday. This time of the year was the time for doing such things. The early stone fruit crop was almost finished, the shearing was over, the land was drying out in the first stages of the long summer. Now was the time when labour moved down into the fertile south where summer didn't begin until after Christmas and there was plentiful work. Now was the time when married couples on all the farms north of the Swan took their annual leave. After Christmas was the Boss's turn. The Boss came last when it came to annual leave, but then the heat was on the land like God's wrath, and it was not such a bad thing to have to wait for that spell on the beaches by the West Coast.

Thus Ben could not offer to stay and keep Denney company, and Denney would not have dreamed of expecting it. Besides, Denney had a very 'proper' streak in her. She wouldn't have permitted him to stay. She would have been horrified if he had mentioned such a thing. Apart from the compromise, what would have become of his forty horses, one hundred head of dairy cattle and the two thousand sheep? Who would have watered and fed and milked while Ben dallied a full night on Denney's side of the range? No farmer, lover of his lands and measurer of the stored hours of work thereon, would dream of leaving his property untended. Only death would have divided Ben from his land, as only death would have divided Denney from her land. This was never said but mutually understood in all their relationship.

Thus Ben, his long legs stretched before him, his weathered face looking darker in the shadows from the vines that shaded Denney's verandah, felt that Denney's only salvation from a possible visit from a wanted man was in going to her neighbours after sundown.

If she felt nervous at any time, Denney assured him, she would do just that. By the placatory note in Denney's voice Ben was uneasily certain she would do no such thing.

On the long, lonely, moonlit ride home through bush and gully and over the hills Ben thought savagely of the vagaries of women.

Why he had taken Denney's possible troubles on his shoulders he could not say. He thought she was the zaniest thing that had ever promenaded a beautiful pair of legs down the sidewalks of the market. Like the Galahads, he was human and would have liked to offer a faint but admiring whistle. He didn't do it, but that was partly because Ben was not the whistling type and partly because there was something steadfast in Denney's blue eyes when he looked at her, and something gallant about that figure with the shoulders back and the right arm that swung free as she walked.

Nevertheless he had to spend the best part of the night riding back to his forty horses, one hundred head of dairy cattle and two thousand sheep, because he had felt that someone, no matter how vainly, should try to persuade her to spend a night or two with her neighbours.

As far as Denney was concerned some inner and final reservation, which she never admitted, would not permit her to acknowledge that she and Ben quarrelled. They merely argued.

When Ben rode away on this particular night Denney, washing up the tea things in her kitchen sink, cracked a valuable cup in the stress of the argument she was still having with Ben, in her head.

'Me afraid of a murderer?' she exclaimed. 'What sort of a person does he think I am? What if a fire broke out in my trees? I wouldn't be here to see it. I would be burnt out before breakfast. He knows as well as I do that the fire hazard notices are up all over the Road Board district.'

'But aren't I afraid?' she said later and mournfully as she locked every window, the three outer doors and her bedroom door leading into the passage. She had the grace to laugh at herself, but all the same no low killer of women was going to drive her from *her* farm. The farm these two hands of hers had built!

Then she remembered McMullens's old suit of clothes in the back verandah cupboard, the food, and the ten shillings had to be put out again. She unlocked the barrage of doors to put these things out for Jack Smith, should he come that way.

Thus reassured she locked herself up again and went to sleep. She was still arguing with Ben when she fell asleep.

On Monday market day Denney got up at four o'clock. There were a dozen things to do before she pulled out the already loaded station wagon. The horses had to be fed and loosed into the big paddock. The fowls had to be fed. Water had to be put in the right places for horses, fowls and the goat. And the goat had to be milked too.

She herself had to be fed and she never left her dishes unwashed, her floor unswept or her bed unmade.

Then she had to dress herself correctly. There would be morning coffee at Luigi's with Ben. And afternoon tea at Vicky's in Pepper Tree Bay.

There was so much to do that, except for the unlocking of doors, Denney forgot about the murderer.

She even forgot about the treasure heap on the back verandah until she was five miles down the Kalamunda Hill heading for the coastal plain.

Were those clothes still there, or weren't they there? Well, she couldn't go back and look now. She'd be late for the early market and it was the early stuff that got the good prices. The only thing that perturbed Denney was the thought the policemen searching the district might turn up and see that pile of clothes, food and money. How would she explain that to them? Instinctively Denney knew that the police wouldn't like that idea at all. She would have to think up something in readiness for *them*.

Down on the flat Denney raced her station wagon towards the main road leading across the Causeway and into the city. The sun was breaking the Hills line behind her and the leaf tips on the gum trees were touched with gold. The dried grasses by the roadside smelt warm and pungent from yesterday's heat. The low grey scrub trees on the sandy plain stood in drooping silence, their enduring heads waiting for another day of sunstroke and thus on to eke out their lives for another hundred years. They were hideous, those little grey trees, yet Denney revered them. They endured the insufferable, and they survived when nothing else could survive in that waterless sand.

When she came to the river she saw that the sunrise had shot the great expanse of water with a hundred colours. On the far side the city of Perth stood as still and silent as that more famous city viewed from Westminster Bridge by a poet of greater renown than Denney.

Over the Causeway she drove, heading straight into Adelaide Terrace where once had been the great houses of the pioneering families and which houses, newly façaded, now represented the executive side of industrial enterprise. The old Terrace had kept its serene dignity nevertheless. Progress had not destroyed the historic trees planted in the fore gardens of the big two-storeyed houses. Enough of these houses still kept their colonial mansion appearance in spite of the cleverly designed nameplates that boasted of oil, or radio, or motor vehicle.

It was a lovely street. Denney did not know whether she liked it best in the first glow of early morning or when the shadows came stealing across it late in the afternoon.

She swung right into Plane Street, shadowed by the great trees after which the street was named, round the circus of St Mary's Cathedral, past the Royal Perth Hospital, into Wellington Street. Now bushland, river and old dignity were left behind. Denney's station wagon took her post-hasting through the heart of the city to the markets.

She swung into the north-south roadway that bisected the markets and Ben Darcy put up his hand in a halt sign . . . 'Like the policeman he was born to be,' Denney thought. Then was sorry for the thought. Ben was what he looked, a tall, slim, hills-ranging farmer, the sun burnt deeply into his face and the open air giving him a strong lithe grace as he moved. His eyes were the clear eyes of a quiet but honest man. There was an inflexibility of will in their depths. She had been wilfully unkind in that thought about a policeman and because of it Denney felt suddenly softened.

She braked sharply and Ben came round the front of the car and opened the driver's door.

'Move over,' he said. Denney did so, obedient as a small child. Ben let out the clutch and moved the gears. He manœuvred the wagon into the side lane between the auction floors. 'I'll move your stuff out. I'll meet you at Luigi's. Ten sharp.'

'What about your own stuff?' said Denney. She wasn't sure she didn't like this strong man act Ben was putting on. She'd think about that later.

'Whose wagon do you think this is?' she began, intent on establishing her own dignity.

'Just do as I say, Denney,' said Ben quietly. He was out of the car now and was already unloading cases of apricots, crates of lettuce, broccoli and rhubarb. 'Just do as I say for once. My time's important too, and I've something to say to you later.'

'Don't forget the eggs have to go over the road,' said Denney, tossing her handsome head. Well, if he was going to insist on being a common labourer tossing fruit and vegetables about on an auction floor, it was his own look-out. And he could move her wagon out of that mêlée for himself . . . since he had got it in there. Huge trucks laden to the heavens with vegetables were grumbling into the laneway to jam the traffic . . . perhaps for an hour.

She walked away, one arm swinging irrepressibly, replying with a gay 'Hiya!' to every 'Hiya Denney! How you doin!'. Really, she was thinking, one of these days these Galahads will learn to call me by my right name!

She decided, this morning, to be annoyed with people who did not treat her with the proper dignity due to her position in life.

She was no common vegetable monger. Her father had been a clergyman. A high ranking one too. He'd founded a school. She didn't remember her father much and she couldn't stand what she did remember of him, a great swashbuckling Irishman with a walking stick that struck terror into the hearts of his daughters. He had repeatedly remarked that his fourth daughter, Denney, was a wild one and sure as God was in Heaven would end her days in trouble. This sort of declamation on the part of Denney's father had always been followed by a dissertation on what happened to the wild Irish when they weren't tamed with a walking stick. Though resident in Australia he remained for ever an Irishman.

'Like your Uncle Rory,' he would say, 'you'll come to no good.' And he would belabour Denney with that walking stick in a manner which he himself would have condemned in another as unchristian and violent.

She had long since forgiven his memory the walking stick and the occasional weals on the backs of her legs. But she had never forgiven him likening her to the wild Irish . . . in particular to Uncle Rory who had cleared out from Ireland to Canada and joined the Mounted Police.

That Uncle Rory subsequently led a life of untold heroism in his new-found vocation was never revealed or discussed, for the simple reason that the Montgomery family had wiped him off the lists of persons known to God and themselves, and so had failed to find out what happened to him after he sailed out of Cork. To have gone to Cork at all, God knows, was a blasphemy for a family whose roots, Australian though it was, were in Down and Meath.

Sufficiently irrational was Denney herself in her thinking this early summer morning that she quite ignored the fact that everybody knew she was 'one of the Montgomerys' but had long overlooked the fact she bore another name. That of her late husband. On deeds, cheques, bills and receipts Denney read the inscription Dennille Shannon Hastings and knew it was herself. For the rest of the time she was just Denney, sometimes Denney Montgomery.

What name she would have demanded of the Market Galahads with their black eyes, black hair, brown sweat-shining muscular shoulders, in lieu of 'Denney' she never thought. In fact, Denney thought a lot but not always to a logical conclusion.

Thus she went on saying 'Hiya there!' as she made a progress of her departure from the markets, stopping only to ask after someone's sick wife or the state of the vegetable crop, or to comment on the iniquity of a government that taxed a poor farmer's income while the rest of the community lived on that same poor farmer's back.

The weather Denney would not discuss. 'The last resort of the intellectually starved,' she said. This was a phrase that came down the years from her father's pointed tongue, but she had long forgotten that. She just liked the phrase and thought it apt. She claimed it as her own.

'I've put the gun you used shooting last Sunday week in the back of the wagon,' Ben Darcy said over the coffee in Luigi's.

'For Heaven's sake . . .'

'Shut up, Denney, for once. And listen.' Ben had not smiled. As a matter of fact he rarely smiled, and when he did the smile came and went at such a pace one wasn't sure whether one had seen the sun rise or merely imagined it.

'You can handle that gun . . .'

'Only when I'm with you. I hate guns. Anyhow, what do I want a gun for?'

'Protection. Now keep quiet while I talk. Don't load it. Even I wouldn't like the thought of you with a gun loaded. You'd be fool enough to shoot. There's a box of cartridges, but you're to put them down in McMullens's shed.'

'That's logical,' said Denney. 'I'm to have the gun but I'm to put the bullets somewhere where I can't reach them when I want to shoot.'

'Exactly. You don't have a licence to carry a firearm. That's my gun and I'm leaving it with you so we can go shooting again. See? That's why there have to be cartridges somewhere about. One doesn't go shooting in the hills with a gun and no cartridges. But the gun you keep up at the homestead for protection.'

'Look, I'd as soon sleep in the room with a snake as a gun. And what makes you think a gun that won't shoot is going to be any protection? I suppose you're still thinking of Jack Smith. Do you suppose his name really is Jack Smith? Sounds phoney to me. When I was on the paper I found the entire outback – you can fit Europe into our outback, you know – is peopled with Jack Smiths and John Smiths . . .'

'When you pause for breath, Denney, just start drinking coffee, will you? I might finish what I'm saying.'

'All right. Go ahead. I'll listen if you're interesting. But please explain why an empty gun would be a protection?'

'Because the other fellow, at whom you point the gun, will not know it is empty.'

'He'll know I'd be no good at shooting even if it was loaded. My hands would shake enough to rock the china on the dresser.'

'Exactly,' said Ben Darcy through his tight unsmiling lips.

18

'That's why a man is always afraid of a woman with a gun in her hand. She might just be fool enough to shoot. So he'll skip.'

Denney's blue eyes opened wide with indignation.

'I like that,' she said. 'Next thing is, you'll say women shouldn't be allowed to drive cars.'

'I don't have to say it. I think it.'

'And what,' said Denney, putting her elbows on the table and leaning forward to gaze into Ben's eyes. 'And what would have happened to the invasion of Normandy if women couldn't drive cars?'

'That was a wartime emergency.'

'And it's an emergency when I drive my vegetables, not to mention the fruit and the eggs, to market twice a week.'

'Very well, I'll concede your point,' said Ben. Denney noted, deep in her heart, that he was chivalrous enough not to mention that she never drove those products of the land right into the mêlée of trucks in the market. She always allowed herself to get into the kind of mess that brought a Galahad forward to her rescue. But she would never have admitted that she had noted this, and even suffered an indefinable pang of something unnamable stirring amongst the chords of her heart.

'Let's get back to the gun,' said Ben. He poured out some more coffee for them both because Denney in her pseudo-indignation had forgotten to do it. 'Keep the gun up at the homestead and if anything bothers you, grab hold of it. But, by golly, you leave those cartridges down at McMullens's. Have you got all that straight, Denney?'

For a moment his brow puckered in anxiety. He looked at Denney. Sometimes he thought he was dealing with a child when he dealt with Denney. At other times when he was aware of those square shoulders and the sheer courage of the way she carried them – when he knew that other people turned their heads and followed her with their gaze – something else bothered him. He never cared to investigate it.

'God almighty!' he said, putting the cup down because the coffee had burnt his lips. Then he addressed the cup quietly. 'You need someone to take care of you, Denney. You're irresponsible . . .'

Denney did not catch the faint tender nuance of his words because she was indignant about that word 'irresponsible'. This was a word that belonged to the Reverend Joe – Uncle Rory – wild Irish theme and was calculated to rouse traumatic reactions that even Denney did not understand.

'I have worked with my own two hands . . .' she began. 'I have felled trees and cleared scrub and wielded pick and hoe . . .'

'Don't be dramatic, Denney,' said Ben. 'You hired the bull-dozer outfit, staged a bushfire and finally hired McMullens and his wife to help you. Oh yes, for the rest you've worked hard. Like the rest of us.'

His words died thoughtfully away as he bit on a biscuit. Denney's indignation had for once silenced her. Besides, underneath all this scurry and flurry of words she was touched that Ben was so anxious for her. She knew his dilemma. She would not stay away from the farm, she would not go to the neighbours. He could not leave his own property and come and protect her. And if he did, it would compromise her. Denney was old-fashioned enough to deal in words like 'compromise' in connection with the relationships between a man and a woman.

Ben Darcy considered it very unlikely that this wanted man would show up anywhere in the vicinity of habitation in the Hills. The chances against it were strong enough for him to decide in favour of watering his own stock and citrus orchard, of keeping the ever-vigilant eye open for that ever-present menace of bushfire.

There was no road over the range and round the gully that could bring him easily to Denney's farm. The shortest route was by horseback over a one-man track through the bush. Even that took sufficiently long that he couldn't manage his own place and his own marketing and spend the darker of the night hours keeping guard over a woman who was too irresponsible to take proper precautions herself.

Denney had already told Ben the police had beaten through the surrounding bush on Saturday afternoon and Sunday morning. That would have cleared the fellow out . . . if he'd been anywhere around.

Moreover, for once, Denney had convinced him as to the nature of the murderer.

'You take it from me,' Denney had said, nodding her head with the wisdom of a reporter-journalist who had once beaten the city block and the two-way path between the newspaper office and the police department in Roe and James Street. 'There are only two kinds of killers. Those who kill for gain . . . and we don't have many of them here. Of course there was

Snowy Rowles, and the gold stealers that shot the detectives . . . what was their name? I've forgotten. Anyhow it doesn't matter. Oh, and there was the man who shot the bank clerk and nipped out of the wrong side of the train with the money bag. He took out his false teeth and put on a false moustache. Can you imagine it? Of course they picked him up on the Trans train, all because he had falsies and no fangs. Gave himself away, the fool.' Unconsciously in this last comment Denney showed herself to be on the side of the pursued. She recovered, however, when she thought of the poor dead bank clerk. 'An only son too,' she said angrily. 'As if any bank's worth dying for.'

'Nothing's worth dying for,' said Ben laconically.

'That's unchivalrous of you,' said Denney. 'Didn't you go to the war and think your country was worth dying for?'

'I went to a war. I shot and was shot at. That's why I don't think anything's worth dying for.'

'You're just bitter,' said Denney in the same tone of voice in which she might have said . . . 'You have a slight cold. You'll get over it.'

'Well, go on about the causes of crime,' said Ben.

'Crimes of passion,' said Denney with triumphant pleasure in the sibilance of that phrase. 'People who love so madly . . . and are done in the eye, or behind the back, by their loved one and get so mad they kill her, or him. Life's not worth living anyway to them. And they invariably kill themselves sooner or later. If not on the spot, then they head for the beach and drown themselves. Of course they have been known to hang themselves from a rafter in the shed or even a gum tree down by the creek. Ben . . . I suppose those nosey police have had the wit to look up amongst rafters and trees?'

Her mental pictures of the end of Jack Smith, the wanted man, suddenly saddened her.

'Poor devil,' she said. 'God knows what he'd been through before he got to that stage.'

It was this sadness in Denney that caused Ben to refrain from mentioning sex crimes and run-amok crimes. From the newspaper accounts of the death of that woman out at the West Coast this particular crime did indeed have the aspect of what Denney called a 'crime of passion'. There had been no announcement that Jack Smith was wanted for killing the woman. But the police had known his name and his appearance in detail, down to the scar on his chin. He had been living in the house with the woman. His disappearance was a gesture of guilt. The police had been beating the beaches, the swamplands north of Perth, and now the Hills. They wanted this Jack Smith very badly, and they couldn't find him. Perhaps, as Denney had said, he had ended his own life. That was the best way out, except it was against the laws of God and the country. The public might like a trial but they loathed a hanging.

'All right,' Ben said later as they finished their third cup of coffee each. 'I'll leave it to you, Denney. But take care. And for God's sake leave those cartridges down at McMullens's. Have only the gun up at the homestead.'

'You've said it three times,' said Denney. She'd leave the gun down at McMullens's cottage too, but she wasn't going to tell Ben that now. It would start another lecture round.

'If the police go through your place looking for this fellow again, and they spot the gun, then tell them it's mine and I've got a licence for it. We're going shooting in the hills on Sunday.'

'Are we?' asked Denney innocently.

'Yes, we are,' said Ben Darcy shortly.

'Okay,' said Denney, accepting this as a quite proper invitation to an outing. 'I'll ride Pericles and bring the lunch.'

'I might come across during the week,' said Ben.

'How'll I know it's you and not the murderer knocking at my door?' asked Denney lightly.

'I'll whistle.'

'Anything, as long as it's not *Comin' Thro' the Rye*,' said Denney.

Long Monday had come to its end with its usual bout of collecting dockets through the market clearing house, a burst of shopping and a round of tea drinking with the family. To the family she told, amidst tearful laughter, the story of the gun without the cartridges that was to frighten away Jack Smith.

The family laughed uproariously. Later, however, in the privacy of the bedroom where lipstick and hats were being applied, each asked Denney with assumed carelessness whether she would care to stay down for a day or two. There was a spare bedroom and surely the place in the Hills could go without watering for two days?

'I cannot, and it cannot,' said Denney. 'Two days in this blistering heat? Hell, the whole place would be dead, including my darling Rona and Horatio and Pericles.' Rona was the goat; Horatio and Pericles, the horses.

'Poof!' she added with final bravado. 'I'm not afraid of a murderer!' And she meant it. She was enjoying the melodrama of the situation.

As she got into her station wagon and drove away she muttered to herself . . . 'I can't stand scorpions, snakes, guns and bushfires. But this Jack Smith? Poor devil. He's hanging from a tree-top somewhere. I just hope it's not on my farm. As for me? Frightened off my property by a mere murderer? Not Denney!'

CHAPTER TWO

Thus, as she sped along the last lap of the gravel road beside the old railway line up on the spur of the ranges, she thought of many things, but not at all of Jack Smith.

From potholes in the road to the Road Board secretary her thoughts leapt to the gun when she heard the rattle in the back of the car.

'And that's going to stay down at McMullens's house, for sure!' she said emphatically.

She swung on to the track that led along her north boundary fence to the gate through which the mounted police had entered yesterday.

The sun, out beyond the coastal plain and across the Indian Ocean, was going down. Denney, as she drove, had her back to this crimson blaze of glory, but she could see its reflection on the eastern skyline. The gum leaves in the tall trees caught the gold in their crowns, but below them the undergrowth was hushed and still in the muted warmth of early evening.

Poetry was not with Denney at the moment, for she was late.

'Damn fowls will be roosting,' she said. She began to list the chores to be done. 'Turn off the windmill first. Then feed the feathers. Next Rona and the horses. Will milk Rona in the shed after finishing. Got to water the pot plants and maidenhair under the tankstand. Set the west sprinklers going. Maybe I'll eat some time before tomorrow morning.'

She drove the wagon over the cow-catcher through the gate

23

and straight up to the house standing silent against the darkling fringe of bush.

Denney loved the bush. She had refused to have it bull-dozed away from all four sides of her homestead. Three sides, yes . . . after all, she did have to grow things. But behind the house, on the north side, the bush stood as God had originally made it. White man's hand had never touched it.

Jarrah trees grew thick and tall here and there. There was an occasional whitegum, and in the shallow gully were the swamp banksias that had first given away the secret of under-ground water. There had been plenty of these last trees on the acreage she had cleared. That's how she had known it was good land. Only here and there in the Hills was there a patch of loam amongst the gravel laterite. Denney had known about this land years ago when she was a child. In school she had been taught about tree types as good landmarks. She had re-membered . . . and later she had bought. It had been Crown land thrown open for bidding, and Denney had known all about the strip of swamp banksia long before any of the speculators came that way. She bought the land at the upset price. She had cleared the gully flanks, but the jarrah bush behind the house she had kept sacred for its own beauty's sake.

There was nothing frightening about the bush to Denney. To her it was a friend. In winter it was thick with wild-flowers long after the wildflowers had gone from Kalamunda and Gooseberry Hill. Tiny creeks seeped out from between granite and outcrops and ran sparkling and free down to lose themselves in the earthy crevices lower down. Blue sarsparilla twined itself madly amongst the bushes of the undergrowth. Zamia palms stood here and there more beautiful in their wild cultivation than any regimented pot plants. Red runner and sticky-faced fly-catching plants crawled over the damp gravel earth. Donkey orchids stood bravely unafraid of being plucked on the bushland behind Denney's house.

In summer all was dry and crackling and, as some said, a bushfire menace. But Denney liked the smell of the dry crackling bush and she claimed it as her friend. It would never do her harm. This was her belief and nothing but a bush-fire would shake her from it.

So far no bushfire had happened.

She drove round the side of the house and down to the gal-vanised iron shed that served as a garage. She could drive easily into the middle of the shed tonight because the Mc-

Mullens, when they had gone away for their holidays, had taken their utility truck with them.

She did not notice or think about the silence all around her. The bush in the summer time was peace. Nothing stirred. All the myriad of tiny life that lived in its undergrowth had gone to bed. The magpies and the kookaburras had gone to bed.

'And so have my blasted fowls!' thought Denney. If there was one thing she hated more than another it was feeding the fowls after they'd roosted.

'Spoils the laying,' she said. She hated the sound of flapping wings and thudding bodies when one or two of the more wakeful birds decided that a late meal was better than a hungry night.

She unloaded her shopping from the back of the wagon and saw the gun.

'Damn you,' she said. She picked it up gingerly and took it, together with the box of cartridges, and stood it against Mc-Mullens's locked door on the little wooden lean-to that served as a verandah. She put the cartridges on the doorstep.

'I'll put you away later,' she promised. Then forgot about them.

Her parcels she carried up on to her own back verandah. She pulled her dress over her head without going into the house and went round to the windmill in her slip.

She turned off the mill. Then went to the shed and filled two dippers with wheat.

When she had fed and watered the fowls she ran water into the troughs for the horses down by the paddock fence. She let chaff flow into the feeding trough through the chute from the storage bin above.

The horses were standing silent and sleepy, flank to flank, in the corner of the adjacent paddock.

'Come on, darlings,' she called. She knew they'd come and she had too much to do to wait and see them coming.

She went up the path towards the house again, and around the earth path to the west side. She turned on the sprinklers. Not once did she think about the treasure heap of old clothes, food and money she had left out last night to speed Jack Smith on his way should he come nosing around.

'You can drink all night, my sweeties,' she told the fruit trees. Then she went back to the small yard where Rona was kept.

'Just wait a minute, angel. I'll get a small bucket and you

25

can eat and I'll milk. That's what you're waiting for, isn't it?'

Not until she had finished did she open the back door and light the Aladdin lamp. The house was airless from the long day's heat and she opened all the doors and windows. Crouching down before the wood stove in the kitchen, she set fire to the kindling she had set ready in the early hours of the morning.

'You . . .' she said, addressing a pot of stew and the kettle, 'can get hot while I have a shower. And don't boil over or burn.'

She went into the wooden bathroom at the end of the back verandah and had a cold shower. When she had finished she put on her panties and brassiere and a housecoat from behind the door. She brushed her hair, put lipstick on her mouth, but no powder, and lastly slipped her bare feet into a pair of scuffs.

This was a nightly routine that Denney never failed to follow. Who knows? A visitor might come. Denney would never be found at six in the morning or eight o'clock at night without lipstick on, her hair done, and at least some underclothes under that housecoat.

Only once or twice in all the years that Denney had been in the Hills had an unannounced visitor come. Once it was someone who had taken the wrong track and was mislaid. Another time it was a group of friends from down on the plain out on the spree. The maddest thing they could think of doing was driving into the Hills to Denney's house . . . and bringing their beer with them.

Denney had not been caught without her lipstick. Like the Spartans before Thermopylæ, she was always prepared.

She had occasional morbid thoughts such as . . . 'Supposing I die in my sleep?' On those occasions she tidied her cupboards, made neat piles of her underclothes in her otherwise somewhat untidy drawers, threw out old clothes rarely worn from her wardrobe, and swept her room, specially under the bed where she didn't often have time to look. She put a further dash of lipstick on her mouth. 'Just so I don't look too awful when they find me.'

On those occasions she usually had a glass of beer or a phenobarbital before she went to bed.

In the morning she had forgotten all about her own funeral, though it had taken her some time to get to sleep for thinking tearfully of its details.

In the mornings she always had too much to do . . .

This night, bathed and lipsticked, Denney went back to the kitchen and the stirring of her stew.

Denney's chores and the business of bathing had taken up two and a half hours. The watering of the pot plants and the oleanders and hibiscus on either side of her front doorstep had taken up a good deal of this time.

'They don't make any money for me yet, poor pets,' Denney reflected of the shrubs. 'But in a mad moment I planted them and now I can't let them die. I just can't bring myself to let them die.'

Denney had a horror about killing anything. Even a scorpion, or a sand snake crushed beneath a stone or under the heel of her brown elastic-sided stock boots, gave her the guilty feelings of a murderer, quickly come and quickly gone.

It was a matter of self-defence, she reflected. 'Them or me. Well, it's just got to be them.' Nevertheless she was aware she was taking life. She had a vague feeling that in the next world she might be taken to task for it. Life was life in whatever form it was, and Denney did not like destroying it.

She liked to go shooting with Ben, but what she loved was the outing on horseback through the bush in places where possibly no human being other than the black natives had ever passed.

Ben and Denney knew gullies and creek beds, groves of black butt and jarrah deeply bedded in the sweet-smelling grey undergrowth that had no tang of memory about them to reveal that anyone else in the world other than Denney and Ben, their two horses and Ben's dog had ever passed that way before.

Most of Denney's shooting consisted of missing. Even Ben was satisfied with one 'roo. After that he gave up his shooting time to marksmanship . . . a black stump across the plain, a banksia nut on the tree by the granite cliff, a white stone in the creek bed. Denney suspected that Ben too had feelings about taking life wantonly.

Denney was stirring her stew when she heard the whistle. It came from her front verandah.

'Silly ass,' she said, still thinking of Ben and putting down the spoon with one hand and pushing back a lock of hair from her forehead with the other. 'He couldn't have gone home at all. Must have come up from Perth in the utility. What does he think I'm made of? Murderer's bait?'

27

She wiped her hands on the roller towel behind the door before she went out into the short passage that led past her bedroom door on one side and a small, never used sitting-room on the other side.

She was glad and mad. She was glad to see Ben. They'd crack a bottle of beer together, but all the time he would have the look in his eye that said his own farm would suffer for this. When was he going to catch up a lost night and a lost half-day? All this because Denney was unaccountably irresponsible. The fact he thought she was irresponsible was what made her mad. Didn't he know she would as soon quit life as quit her farm when its very life blood flowed daily from her ministering hands?

These reflections, as she went down the passage, were a nice mixture of the poetic and the journalistic.

She turned on the passage light, then, as she opened the door with her right hand, she looked down to make sure she had buttoned up her short housecoat. Below its hem she saw her white shining bare feet in their red thonged scuffs.

Then she looked up and saw, in the shaft of light flowing out into the night, the man standing eight feet away on the edge of the verandah, the gun held menacingly before him.

She thought . . .

Is he man or boy?

Whichever he was, Denney knew he was Jack Smith. It could be none other.

Her heart gave one painful thud and then stood still. It was extraordinary that she spoke, moved a hand, for she was certain her heart had stopped.

Flashing thoughts interweaved themselves like point counter point in her head.

'This is it! How funny. But of course it's not funny. Not even funny peculiar. And he whistled. That was Ben's way . . .' Tears of self-pity surged momentarily behind her eyes. 'Ben, *dear Ben*! What will you do when I am gone? No one to bully and no one to love. I suppose you do love me.'

Aloud she said:

'*Jack Smith.*'

'No,' he said. 'I'm his twin brother. Move back down the passage, lady. I'm coming in.'

'What's the good?' said Denney. 'I haven't anything.'

Then she recognized the clothes. They were too big for him, but there was no other coat as violently green as that in the

28

world. So he had collected them! The food and the money too. Why hadn't she remembered to look when she came home?

'Too busy again,' she thought with a sudden weariness at her own folly. 'And all I did was leave out treacle bait for a viper.'

He was young, and he looked thin enough to be hungry. His hair was fair and a lock fell across his forehead.

He came slowly across the verandah towards her.

'Move back, lady, or I'll shoot. Right back down that passage where you come from.'

Denney saw his hand tighten on the barrel. He had killed one woman, he might as well kill two. He could only hang for one, not both of them. She'd said that to herself before. She'd said that to Ben.

Denney turned round, her back to him, and walked down the passage. A plague of ants seemed to criss-cross her back as if it, with independent feelings and thoughts, waited for death too.

She had no defence. There was no possible defence when you were alone in a house six miles from the nearest neighbours and the man held a gun in his hand. She wondered if it was loaded.

She heard him coming slowly, cat-like, down the passage behind her. At the kitchen door she stopped and turned her head. Fear and self-reproach made her angry and anger turned her back into the Denney Montgomery the Market Galahads, the family, knew.

'Where did you get the gun?' she asked.

'Down that house the other side of the shed,' he said, making a backward gesture with his head. This gesture also served to toss that lock of long hair out of his eyes.

He looked effeminate. Not big enough or strong enough to kill a woman.

'He's only a kid,' Denney thought with scorn. 'A little sawn-off pussy-faced kid.' She went into the kitchen.

'Right over there by the wall,' he said, sidling round the door into the kitchen after her. He made a poking movement with the gun to give her direction. 'Now reach up behind and pull that blind down.'

Denney did so.

With one foot . . . the gun still pointed at Denney . . . he kicked a chair out from under the table in the centre of the room. He caught it with his left hand and with a flick had it against the wall behind the door. He kicked the door closed behind him. Then he sat down on the chair. He had kept his eyes on Denney.

Now he relaxed, the gun across his knee but his hands at the vantage points for shooting.

'That's good,' he said. 'That's bloody good. A fellow's been standing two hours watching you and your antics.' He glanced down at a flamboyant watch in a chromium case on his wrist. Denney stirred, but in an instant his eyes flicked up again and his hands tightened on the gun.

He had blue eyes. His face was effeminate in its fairness and with its full red lips. He was good-looking and he was incredibly young. Denny was sure she had read in the paper that he was twenty-three. Perhaps it was the too-big clothes on him that made him slighter, younger than his years.

And she couldn't see any scar on his chin. The police descriptions had very clearly stated there was a scar. That was the chief identification mark . . . the reason why Jack Smith could never try to lose himself in a crowd or knock at a door in open daylight.

'What did you mean? You are your twin brother?' Denney asked. One moment she was so calm and objective she might be at a boring Sunday-school party. The next, sheer terror shook her. Then suddenly she was calm again. She was like two persons each operating in one framework. First one voice spoke and then the other.

Desperately: *I'm alone in a house with a murderer.*

Then the other: *He's young. And he's tired . . . he's hungry. He has a pretty face. Heavens, what an awful thing to say about a man! Man? He isn't even a man's pants.*

'So I am my twin brother,' said Jack Smith. He made a motion with the gun again. 'Get that stuff that's smelling on the stove. Stew. God, I reckoned I'd had the last of the stew in Nashos. But that smells good. Stick a plate on the table. And for God's sake hurry.'

The stove was against the wall adjacent to Denney and she turned towards it. She lifted the spoon and stirred the stew again. If she had looked out of the corner of her eye she would have been able to watch Jack Smith, but she didn't want to do that. She knew without looking what he looked like, a flame of hunger eating his eyes so that they wouldn't be blue any more. Her hand, as it stirred, shook; and she felt very sick. It would be pleasant to faint: an escape from reality.

'Two plates,' said Denney. 'I'm hungry too.' She was astonished at the words she uttered. Then the words themselves gave her courage. 'There's enough for two and then some . . .' she said crossly.

'All right! Two plates!' he said. 'Put mine on the end of the table and get back there to the stove. Right. Now get yours. Put it on the other end of the table. You can sit down. Put your hands on the table so I can see 'em.'

By twisting one foot round the leg of his chair he eased it forward. With his left hand he picked up the fork Denney had put beside the knife on his plate. His eyes seemed to smile savagely at her. His right hand, finger near the trigger, held the gun, resting on the table but pointing at her.

'Good job it was stew, eh? I don't have to cut, see? Don't have to use two hands,' he said.

Denney was sitting on the chair at the other end of the table now. It was a big table and he was a long way from her.

She remembered violent scenes she had seen on the films wherein the hero at one end of the table up-ended it against his opponent. She remembered it but did not think about it. She could never do it, she knew. Up-end the table, yes, but struggle for the gun, best him in a physical battle? No. Her spirit was calm now and most of the time her heart was beating normally, but her knees were like water. Her feet under the table where she crossed her ankles were shaking so that it was a wonder they couldn't both hear her feet beating a tattoo against the linoleum-covered floorboards. She rested her elbows on the table and clenched her hands under her chin. Her large violet-blue eyes looked at Jack Smith. She might as well look at him. She might as well know what he was like.

She had polished her linoleum floor yesterday. The thought of the mess her shot body would make on that floor brought tears of pity to the edge of being shed.

'Got any cigarettes?' he asked. His mouth was full and the fork, loaded, was half-way to that mouth again.

'Yes, in the dresser drawer,' said Denney, not turning her head. He could see the dresser for himself. It was against the wall opposite the stove and at the side of them. Beyond it, just to the right of Denney but a little behind her, was the door leading to the back verandah. She had closed it when she came in from the shower.

She knew that if she attempted to make a dash for it the odds were too heavily against her. The greatest of those odds were her watery knees and trembling legs. They would betray her. They were too weak to carry her as far as the door. If she stood up to go, she would faint.

Yet she could look at him with this absurd objective calmness.

'Get 'em,' he ordered, nodding his head in the direction of the drawer.

Denney pushed her chair back and was astonished that her legs carried her unfalteringly to the dresser. She opened the drawer slowly and took out the cigarettes.

That back door . . .

But she couldn't do it! There was the back verandah to cross . . . the path . . . the unsheltered gravel yard. The light would flow out there just as it had flowed out of the front door to show him waiting, gun pointed, on the edge of the verandah.

She was thinking of this so that unthinkingly, after she had taken out a packet of cigarettes and closed the drawer, she crossed the kitchen behind her own chair and took a box of matches from the shelf over the stove.

With his right hand he followed her movement, pointing the gun.

'Put the blasted gun down,' Denney said in sudden violent, despairing irritation. She threw the cigarettes and matches down the length of the table to him. 'I want my dinner too. It's getting cold. I'm just as hungry as you are. I haven't had anything but three rotten cups of coffee this morning and two cups of tea this afternoon . . .'

He did not relax his vigil with the gun, but Denney sat down and picked up her knife and fork and began to eat.

He watched her, cat watching mouse: Denney, chewing rhythmically, looked down the table at him, her eyes insolent and challenging.

'There's some more in the pot, if you want it. Get it yourself,' she said. The venom in her voice surprised her. Well, what was he anyway? A miserable little sawn-off shotgun of a hermaphrodite. This word, forbidden in the polite circles of Denney's family and friends round the Bay, pleased her. She couldn't pronounce it correctly in her mind, but the mental uttering of it gave her an inexplicable and pleasurable relief. She not only, by this mental utterance, got her own back for the fright he was giving her, but it renewed her sense of her own vitality. She was tall and strong – and yes, she had a certain type of beauty. She was afire with the gift of life, of feminine wiles. She did things. She got somewhere. She made the earth . . . this little bit of Hills land . . . to flower. Here she was being held up at gun point by this lily-livered pink-faced squirt!

'Get it yourself,' she said again.

' 'Cept that bread on the verandah this morning, I haven't eaten for two days . . .' he said. 'I can't hold any more. Stummick's shrunk.'

'Then light a cigarette. You can put down the gun. I'm not going to run away.'

'You can't,' he said sneeringly.

'Okay, I can't,' said Denney. 'When I've finished this I'm going to make some tea.'

He pushed his chair backwards against the wall again. The gun lay across his knee as, his eyes unwaveringly on Denney, he struck a match and, extracting a cigarette with the fingers of one hand, he put it to his mouth and lit it.

'What's your name?' he said.

'Denney.'

'Okay, Denney. You can smoke.' He threw the cigarettes and matches, one after the other, across the space to the table. They slid with absolute accuracy down the table and stopped beside one another two inches away from her plate.

He moved his hand with a quick flicking gesture. Denney noticed how slim, long-fingered yet steel strong those hands were. He had a number of different mannerisms with them. They had a language of their own. There was something delicate, like a ballet dancer's hands, about them. Yet they were also very strong.

That was perhaps how . . .

Denney had another moment of that cold sweating fear that kept seizing her at intervals. For a moment she wanted to be physically sick. She wanted to bend her head and vomit on the floor.

Instead she pushed back her chair, stood up and turned her back to Jack Smith as she went to the stove, and lifting the tea canister and the teapot down from the shelf above the stove, began to make the tea.

'Where were you when I came home?' she asked, without turning her head.

'In the orchard.'

'Not in the bush?' she asked, surprised yet relieved. She couldn't bring herself to believe that the bush, *her* bush, would give sanctuary to a foe.

'No,' he said with a laugh that was also a sneer. 'That's where they'd look. That's where they'd find tracks. The sods. When there's bush there they don't think about open orchard.'

'Were you here when the police came through yesterday?' Denney turned her head and looked at him with genuine surprise, anger forgotten, curiosity roused.

'Yeah. Down the orchard. Lying down in the peas. I watched 'em.'

'You've got a nerve,' said Denney, her eyes indignant with this impertinence.

He grinned. Suddenly the sneer had gone out of his face and he was a good-looking boy, except for the weak chin which receded into the open neck of his shirt collar.

'I was too shrewd for the bush,' he said. 'All those copperheads think of is the bush, the bush, he's run to the bush.' Suddenly he broke off, then was mimicking the radio announcers. He waved his left hand in the air, making elegant flicking ballets dancer gestures with the fingers. '*The police have, early today, closed in on the eastern Hills district. Early last night a shop was ransacked in Kalamunda, and a Holden car was stolen from Railway Parade, Gooseberry Hill. It is thought the man wanted for questioning in connection with the Seaton murder is hiding in dense bush at the back of the range.*'

'Did you?' asked Denney. 'Did you break in? Did you steal a car?'

Jack Smith's volatile eyes changed expression. The blue irises became stony agates.

'No bloody fear,' he said. 'I don't leave any trail behind me. That's what those coppers are. They got you so they got you for everything. Don't matter who steals a raking car; who cracks in what shop . . . *I* done it. See? Anything that gets done now, *I* done it. See?'

He had a curious way of lapsing from a normally educated speech to a semi-literate one. Denney had a feeling that the educated speech was his natural one. The other had been picked up. From associates? The films? Cheap paperbacks?

Denney put the teapot on the table, went to the dresser and lifted down cups and saucers. She poured milk into the two cups. She had been digesting what he had said.

'How do you know what they said on the radio?'

He put his left hand in his pocket and pulled out a transistor set. He leaned forward, across the gun, and put it on the floor. With his eyes watching Denney he adjusted the dials with the quick, easy dexterity of those long, slim, steel-strong flickering fingers. A volume of hit-tune music filled the kitchen. He toned it down. Then switched off.

'Where'd you get that?' asked Denney.

'Stole it. That's what you think, eh? You're the same as the rest of 'em.' His voice was arrogant, and thinly bitter. 'Stole everything. Never done a day's work in me life, eh?' He had forgotten his gun and his right hand was making those curious staccato gestures that Denney had seen the gangsters make on American films.

'So what!' he said. He gripped the gun again and moved it a fraction of an inch.

'I don't know anything about you, so how could I think you stole it,' Denney said, pouring out the tea. She pushed a cup half-way down the table. 'Come and get it,' she said.

Still standing, she extracted two cigarettes from the packet and slid the packet down the table towards him. She turned away to the mantel over the stove to get another box of matches. She heard him stand up, take two steps across the floor and reach for the cup of tea. Her back felt that brigade of ants marching across it again. When she turned round he had picked up the cigarettes and matches and put them like two biscuits on the side of the saucer. He was backing to his chair, the tea in one hand and the gun in the other.

'Oh, for God's sake put that gun down,' Denney said, relieved she was alive, tired of being frightened one minute, indifferent the next. 'We might as well have our tea in peace.'

He put the gun down on the floor beside him. He laid it pointing in Denney's direction, the position such that he could, in an instant, drop his hand on to the effective part of the barrel. He practised doing this several times, watching her with hard smart eyes while he did it. Then he picked up the cup and saucer from the floor and slumped back in his chair.

Denney lit a cigarette. She used her left hand to smoke it and used her right hand to take up her teacup.

'I've been waiting hours for this,' she said savagely. She too was bitter now, as if having to wait so long for her tea was an unwarranted piece of interference on the part of Fate.

'Same here,' said Jack Smith caustically. ' 'Bout twenty-four hours.'

There was a momentary silence. Denney broke it first.

'What did you do with your own clothes?' she asked.

'That'd be telling,' he said. 'Where they won't find 'em, or the dogs smell 'em. If they bring dogs now all they'll smell is what I got on. Boots too. Look, do they have dogs in this State? The police have dogs?'

He stretched his feet out in front of him and Denney noticed for the first time there was something familiar about the boots. McMullens's working boots.

'Did you break in that little house to get them?' Denney asked with rising indignation, ignoring the question about dogs. At the moment the cheek of this pipsqueak taking McMullens's boots absorbed all her attention. Without that gun he wouldn't be worth spitting at. It made him *big*, like McMullens's boots.

'There you go again. Breaking in. That's all anyone thinks. Breakin' in. No, I didn't, if that's any satisfaction. They were in the shed. Where you keep the bloody cars. Bloody garage, you call it, I suppose. Though I seen better . . .'

Again the relapse into coarse speech. It was sharp and sour.

'Where have you seen better garages?' Denney asked. 'The inside of them, I mean. You went to a good school, didn't you?'

'*Schools*,' he said, taking up her last question. 'One school . . . two schools . . . six schools. Either you get pushed out of 'em or your mother gets told . . . *Come and take this bastard away.*' Then, changing his tone to mimicry, 'Of course, we'll hush it up. Let him leave at the end of term. Don't cha' know!'

'But why?' Denney asked, opening her eyes wide.

He shrugged. Even with the cup and saucer in one hand he managed a gesture, fingers spread fanlike and passing quickly across his face. It was one of those curious dancer-like gestures, the fingers stiff yet peculiarly fluid, the hand moving like a fan before his face.

'Because I ain't any good. My stepfather, he said that. Ain't any good. Won't never be any good. Rotten to the marrow. Got it?'

Denney began to see now that the semi-literate speech and the hand gestures went together. They belonged to a personality that was playing a part. When he spoke correctly he was

36

a good-looking boy with an uneasy smile and a weak chin, and no character. When he was bitter, coarse, illiterate, he was the chain gang criminal, big with McMullens's boots on and Ben's gun in his hand.

'He's not any different from me,' she thought. 'I'm two persons too. There's me, sitting here, and there's me running through the bush. Stumbling, falling, cutting myself . . . the tears running down my cheeks. Running from a murderer with a gun.'

'You had a stepfather,' said Denney, sudden pity softening her voice, because of this fellow feeling of being two people, one brave, one cowardly.

His ears caught the subtle change in her voice. The pretty-looking boy with the uneasy unhappy smile came back.

'Yes,' he said. 'My father was killed in the war. My mother married again and this fellow . . . this one she married after the war . . . he had a stick in his voice. You know the kind. *Got-to-thrash-it-out-of-him* kind of voice.'

'But thrash what out?' asked Denney.

'Dunce. Couldn't add up. Couldn't spell. "He's just a lazy bastard," my stepfather said. This fellow with a stick in his voice. "We'll thrash him and make him work." ' He suddenly stopped as if remembering something. Then added. 'Me, and my twin brother.'

Denney picked up the second cigarette from the table and tapped it down as she reached for the box of matches which he leaned forward and sent flying down the table to her.

'Let me get this twin business straight,' said Denney, frowning. 'You have a twin brother?'

'Yes, that's right. Maybe that's him breaking in and pinching cars. Maybe that was him . . .' He stopped short. Hunted eyes suddenly became crafty agates again.

Denney knew what he had been going to say. *Maybe that was him who had murdered Beryl Seaton; plunged a knife in her heart.*

'And you're covering up for him,' said Denney. She struck a match and lit her cigarette to hide that, at the thought of the murder hovering in the air, terror had temporarily revisited her.

She was looking at the lighted flare of the match and the tip of her cigarette, but she knew that he relaxed back in the chair. Before she looked at his eyes again she knew they would be expressionless, perhaps hiding contempt for her, but also hiding reality from himself.

'Go on, and tell me some more,' she said, putting the dead match in the saucer.

'What more?' he said, 'Thrash him here, thrash him there . . .'

He took a long drag of his cigarette.

'One time I left my coat at school and he came in when I was in bed. An' he pulled me outa bed and started thrashing me, and I was asleep and didn't know what for. Then in the morning he thrashed me some more to make me remember to bring that coat home. An' I yelled that much my face was all dirty. Then when I got to school I got some more cane from the boss because I'd come to school dirty.'

Jack Smith looked up at Denney, his eyes cold and hard.

'See what I mean? Thrashing was all the go those days. If he didn't hoe into me, him with the stick in his voice, then they did it up at that school. An' after school it was the big boys. Tied my bike up on the top of a tree so I couldn't get it, and when I got home I got another thrashing for not bringing that bike home. An' took me pants off, the big boys did, because I was a little squirt, and chucked 'em in the incinerator.'

He drew fiercely on the cigarette again.

'Go on,' said Denney. Her own eyes were dark and angry with the old burgeoning feeling that those of Irish descent have when they hear of wrongs to the one underneath. To Denney, Jack Smith wasn't a man on the run right now. He was that small boy of long ago who found in all mankind only enemies.

'Go on,' said Denney again.

'Well, that day, the day I got thrashed for me coat, I couldn't find the coat anyplace. So I took another. They were all the same coats, those days. You know, black and shiny on one side an' black and dull on the other. All the kids had 'em. I reckoned someone had took my coat, so I took someone's. See? Fair enough, eh? An' that way I wouldn't get another walloping when I got home.'

Denney nodded.

'Well, the next day that kid's ma came up to the school with the cops. Someone had took her Ikey's coat, and it wasn't the first time. So they collared on to me. So I got it. See?'

'Got what?' asked Denney.

'Down to the police station. Up to the Kids' Court. *On*

probation, the magistrate said. Then they hopped into my step-father. Him with the stick in his voice. *You don't train this kid proper*, they said. *You oughta use discipline on your boy. If he comes here again he goes in the jug. What's more, you pay two quid so this other boy can buy another coat.'*

Denney's eyes flickered, partly because there was smoke in them and partly because anger had filmed them over with a stinging dew.

'So my stepfather,' said Jack Smith, 'he took me home an' he thrashed that coat, and that two quid, in me and then he thrashed them out. So I quit. Cleared out. Hopped it.'

'Where did you go?' asked Denney.

'In the bush. Three days I went in the bush, then I got kinda mad because I had no one to talk to. I can't stand no one to talk to. So I thought I'd go home and see my mother. The cops were all over the place looking for me. So they took me up to Court again because my stepfather he said I was uncontrollable an' the State could have me. So the magistrate said I was uncontrollable and he'd put me in a Home.'

Jack Smith stopped. He ground out the last of his cigarette and reached for another. He lit it slowly and flicked out the match with a delicate dandified movement of his wrist.

'That was a good Home,' he said. 'Nice place. Good food. An' the teachers were pretty decent. Only I didn't stay. I cut out again.'

'Why didn't you stay?' asked Denney.

'The other fellers. They came at the same ol' gag. I was a little squirt. *Take his pants off*, they'd say. *An' chase him round the muck heap*. So I quit. After that I was always in an' out one place an' another. An' I always quit.'

He paused.

'Then I went home again, for a spell . . .'

It was a long story of brutality endured in childhood; of teachers who scorned and were held in scorn : of fellers down at certain milk bars who had started off by calling him a pansy, a queen, a queer. But when he could show them he could bend a bottletop between his forefinger and thumb, cut, bite and bend a threepence between his teeth; could knot a rope like a hangman's noose, could undo any knotted rope – they'd learned. By God, yes. They'd learned. He could flick a bicycle chain. He was smarter than they were. He'd shown 'em.

This story Jack Smith told sometimes in the milk bar vernacular, sometimes in the voice of a boy who had gone to a good school.

'My stepfather, him with the stick in his mouth, he put me on an aeroplane to go to New Zealand. We were living in Sydney then. And they turned me back. Yeah, that's what they did. They weren't goin' to give me any break. *Clear out of here. We don't want your kind of rot in this country. You get back where you come from. Sydney slums.*'

'Did you live in Sydney slums?' asked Denney.

The packet of cigarettes had flown backwards and forwards across the air and down the length of the table. The pile of butts grew in Denney's saucer and were scattered, crushed by McMullens's boots on the floor around Jack Smith's chair.

Once or twice in the recital he remembered the gun, and he would break off to practise a quick drop of his hand to get it at lightning speed.

Denney did not blink an eyelid. She was absorbed in Jack Smith's story, which she knew instinctively and with absolute certitude was true. It had all the authority of truth about it. In the narrative he spoke simply, fluently. When lapsing into pits of bitterness, or reporting something said, he spoke like the stereotype of all juvenile criminals.

As his story progressed Denney could see it all. He had become a petty criminal from consorting with petty criminals. They had been the only members of society who had accepted him. He was discarded and despised by his own kind, so he went where he was no better and no worse than others in the group.

They had called him a pansy and a queer, but he had done things with his steel strong fingers none of them could do. He taught and found respect for himself because he could do something no one else could do.

'Did you live in Sydney slums?' Denney had asked.

'By crikey no,' he said. His face twisted with a wry sardonic bitterness. 'The North Shore, if you please. The very best la-di-da toney place. Toney friends too. Mrs This and Mrs That. *Oh, my dear, what a lovely handsome boy you have! Such lovely skin. And that fair hair! He ought to have been a girl.* And my stepfather. With a stick in his voice. He'd say . . . "By God, I'll thrash that stuff out of him. I'll thrash a bit of manhood into him. Him and his flash clothes and flash watch. He's no good, I tell you." [1]

'Did you have flash clothes and a flash watch?'

'In those days? Yeah. My mother, she gave them to me. She was always crying. In the end she'd give 'em to me. And she'd say . . . "For God's sake keep out of your father's way." In the end I got out. Right out. Me and some mates, we went to Victoria, and my pal . . . his name was Jeanes . . . he'd pinched the car. They caught us on the border and we got clapped in the delinquent jug. The delinquent jug! I ask you!'

Again that quick mesmeric gesture with the hand.

'You ever been in the delinquent jug?' he asked.

With solemnity Denney shook her head.

'Thought you mighta been. You just mighta been. You got something. You don't put on that *stink under your nose look*. You don't start that *tell-me-what's-troubling-you-boy* hogwash.'

'Me in the delinquent jug?' asked Denney, indignant. 'I never thought of such a thing. Though mind you . . .' She paused, wrinkled up her brow and sought in the packet for another cigarette. 'Now I come to think of it I guess my father thought that way. Only we didn't call them delinquents those days. Just larrikins.'

'I guess it's the same thing. What your father think about you going in the delinquent jug?'

'He used to say I'd come to no good. He often said it.' [1]

'What for? Did he belt you?'

'Yes, across the legs with a big stick he always carried. A walking stick and it was heavy. And he had six foot two of big man behind it.'

'What for? What did you do?'

'I used to run away. Not far . . . just down to the river, or up to the railway station. He said he'd thrash it out of me.'

'Did he?'

'No, he didn't,' said Denney. 'But I didn't end up in the delinquent jug.'

'Maybe you aren't your twin brother,' Jack Smith said, heavily sarcastic. 'It's what your twin brother does that catches you. All the time you're fronting for him. Then you get caught with what you do and what *he* does.'

'Did your stepfather thrash your twin brother too?'

'Yeah. Me and him. Him and me. Didn't matter anything to him. Just bash us about. That was his kind. Never spoke but he didn't have a stick in his voice.' [1]

He fell into a ruminating silence. Denney stood up and Jack Smith bent and reached for his gun.

'Drop it,' said Denney in a tone as caustic as his own. 'I'm only going to make some more tea. How long do we stay here? All night?'

'Till I done talking. I haven't had no one to talk to for three days. I get mad out there in the bush on my own. I just get plain crazy for some cow to talk to. I get sand in my head. Right inside. In the brainbox. You ever get sand in your head?'

Denney nodded. 'When I get mad,' she said. 'So I stop getting mad.'

Denney was at the stove again. She bent down and pushed the half burnt wood-ends together in the fire shelf so as to bring the simmering kettle to the boil. She picked up the teapot and emptied the tea-leaves into the drainer in the sink. She walked over to the dresser and took a packet of biscuits from the cupboard underneath. She broke the paper off the packet and set the biscuits out on a plate.

She took down a tray and set a cloth on it and two fresh cups and saucers. Not once did she look at Jack Smith, but all the time she knew he was watching her, his hand ready to drop on that gun. She took a new packet of cigarettes from the drawer in the dresser.

By this time the kettle was on the boil and Denney made the tea. She carried the tray, beautifully set out, to the table.

'What you do that for?' Jack Smith asked, his voice heavy with suspicion and his eyes on the tray with its cloth and clean polished china.

Denney shrugged.

'I don't know,' she said. 'Guess I was treating you as a visitor.' She began to pour the tea. 'Do you know what?' she said. 'My mother and my sisters always put a cloth down when they have a meal or tea . . . even if there's no one else. I suppose I got the habit from them.'

Jack Smith's face was working with a sudden uncontrollable emotion.

'My mother too,' he said. His eyes were full of tears. Then he reached for the gun and raised it. 'By God, I'll blast the soul out of you if there's any more mother talk. What you take me for? A pansy, hey?' His lips twisted with a bitter hatred. A minute before their expression had been deadpan.

'All right,' said Denney, pushing a cup and saucer as far down the table as she could reach. She pushed the sugar bowl and the plate of biscuits after it. If she had looked up she would have been looking straight into the barrel of Ben's shot-gun. This was the weapon he had lent her with which to pro-tect herself: the one she had potted at 'roos and, failing 'roos, then crows and black stumps and bottles set up on the fence post. She had liked potting at stumps and bottles. Then she didn't have to kill. Everything, even a maggot-laying fly, had a right to life, Denney thought. She had to be very mad and have a bucketful of sand in her head to kill flies without feel-ing.

She was neither calm nor terror-stricken now. Looking into the barrel of that gun she had an extraordinary sense of fatal-ism. It was something quite foreign to her temperament and she had a certain sense of interested wonder that this was how she, Denney, would face death when the time came. Who'd have thought it?

'I didn't know I had it in me,' she said to herself. 'Nothing matters any more. Funny, but if I live through this nothing will ever matter quite so much any more.'

There was a long, tense, silent minute and Denney thought that in that minute her life was truly in the balance. She went on pouring tea.

'Okay,' Jack Smith said in a mollified voice, and he put down the gun on the floor again. He stood up and crossed the intervening space to the table and reached for his tea. He took a handful of the biscuits and put them in his coat pocket.

'Aren't you hot in that coat?' Denney asked. 'Why don't you take it off.'

'Take your coat off and you might as well take your Thomas off,' Jack Smith said coarsely. 'Me? I like to stay armoured.'

He sat down, stretched his feet out in front of him and began to drink his tea. Denney noticed he held his cup cor-rectly. He drank neatly and noiselessly.

She sat down in her own chair and drew her cup and saucer towards her.

She felt very sick now. She was certain her face was white. She would have to keep it downbent. Light a cigarette. There was water in her knees again and her feet, crossed at the ankles, shook so that once again she thought he must hear them beating a tattoo on the floor.

So she had been frightened, after all, when he'd pointed that gun at her! That calmness, it was only a front. But where did it come from? How did she manage it?

Denney took half the remaining cigarettes from the packet and pushed the packet down the table towards him. Jack Smith was silent, and Denney lit a cigarette.

Now she felt desperately tired. Sheer physical fatigue overcame her like a sudden assault. She'd been up since four o'clock in the morning. What was the time now? She looked at the clock over the kitchen stove. Eleven o'clock. Was that all? She thought she and Jack Smith had been sitting here in this kitchen for a week.

'Bloody timekeepers,' said Jack Smith, seeing her look up at the blue-and-white enamel clock.

He bent down and juggled with the dials of the transistor set again.

A man's voice filled the room and Jack Smith toned it down. It was the late evening news.

'The Minister for Works announced that water restrictions would be in operation as from seven o'clock tomorrow morning. A ban on all sprinklers or running hoses is imposed between seven a.m. and seven p.m. Residents of the metropolitan area are reminded there is a twenty pound fine for violation of the ban.'

A long pause. One could almost hear the announcer taking in breath for his next item of news.

'It has been learned that the police hunt for the man wanted for questioning in connection with the murder of Beryl Seaton has been moved from the Hills district to the Chittering Valley. Two shops were ransacked late this afternoon and early this evening on the Chittering Road. Crumbs were found where the wanted man had probably eaten. Also a pair of brown shorts thought to belong to him. The Holden car stolen last night from Kalamunda was found smashed on the York Road and a Holden utility truck was stolen from Allen's garage four miles farther along the same road. Residents are asked to look out for a dark grey recent model Holden utility numbered X129467. The wanted man, Jack Smith, is fair-haired and has a scar on his chin. He is twenty-three years of age and when last seen was wearing a brown khaki shirt, brown shorts and sandals with grey socks.'

Denney watched the smoke curling up from her cigarette. She had meant to look for that scar before but had forgotten. Jack Smith held his weak receding chin well down into the neck of his shirt.

He bent down and switched off the transistor set. He sat up again.

'See what I mean?' he said, shrugging and making that curious stilted eloquent gesture in the air. 'Now I've tooken two bloody cars. Now I've eat crumbs and left em' laying around. Now I've lorst me brown pants. Me shorts. Me bloody lousy shorts. An' I'm out on the Chittering Road. Maybe I'm at York, wherever in hell that is. Say *you*! What you say your name was? Denney. Say you, Denney. Where the blazing hell am I anyway? Where's this place we're at now?'

His voice was rising in a crescendo of passion.

'You're here at my place,' she said. 'And they're a damn lot of liars and if ever I meet up with them I'll tell them so.'

Suddenly Denney too was indignant. She looked up at Jack Smith, her own eyes angrier than his.

'You've been here the whole time. You couldn't have smashed a car and stolen another. I never heard such rot in my life . . .' Her own voice was rising with vehemence. The Irish in Denney was coming out. The thing in her that made her move in, battling for the Market Galahads who had suffered an injustice, was at work. Denney, as Ben had once said, was always on the side of the man underneath. Always on the losing side. The defender of the underdog.

Her father might have bequeathed to her a memory of lashes on her legs, but he had also left her his Irish legacy of fighting lost causes.

Jack Smith's passion ebbed away with Denney's rising indignation. He watched her, curious and pleased.

'See what I mean? Every time I was in the delinquent jug it was the same. Anything gone . . . anything broke . . . anything to blazes. That was me, Jack Smith. Jack Smith, he'd done the lot.' He paused. Then added, 'Me and me twin brother.'

Denney, recapitulating Jack Smith's long story in her mind, missed this particular reference to the twin brother. Suddenly the long repertoire of offences committed against him had the tang of verisimilitude about it.

Give a dog a bad name. Maybe he had been difficult. He hadn't done well at school. His stepfather was a hating and hateful man. He'd done something wrong. After that they'd hounded him . . .

'Yes,' said Denney, breathing the fire of indignation with each word. 'I can see what they've done to you. The fools. Oh,

45

I'd like to get my hands on them.'

Jack Smith had given up all claims to indignation to Denney. He leaned back in his chair, stretched his feet out in front of him and sank his chin on his chest.

'You can see, can't you?' he said, speaking in reasonable English again. 'Nowhere to go. No one to turn to. Nobody cared a damn.'

'Well, I care a damn,' said Denney. 'I'm not going to let them fasten that one on you. That's for sure. I'll go in the Court myself. I'll . . .'

'There isn't going to be any Court,' said Jack Smith. 'I'm not going to get caught.'

'What will you do? Where will you go?'

'I'll stick around here for a while,' said Jack Smith easily, pulling in his feet. 'One thing, the heat's off up this way.' He looked at Denney, his eyes bright and careful. 'Who comes round here tomorrow? Who comes round here any day?'

'No one,' said Denney. 'That is . . . I have a friend. He might come . . .'

'He'd better stop away. He'll get a blast of pellets in his moniker.'

This was a new fear. Jack Smith might shoot Ben, or any other passing caller.

So vivid was Denney's imagination that she saw Ben, his tall slim leathery figure, dressed in his khaki drill clothes, the old wide-brimmed stetson hat set carelessly at an angle on his head, walking up the path from her homestead-gate. In this picture Ben too was carrying a gun. His .303, carelessly slung under his arm.

This mental picture of Denney's was partly unreal because Ben, when he did come, would bring his horse right up to the tree outside on the gravel square, and if he carried his gun it would be left in the leather socket across his saddle. If he came by the long way from the city it would be in his utility, and he would drive through the gate, across the cowcatcher and right up to the front verandah.

But the picture of Ben walking up from the gate persisted in Denney's mind. In her fantasy she heard the sound of Jack Smith's shotgun exploding its cartridge and saw Ben's face suddenly blown into a bloody mess by a spate of pellets. She saw him crumple and she saw him lying on the brown gravel track half-way to the homestead. He lay back, his head on one side, one arm across his chest and the other still holding the gun which lay alongside him. Mercifully, in this picture, the stetson hat had fallen forward and it covered the terrible thing that had been his face.

'Listen,' said Denney, like a mother putting a logical argument before an obtuse child. 'Ben Darcy . . . he's my friend. He would never hurt you. Why don't you go off along the ridge of the range? There's valleys all along there. You could stay hidden for weeks. Even months . . .'

'Too lonely,' said Jack Smith. 'If I had a cobber it 'ud be all right. I gotta have someone to talk to. If I don't talk I go mad, see? I mean, I might go mad any time. I can't stand having no one to talk to. I gotta be with people, see? I get sand in my head. In the brainbox. I gotta have someone . . .'

'Yes, I see,' said Denney. Oddly enough she could see. She saw right into the heart of Jack Smith. If he was desperate he was desperate from loneliness. He'd been that all his life. That's what had driven him into the company of petty juvenile gangsters.

Jack Smith, his ears finely attuned to every shade of meaning in a voice, knew that Denney did see. He knew that her sympathy and indignation were genuine.

'I'm going off,' he said unexpectedly, stooping down and picking up the gun. He put the packet of cigarettes and the matches in his pocket. He moved to the table and scooped up the rest of the biscuits and put them in his pocket too.

His eyes glanced round the kitchen. At first Denney thought he was looking for something, but then she decided he was familiarizing himself with the room.

He had sat in this room and had been given tea and cigarettes. He had talked and been listened to. The room meant something to him.

'I'm going off,' he said again. He brought his gaze back to her face. 'Don't you go away,' he said. 'I'll be watching. I won't take my eyes off this place. And I'll have the gun . . .'

'I won't go,' said Denney. 'I don't think anyone will come. But you mustn't mind if someone does . . .'

'I'll mind,' he said threatening, and jerked the gun up and down. He carried it under his right arm now like the mental picture she had of Ben carrying his gun as he walked up the homestead path.

'Anyone come here and you might talk,' Jack Smith said through half-closed lips which Denney knew at once was an expression he had taught himself. He had all kinds of façades,

47

this weak boy who looked sixteen and was twenty-three. Was that another official lie? None of his façades quite rang true, not even his real self, which was the youth whose face had crumpled when Denney had introduced the mother-talk.

'You'd talk. Even you'd talk,' he said menacingly. That 'even you' somehow put Denney on a different footing from all other people.

'Why don't you go away in case someone comes?' said Denney. In a surprised kind of a way she realized his last words had given her a reprieve of life. If he thought she would talk he assumed she would be alive to talk. He wasn't going to kill her. Not tonight anyway.

Such was his loneliness he would have to satiate himself with tea and cigarettes and talk first.

'They won't come,' he said. 'They won't dare, I'll be watching.' He backed away to the door now and, putting his hand behind him, turned the knob and began slowly to open the door. 'They'll know better,' he said. 'They'll stay away. Me and my gun . . . They got no chance against me.'

That was what he wanted, so that was how it would be. He was God because he had a gun in his hand and McMullens's boots on his feet. In this role of God he warned the world to stay away from Denney's farm.

'I see,' said Denney. She was still seated at the far end of the table, the tea-tray in front of her. She lit another cigarette and still her hand was steady. 'What do you want me to do, Jack?'

'You stay right here. Don't you go anywhere. I'll be watching . . .'

'But my fowls . . . my horses. The watering . . .'

'You can do all those things. Like you were doing when you came in tonight. You can do them. But I'll be watching . . .' He patted the gun barrel with his free hand. 'Don't you forget this fellow. One false move . . . and he talks. He talks very pretty when I want . . .'

'I won't go away,' said Denney. 'What will you do for food?'

'I'll be here tomorrow night. You get it ready. I'll be here. I'll whistle. You'll know.'

He backed into the passage. Suddenly he turned and with quick light steps went down the passage. Denney heard the front door, and then the wire door, bang behind him.

After that there was silence.

Denney sat quite still where Jack Smith had left her . . . behind the tea-tray that was set with a cloth.

In a dazed way she glanced round the room. Had she dreamed it all?

But there were the used cups, the trodden cigarette butts; the chair by the wall where he had sat.

'This happened to me,' she said. '*Me.* Why me?'

CHAPTER THREE

Denney did not escape through the bush that night. While she had been gathering the dishes and washing up, later locking the doors and windows, she had been planning it. In her imagination she saw herself creeping like a snake along the ground . . . inch by inch down past the garage . . . McMullens's cottage. Past the almond trees and the grape vines and the fowls' roost. Under the wires of the horse paddock . . . into the bush. Into the dear and blessed camouflage of the bush.

But how did she know he mightn't be waiting just there for her? He had said he'd hidden in the orchard. But he wouldn't hide in the same place twice, surely? This time it would be the bush, just as the bush would have been Denney's own cover.

On each of the three other aspects of the farm there was too much open space to cover. There was a bright moon. Denney had seen it when she had pulled down the blind for Jack Smith. A bright white moon that turned the stubble of the oat paddock into silver and made the orchard trees cast long, thin, straggling delicate shadows on a white ground.

The moon would be shining full on her back verandah and door, too. There would be no escape that way. From the front verandah . . . the way Jack Smith had come and gone . . . there would be the short cover of the oleanders and hibiscus. After that only the orchard.

Denney's courage faltered and died in the face of the shadows, the moonlight patches of open space, the still secretiveness of the silence all around her; the watchfulness of the barrel of that shotgun.

'I'm not very brave,' she thought. 'I'm not even brave enough to run away. In the morning . . . tomorrow. It will be easier to get near the bush and I can see what I'm doing. Then make a run for it . . .'

She locked all her doors and as she did so wondered if a shotgun could blast open a lock. She wasn't at all sure about that. Anyhow, even if the gun failed, he, this Jack Smith, could find at least three axes down at the workshed. What he would want three axes for, Denney thought with indignation, she couldn't imagine. One axe was enough for any door, wasn't it? Denney winced. Then suddenly she felt very sick. Her heart had been beating so fast for so long she had begun to accept it as normal. Now it made her sick.

She took a light blanket from her bedroom and lay down on the sofa in the little-used sitting-room. Why she thought she would be safer there than anywhere she could not imagine. There was nowhere but the floor to lie down on in the kitchen . . . and the bedroom had to be avoided at all costs. If he did come back . . . a bedroom would be a fateful scene of action. It had possibilities inherent in its nature that Denney couldn't bear to contemplate.

She lay on the sofa fully dressed and listened to the silence.

Every now and again the framework in the house cracked as the timber contracted in the cool of night after the heat of the day. Denney, who had listened to those cracks a thousand times unmoved, now started with every one.

She was alone on a lonely farm, and somewhere outside a murderer was lurking with a gun under his arm.

Denney sweated in terror as she had not once done while Jack Smith was in the house.

Then she began to think of his face as he had sat there in the chair, his back to the wall, his chin sunk on his breast. She began to think of all the things he had told her. The step-father made her gorge rise, so did the school teachers and the officers in the 'delinquent jug': the other boys who had called him a pansy, a queen, a queer.

Her heart swelled with indignation, even pity. She began to think of the things she would have done for him if he had been her son, instead of some other feather-brained woman's son.

Denney in the softness of her sorrow for Jack Smith, the pretty boy, fell asleep. Pity, light-footed and unheralded, had driven fear from her heart.

In the morning she didn't know why she was where she was —

half-slipping from the sofa in the badly aired sitting-room.

She had been hearing cocks crowing in her sleep for a long time, but had refused to wake up and listen to them. All the farm noises were stirring the warm still air of the hot summer morning.

Then she remembered.

'My God!' she said, throwing off the blanket and getting up dishevelled. 'I've overslept. I left the water on in the west orchard all night. There's everything to do . . .'

The memory of Jack Smith knocked at her mind with the threat of fear in the offing.

'I'll have to think of him later,' Denney thought desperately.

She unlocked doors in feverish haste and flew into the bathroom. She washed her face and put lipstick on in front of the little mirror in the door of the wall cupboard where she kept her cosmetics. She ran a comb through her hair.

There wasn't any time to change or have a shower. There were hungry animals outside. There were all the delicate ferns drying out in the mounting heat of the sun. There was the picking to do before the sun had blistered the bloom from the skins of apricots, peaches, tomatoes . . . Rona would be in pain from an overloaded udder, the horses restless, the fowls put off their laying . . .

Feverishly adding up all she had to do in record time, Denney raked the ashes in the stove and set a small fire going. She filled the kettle and left it to boil and then went out on to her back verandah. She ran down the steps and down the gravel path to the feed bins for Rona and the horses. The fowls' mash could heat up on the side of the stove and the fowls would have to wait.

She took a bucket and milked Rona and then let her out in the pea paddock. She took a basket and collected eggs and then had to take them to the shed to stamp them and pack them in the papier-mâché trays, one upon another, and so into the box ready for market. She had to lift down those boxes one at a time and place them in the canvas cooler below the bench.

Time was flying onwards, but she managed to pluck the tomatoes from two of the rows before running back to the kitchen for tea for herself and mash for the fowls. The fowls were making enough racket down at the gate to rouse the dead from their graves.

Denney hardly thought of Jack Smith at all. He was there, at the back of her mind, and she would deal with the thought of him presently.

For the moment she had to do all her own work and all the work usually done by both McMullens and his wife. Most of it had to be done before the sun ruined the day's harvest.

Where was he? Down in the orchard? Down in the bush?

Well, she couldn't worry. She just couldn't worry. There was too much to do. Her farm . . . her beloved farm . . . this thing she had created out of the earth herself when everyone – yes, everyone, and that included Mama and the four sisters, not to mention all her fellow journalists on the paper – had said it was impossible. They had said she was mad, irresponsible. They had said she would get sick of it and that the work would kill her. The place would go to rack and ruin.

They had given her one year . . . and then two years.

Six years had passed and Denney knew she would never leave her farm. She had made it . . . out of her two hands. She'd shown them she could do something.

They'd thought she was just a girl around town beating up the bright spots to hide the memory of that short marriage that had ended so swiftly and so surely with John's death.

They had said she didn't know how to work with her hands. Montgomerys always worked with their heads and not their hands.

They had said it was too tough a job even for a man. They had said the sun would kill her . . .

They had said everything except that she would stick to it, or make a success of it.

Denney had been going to show them, and was still showing them. That was what Jack Smith felt like when he bent bottle-tops with his thumb and forefinger. When he bit threepences and doubled them up between his strong teeth. He'd show them he could do something that would earn awe and admiration . . .

As Denney worked at double speed at the day's chores she nodded her head in understanding of Jack Smith's feelings. She knew just how he felt. She knew it as a surging through the bloodstream as anger and determination made a marriage between themselves. She knew the sense of injustice because nobody believed. No one had faith . . .

'But, after all, he did kill a woman,' said Denney to herself as she stopped still in her tracks half-way between a young apricot tree and the case in which she was packing the newly picked fruit. 'He did kill her, or why else do they want him? And what was that talk about a twin brother? Could there be a twin brother? Would it possibly be a twin brother who had done all those things he had described? And was he making tracks – red-herring tracks – to draw off the hunters?'

Denney put an apricot in her mouth and ate it unthinkingly. She shook her head.

It would be too likely an explanation. It would be too much the explanation she herself wanted.

But she would keep it in mind.

She stood still and looked around. Where was he? Was he watching? Was he sleeping?

All the birds and animals and ferns were fed and watered now.

If she left the farm now she would lose some of the fruit, but that didn't matter beside the prospect of staying alive.

If she went towards the bush . . .

She would have to do it carelessly . . . in case he was watching. She could pretend to be picking up bark. She used bark for her hanging fern pots. Sticks or bits of wood wouldn't do because there were piles of it up by the back door. He would know it was a ruse.

She could take some wire frames over to the big log by the edge of the bush and laboriously and obviously layer one with bark. She would pick up the bark . . . and layer it carefully. She would weave it in and out the wires and hold the basket up high as if looking under it. That way he would see how harmless was her occupation near the edge of the bush. She could work nearer and nearer that edge. It was better escaping this way than in the dark of night. One could see.

Then make a run for it . . .

She made no attempt to explain to herself her shifting emotions concerning Jack Smith. She acted as she thought, impulsively. When he roused her pity she felt pity to the exclusion of all other emotions. When she was indignant on his behalf, then she forgot even pity.

When she remembered he was a murderer and might murder again she became terrified and tried logically to lay her plans for escape.

Good God, she must have been mad to have sat there in the kitchen drinking tea and smoking cigarettes with him! He might have raped and shot her any moment.

As the word rape impinged itself on Denney's mind the rest of her thinking processes ran off at a tangent.

Could he rape a woman? Wasn't there something odd about him? Those boys at his school had called him a queer. Was he? Was that what made him so youthful, so soft-skinned? His hair to fall fair and curled in a stray lock over his forehead? The full mouth, and the moment of tearfulness?

What about the woman he had killed? Why had he done that? Weren't all those crimes crimes of passion? Hadn't the police, and the newspaper reporters, said that many times when she had worked on the newspaper? Hadn't she told Ben that herself, and hadn't he agreed?

Denney had some more tea and then damped out the fire in her stove. She tidied her house because, except for under beds and wardrobes, she always did this when leaving it. She couldn't bear the thought of her sisters, any one of them, arriving on an unexpected visit and saying with raised eyebrows and sorrowful tones . . . 'Denney, of course, never was anything of a housekeeper.'

Denney knew them all so well, she knew that if they came they'd be no sooner here than they would remember a hundred and one things they had to do before going home again. They would come, gulp down tea, borrow cigarettes if they hadn't brought any, or give her some if she was out of them, and say . . . .

'Well, I can't stay, my dear. I just wanted to see how you are.'

As if she wasn't always all right, and as if they weren't always, one and all of them, in a tearing hurry.

Still, they did come, and they did care about her . . . all by herself out there in the bush. And thank God, they never had time to look under beds or in the refrigerator. Not that they would, Denney reflected, even if they had time. They were really very kind. They meant well. They would have looked after her if she had been ill. Denney, thinking of them, had fleeting mental visions of them.

There was Theodora, with her school-ma'amish glasses: Vicky with her latest hair-do and a slashing new dress: Mary with her patient considered advice about legal forms . . . investments: Gerry with her hearty, almost fruity, laugh and her devastating tales of the rotten advice she was always given by her friends on the racecourse.

Denney, as she gulped down tea and made a final round of

her house, thought of them all one after the other. She had a lump in her throat as if she was saying farewell to them as well as to her house. She felt like a person going on a long, long journey to unknown places from which she might never return.

Even Denney's imagination stopped short at concluding that journey in her mind. It would have meant that she visualized herself running through the bush . . . a spate of the shotgun's pellets in her back. No, Denney could not face the prospect of being shot in the back, so she ignored the prospect of being shot at all.

She was temporarily leaving home and she had to think it all out calmly and collectedly, like an intelligent criminal on the run. The unintelligent ones always did something silly. Denney had always had a secret sympathy with the criminal on the run. She had taken a vicarious pleasure in the bravery of his privations, the skill of his elusiveness. It was all based on some psychological dream of escape from authority. Had it been the Rectory life that cabined and confined? The father with the heavy walking stick? The iron bars of the iron cot she and all her sisters had used, one after the other, in infancy?

Or was it her Irish forebears who were, as her very Irish and therefore self-diagnostic father averred, 'agin the government' on principle?

Was she no more than a congenital anti-social zany?

Denney winced.

Whatever she was, whatever the causes, her actions were compulsive, and reason could not halt them. Reason was a weak sister with a nagging voice of whom no one took any notice.

Thus Denney continued to reason in her own way.

She wouldn't lock the door as she went out, for instance. Then, if Jack Smith was watching from the orchard or the bush, he wouldn't guess her intentions. She would have to wear the old straw working hat with a hole in the left side of the crown. A piece of hair always wormed its way through that hole.

She must eat well before going and not carry anything with her. She would drink well, too. Once she was deep enough in the bush, she could double back to the neighbours on her south side. They were the brutes who starved their dog on polony and bread scraps. Well, for once they would have to put up with her and she would have to put up with them. She could look the other way every time their dog, skin and bones, came near her. She could make up for that by surreptitiously feeding the dog under the table when the time came to be given a meal herself. They wouldn't have the nerve to serve her with polony.

Of course, if the dog barked and snarled at her that was another thing altogether. She would withdraw her sympathy at once, and permanently. Denney hated snarling dogs. Cheek of them, she thought, when you come to think how they sponge on the human race.

'Of course everyone thinks I'm bird-brained. But I'm cunning too,' thought Denney as she finally went out of the kitchen door, closed it carelessly behind her and walked across the narrow wooden verandah and down the steps to the gravel square below.

It was here, row upon row, under the protection of the verandah floorboards, that Denney's ferns and pot plants stood. Drops of water now rested on their leaves and the dark earth in the pots was black with moisture.

She did very well with her pot plants about Christmas time on the market. Nevertheless, parting with one, let alone several dozen, was like parting with her heart's blood. Looking at them she felt as if she was taking farewell of them, just as a few minutes earlier she had taken farewell of the rooms in her house and the ghosts of her sisters who sometimes sat in them.

'I'll give you one more drink,' she told the pot plants. 'I might be away all day . . . and it's going to be a scorcher.' She corrected that. 'It's a scorcher already!' She went back up the verandah steps to look at the thermometer.

It read ninety-five degrees in the verandah shade. It was not quite eleven in the morning. The east wind was still moving the tree-tops in the bush beyond her house. It would be a hundred by noon.

Denney went back down the steps and along the path to the tap by the galvanized iron shed that housed the tools. She had already used this tap and, as the washer was worn, each time she used it a thin stream of water ran down the hose and spread in a wide patch over the brown gravel earth.

Denney looked at this patch of waste water and felt remorseful that she was about to add to it. The water came from her storage tank on the south side of the house and it was more precious than money. It cost more than money, time, sweat, and indignation, to pay for and cart water if the storage

56

tanks ran too low.

The reticulation plant having been at work all through the late night caused her a slight flare of temper as well as compunction.

'That Jack Smith! I'd like to make him pay for it.'

Nevertheless she turned on the tap, lifted the hose and drew it snake fashion back towards the rows of ferns and pot plants growing under the foundations of the verandah. She lovingly trickled water into each pot . . . the begonias first, then the hydrangeas, the paulus, the aspidistras, the geraniums and the fishbone ferns.

She held the hose with one hand and pushed her straw hat farther on the back of her head with the other hand. It itched against her scalp where the broken straw around the hole spiked her head. Perspiration stood in small beads like a gentle dew on her forehead. She adjusted a spray nozzle to the hose end and fixed it on an iron rod driven in the gravel. Thus a fine spray would play on the maidenhair ferns.

She would let them glory in that . . . there was a rainbow shining through the water . . . while she set about gathering her wire baskets, the necessary tools, and carrying them down to the old log whose flat top served as a work table twenty-five yards this side of the bush fringe.

She made a great rattle and to-do pulling wire frames down from the shelves in the toolshed. She carried them outside and placed them in two piles on the gravel square where anyone, particularly Jack Smith, could see them. That is, if he was looking.

She brought the tools out and laid them in a row on the gravel. There were knives for slicing and peeling zamia palms; tiny hatchets for breaking, and saws for separating, the jarrah bark; a razor knife for peeling the thin fine leathery bark of the wattles.

She put a canvas shoulder bag across one shoulder and then placed the tools in it. She stooped down and lifted one pile of wire frames and carried it, like Malays carrying their wares, on her head.

She walked across the tomato patch and the pea and bean crop towards the log and the bush fringe.

Twenty-five yards from the log her nerve failed her. Denney complained to herself that she had palpitation of the heart and water in the knees. She must remember some time to see a specialist about those palpitations. She had noticed them on other occasions, such as when someone took her into the bull paddock on Royal Show Day, for instance, and told her to hold the rod attached to the bull's nose.

If she remembered right, she got water in the knees that day too. She'd have to see another specialist about that. Robbers! Once you got into the hands of one specialist you had to run the whole gamut of the Terrace.

Denney put the wire frames down on the ground and moved her straw hat to another angle. That changed the area of spiking by broken straw on the crown of her head. Her hair was damp under the hat and damp where the little rivers of perspiration trickled down her temples.

This, she rationalized, was where she had to show she was really cunning. An intelligent criminal. She would turn round and casually walk back to that other pile of wire frames resting on the gravel outside the toolshed.

It all went to show she had no ulterior motives in migrating towards the bush. It would prove she was not running away. She was merely about the day's business. In this wish and intention to run away Denney had unconsciously identified herself as criminal.

With this lot of frames she'd get right to the log. Then she'd begin to work. There'd be no hurry about it. Line a frame with the bark lying around the log to begin with. Then move, as if hunting, nearer the trees. When she first got to the trees she could even slit some green bark from the wattle and take it back to the log and work on it a little. Thus she thought as she went back to the shed for the rest of the frames.

Then . . .

God in Heaven!

Denney's heart stood still. Then it thumped. It hurt so that she put her hand to her breast and pressed the place where it hurt.

There, in the damp earth made by the water trickling from the hose, was a footprint.

A man's footprint. The footprint of one of McMullens's boots, worn by Jack Smith. Denney knew that cross ridge of rubber studs McMullens wore on the soles of his boots.

The footprint hadn't been there when she had turned on the hose to water the ferns.

She walked across that wet patch herself with legs so stiff that it was no longer water round the knees that bothered her so much as iron bands. As she leaned forward to turn off the tap her fingers were so stiff they would hardly close on the crosspiece. Instinct made her trample out that one footprint with footprints of her own. Instinct warned her that it was wiser that Jack Smith did not know he had left that trademark and so told Denney he was indeed watching. He was here, somewhere round the shed behind the vine trellis . . . round the corner of the house . . . Behind that gun.

As Denney, bending forward, strained to turn off the tap she thought she could feel him breathing down her neck.

When she straightened up she moved her hat again. She took it off and fanned herself and stared fixedly at the tap, a frown furrowing her forehead. He might well think she was worrying about that worn washer. Her eyes watered with the hardship of looking at that tap, and she could not think coherently.

What had he been doing?

A drink of water, of course. The other tanks were padlocked. He was thirsty, and it was hot.

She had better not padlock this tap or there would indeed be murder done. Even sane people go mad with thirst. It must be at least a hundred in the sun now.

She bent down and picked up the second pile of wire frames and, carrying them on her head, went back across the garden towards the log. This time she did not give way before she got there. She went straight to the log and put the frames on its flat top. Then she recovered the first lot of frames, left twenty-five yards away, and brought them to the log too.

She went back to the log and sat on one of the lower limbs and took out her cigarettes and lit one.

'I would like a little weep,' she said. 'No, a big one. A really big one.' Oddly enough, she who could shed tears of laughter and rivers of liquid salt at the drop of a hat could not, as she sat by the log, lonely and afraid, have her little weep.

Her eyes were hard and bright and the cigarette smoke burnt them. Her heart beat sometimes fast and sometimes painfully slow. She felt Jack Smith's eyes boring into her back and sensed his long, strong, elegant fingers playing with the safety catch on that gun.

'And it's only a blasted shotgun too,' thought Denney miserably. 'Damn Ben for making me take that gun. Now look what he's done to me!'

Neither tears nor coherent thoughts would come. For the

first time in her life Denney, who talked to herself when there was no one else to talk to, was wordless. Her mind was a blank. Presently she began, automatically, to work.

For three hours Denney sat, under her old yellow straw hat, in the blazing sun and worked at lining wire frame baskets with slivers of bark that she picked up around the log. She did not go near the bush. The bush was stiff and silent in the heat. Not a stick cracked nor did a gumnut drop. No lizard stirred.

All the time she felt Jack Smith's eyes on her. She thought she could feel his breath raising the tiny hairs that grew frail and fair at the nape of her neck.

At three o'clock heat, thirst and exhaustion put a period to her self-imprisonment.

She made the double trip back to the toolshed with her finished work. The sun had dried out the wet patch on the earth under the tap and there was now only a jumble of clay gravel where her own feet had annihilated Jack Smith's track.

Denney put her frames away, the finished and the unfinished side by side; and the tools in their proper place in the rack underneath.

Fatalistic, too tired to be frightened any more, she went up the three steps on to the verandah, crossed it, then into the kitchen. If it was her destiny to be shot she could do nothing about it. Her legs wouldn't carry her far enough. The crackling of the dried-out undergrowth in the bush would have shouted her passage between the trees, and her path to escape. She had been afraid to run away.

The kitchen was as she had left it. Jack Smith might have been driven by heat and thirst to find water, but he had disdained food.

He wouldn't come too much into the open, of course. As he watched, so might he be watched. For a boy who had always been bottom in every class in every school he wasn't so very unbright. He wasn't making too many mistakes.

For the first time since the moment when Denney found that track she was thinking logically.

She couldn't escape in daylight. She knew that now. He kept vigilant watch. She was trapped by him and by her own fear.

She hung her hat on the peg behind the door leading in from the verandah and then gathered some sticks and small wood from the woodbox to light the fire again.

Her old wry, life-saving, enduring humour began to come creaking back to her rescue, like the slow return of health to a body that had been near death with a strange malady.

'Might as well have left it burning,' she said of the fire. 'All I did was give myself more work and a long wait for a cup of tea.'

When she had had her tea she sat on a chair pushed against the wall and fell asleep. Every now and again her head would loll forward and she would wake with a jerk. A minute later she was deep in a heavy, doped, merciful sleep.

She was worn out. She had had a long day yesterday and only a few hours' sleep last night, then long hours in the sun. There was no way out from this maze that was suddenly her life. There was no end in view.

So, propped on a hard chair against the kitchen wall, Denney slept through the heat of the afternoon.

She was awakened by the sound of a motor-car passing along the lower road that ran across the mouth of the track that led to her homestead.

In a flash Denney was on her feet.

She had subconsciously been waiting, hoping and fearing for that sound all day.

She went along the passage into the sitting-room where she could look through the lace curtain of the window to the track leading down to her boundary gate.

'Not Ben . . . not one of the girls . . .' she found herself saying, hoping and praying for their safety too. She thought of the storeman in Gooseberry Hill and the newsagent in Kalamunda. Sometimes they came out to the farm with goods. 'Not them either . . .' she thought. 'I don't want them killed either . . .'

What should she do if the car turned up her track? It would stop at her boundary gate. The track went no farther. Would she run down to warn that driver?

Fatal to do that. Jack Smith, if he was in shooting mood, would think she had gone down to tell of his presence. Should she let the newcomer make the distance right to the homestead . . . if he ever got past the hazards of slowing down over the cowcatcher?

Denney had once agreed with Ben when he had said that God had not made her fit to face dilemmas. That was one day when, out shooting, they had cornered a big grey kangaroo. It was a female and had thrown her joey out of her pouch. They had ridden her down in the end because she had had her great balancing tail caught in a rabbit trap. The trap thrashed about on the ground at the end of that tail.

When they cornered the grey she faced about and reared up fighting.

'My God, what do we do now?' Denney had cried. She didn't want to fight a kangaroo and she didn't want to shoot a mother whose baby joey was lying hidden somewhere back in the bush waiting to be found. She wasn't any good at shooting in such moments of stress, anyway.

'Don't shoot! Don't shoot!' she cried to Ben. Tears suddenly ran down her face. Pity for the grey . . . fear for themselves.

But Ben's .303 had spoken, before her words were fully out. The explosion of the gun and the falling crash of the big grey had covered her words.

'I will never speak to you again,' Denney said, tears and anger rendering her face defenceless and childish.

'It was the grey or us, Denney,' Ben said. 'One had to make quick decisions. Those claws would have ripped us . . . and the horses too.'

Denney spent all the rest of that afternoon going backwards and forwards over that track trying to find the joey. She hadn't slept that night or the next night for thinking of the joey waiting in the bush for the mother that would not come.

After three days she knew the joey would be dead and its suffering ended. Her own suffering ended then too. So many things died in the bush. To be dead was to be quiet . . . and out of pain. It was to be asleep.

Ben had said God hadn't built her to face dilemmas. He had also, on that occasion, called her a bird-brain for the first time, further adding that her imagination ran away with her and that women were no good in emotional situations anyway. Denney least of all.

She had not met Ben for coffee at Luigi's on the next market day, but by the following one, Friday, she had forgotten about the big grey in the excitement of having topped the market price with her turkey gobblers. She had hurried to Luigi's to tell Ben the news. In his wisdom . . . or was it kindness? . . . he had refrained from comparing the death of one grey with the imminent death of six turkey gobblers. Nor had he mentioned any lack of logic in Denney's present radiance. He had smiled.

Now, as Denney stood at her sitting-room window and stared between the fine patterns of her lace curtains, she was faced with another life or death dilemma.

The indecision did not last long, for that motor-car, down on the road running parallel with the railway line, was moving fast. It moved on past the opening into Denney's track. Its engine, which had grown louder and louder like the beating of Denney's heart, now faded away in tune with the release of her nervous tension. Presently all sound was gone. A dust cloud amongst the trees in the bush beyond her boundary fence marked its trail, wraithlike as a memory.

Had succour been at hand?

Denney did not know. All she knew as she turned away from the window was that she felt relief. How crazy could a person be? Hope had died, yet now she felt relieved.

There'd be no shooting yet awhile. The evil hour had been postponed. She, or the driver of that car, had a little longer to live.

Denney cooked a small shoulder of lamb in the oven that night. It had been in the bottom of the refrigerator. She added potatoes from the dresser cupboard and parsnips and runner beans from the crisper tray.

She had arrived back at the stage of being able to have a conversation with herself.

'He'll be hungry,' she was saying. 'Anyhow, I am. If the Spartans could comb their hair before Thermopylæ, I can at least eat a roast dinner before Philippi.' She did not remember at what period in time occurred either Thermopylæ or Philippi, or even whether she had ever known. This was an effective way of saying what she meant and it sounded learned. Denney wished she could reel things off like that when she had an audience.

When the fire had settled down to solid coals and her dinner was in the oven she went outside again to her nightly chores. Once again all thought was absorbed in the speed and detail of the work she had to do.

'Water the ferns again, water the tomatoes and the vegetable patch. Feed and milk Rona, feed the horses . . . let them out into the night paddock. My God, they've been in the inside paddock all day. What am I dreaming of? Feed the fowls, collect the eggs, pick any ripening tomatoes. Turn on the windmill, remember to turn it off when the tanks overflow. Don't look for footprints. Don't look, don't think. Just keep going. Remember to get Dodds out from Kalamunda to refill the food bins for her. Life really was hell when McMullens was away. There are enough tomatoes to make another market trip tomorrow. That is, if there's a good apricot picking in the morning. Have to get up early. Hardly ever go to market on Wednesday, only once in a blue moon, and Ben wouldn't be expecting me.'

The market!

A way out! Was it a way out?

But if he wouldn't let her go outside her boundary gate, how could she go to market? In a station wagon too?

She could offer to give him a lift. Where to?

'How crazy can I be!'

Nevertheless she packed the stamped eggs carefully in their trays and added those trays to the box in the cooler under the work bench. She graded and packed half-ripe tomatoes with the greatest of care. She went round the young apricot trees and picked what she could and made a guess at what the picking would be like in the morning. All the time she felt the open mouth of the barrel of that shotgun following her around on the pivot of Jack Smith's hand.

It was very late when she went inside. The sun had gone down and the sky was a dying grey. The bush, like all summer evenings, was very still. It was silent and waiting.

A fowl, changing its roost, fluttered down, then rose again with an irritable squark. A nut fell from a banksia on the bush fringe, the windmill clanked in its slow rhythmical movement where the vanes caught some of the movement in the upper air.

Miles away on the road that led in winding curves down the western slopes of the range to the coastal plain the sound of a car horn broke on the evening air.

Denney knew exactly where that was. The curve below Davies Crescent. There was steep bank on one side that led down to the creek and its veil of scrub, hovea bush and hakea; on the other side of the road was the breast of Gooseberry Hill, bush clad, smelling of dried eucalyptus leaves.

When they were children, the Montgomerys had spent their winter holidays in the wooden house that stood on that hill.

They had hunted wildflowers in the rocky inclines leading into the next valley. They had caught gilgies in the creek. They had waded up that creek until they came to the wire fence of the Chinaman's gardens. If the Chinaman had been working in his gardens he gave them bananas in exchange for their wildflowers.

Now that she was grown up Denney knew the Chinaman had not wanted the wildflowers. He had wanted an excuse to give five little girls their fill of bananas.

The Chinaman and his gardens were gone now. There was no sign they had ever been there. The creek had dwindled, its waters caught by dams higher up, and the bush had taken back its land.

Now, twenty years afterwards, a motor-car had blared its horn on the evening air as it swung round that curve on a bitumen road. In the days of the Montgomerys' childhood it had been gravel and sand.

Yes, something had changed in Kalamunda after all.

Denney showered and put on the same housecoat she had worn yesterday.

She put lemon juice on her hands and scrubbed them, because in her haste to pick the tomatoes and apricots she had not put on her working gloves.

She put lipstick on her mouth because she always did this. When they found her body she didn't want to look too awful. She tidied up her room. She folded up the rug she had used last night and put it neatly on the end of the sofa. She didn't want that to look too awful, either.

She went back to the kitchen and set the table for two. One at each end. She dished up her dinner, making the gravy for the roast extra rich and thick by adding a small tin of mushrooms.

She put the dinner back in the oven to keep warm and then sat down to wait.

She would like to turn on the radio, but she wanted to hear him coming. She'd get a fright if he just walked in unheralded through the door.

Besides, he had said he would whistle.

She would like to do her invoices and bring her books up to date, but she knew her brain wouldn't think for her.

She damped back the stove fire because it made the kitchen too hot, and she opened the window and the inside door.

Then once again she sat down to wait.

She smoked two cigarettes one after the other, and as she smoked she gazed across the room into the dying embers of the fire.

She thought of John, and the night he had died. He had turned over in his sleep and stopped breathing. That was all. He hadn't known there was anything wrong with his heart . . . but it had just stopped ticking. Like a clock that won't work any more.

Denney hadn't been twenty years old and she had had to wake up and find him there . . . asleep. Finally and irrevocably asleep. Never to wake.

Her mind vaulted over the agonizing years that followed.

She thought of the day when she had retraced her childhood's explorations in the bush and found again this piece of land.

She had gone to the Lands Department and learned about the imminent opening up of this land. She had gone to her favourite Member of Parliament and she had got the land at upset price.

Denney didn't worry about doing things like that. She knew . . . because of her life on the newspaper . . . just what land agents had done about land. They had bought up vast acreages at upset or near upset and held them uncut and closed down for decades . . . even generations . . . until boom times made a tiny fortune for them, or their offspring.

What was sauce for the goose was sauce for the gander as far as Denney was concerned when it came to the sitting on the doorsteps of the Great.

In plain fact it was the only time Denney had ever done that for herself. She had done it dozens of times for the friends and acquaintances with which her path through life was strewn. She never discriminated between the injured and the sharp, the lazy and the unfortunate. She believed every hard-luck story that was poured into her ears and she made inroads into the time of Members of Parliament and City Councillors with a brief for every hard-luck story that came her way.

The only time she had ever got in first with something for herself was when she had bought this land.

For a reason Denney could never define, it had meant life or death for her.

She had bought it and fenced it before she told the family. What an outcry there was then!

Denney had gone mad. She had taken leave of her senses. Of course her money, her little pittance, was as good as lost anyway. How was it the Montgomerys had had a bird-brain born in the family? Teapots steamed and teacups clattered in Pepper Tree Bay for months. Drawing-rooms reverberated to heated discussions the length of the riverfront.

'Denney Montgomery gone up in the Hills! What do you think?'

'Well, my great-grandfather came out from England when there were only two hundred people in the colony. He went into the bush where no white men had ever been before . . .'

'Yes, of course. So did my grandfather. Of course, I'm an old woman now and that was a hundred and fifty years ago.'

'Well, what's the difference? The bush is just the same and now there aren't any wild blacks and there are plenty of roads. Not to mention motor-cars and people to help *work* a farm.'

'But they had to do it then. It was necessity. You did it – or you died of starvation.'

'Perhaps it is necessity with Denney Montgomery.'

This brought puzzled brows because clearly Denney, with her large family, was not likely to starve.

Yet it had been necessity with Denney Montgomery, but she would have been the last person to define why. She had to achieve something of her own in order to reassure herself she was not indeed a bird-brain; somebody who was one stop this side of the analyst's couch.

Then Ben had come into her life. Tall, Hills-ranging Ben with his laconic way of speaking, his sun-weathered face with the hard blue eyes that rarely softened. Ben, with his quiet flattening way of pulling her up . . . 'Don't talk rot, Denney. That's your imagination running away with you again.'

Ben, like Denney, didn't like killing things. Not killing for killing's sake, anyway. The war had finished him for that kind of thing. After that he thought even animals had a right to live, unless it was a 'me or you' kind of situation.

'I found out . . . away there at the war . . . that men too are only animals, Denney,' he said in his tight-lipped way. 'Let's leave it at that. If man has a right to live, so has the other kind of animal.'

One 'roo on a day's shooting was enough for Ben and even that he didn't like very much.

'The blasted things eat out the grazing,' he said. 'The jungle law all over again. They eat the grass, and the cattle and horses can die.'

He didn't rear cattle for the beef market; only for the dairy industry. Sheep he reared for wool.

Denney realized that on account of these principles Ben's life wasn't logical, but as she believed and felt as he did she didn't argue about it.

'Sometimes one has to kill,' she said. 'But one doesn't *like* doing it. That's the point.'

Ben agreed.

'One doesn't have to do it needlessly,' he said, then closed the subject.

He shot relentlessly and accurately at black stumps, spoors of cow dung, a leaf in gentle rhythmical flight to the ground. He was a perfect marksman and had twice won the Queen's Cup.

Denney had watched him riding away to those contests, his khaki-trousered legs hanging long in the stirrup, the battered old army hat on the back of his head, his club badge pinned to the faded band.

The first time Denney had seen the men foregathering for the shooting contest she had kept a straight face and only afterwards in her sisters' drawing-rooms round the Bay had she laughed, as they laughed, tears spilling over the long veil of black lashes on the lower eyelids.

'You should have seen them! Old dingo-shooters – a year of the outback on the seat of their pants. Then the army ser-geant. My God, darlings, you ought to have seen him! Not a hair out of place. Pants pressed so they didn't look like pants any more. His boots . . . polished. A lamp-post down his back! And those kids just out of school cadet corps: their broad brims set at a rakish angle trying to bluff someone they were outback stockmen and had nothing to do with aiming at a Commission in the Reserve.

'Then there were all those wops from the Hills. Young and old, tall and short – all got up like bushrangers. And Ben . . .'

'Well, what about Ben?'

But somehow Denney couldn't laugh at Ben. Ben was very serious about this shooting business, and the look in his eye had told Denney he didn't think any of his fellow marksmen were funny.

'That's the way they like it,' he had said in his soft drawl that was more effective than a shouted command. 'That's the way they do their shooting – day to day. They don't dress up to prove they can handle a gun.'

So Denney didn't laugh any more. On the contrary, she waited for someone else to start laughing, and then she let them have a piece of *her* mind. As everyone knew, Denney could do that very effectively – when so moved.

Thinking now as she sat in her kitchen and waited for Jack Smith, murderer, to come to dinner, she forgave Ben the gun he had given her and with which Jack Smith now menaced her.

The nostalgic picture of him riding down on to the plain, his gun slung across his back, his heart intent on marksmanship, brought a lump into Denney's throat.

She knew Ben would think she was a fool now – that everything she did or did not do about Jack Smith would be wrong in his eyes, but that he would love her just the same. How grateful can the human heart be – for just a little love?

Denney thought about her sisters. Like a yacht veering in the wind her mood changed.

In a wry kind of a way she saw herself in Vicky's house . . . or maybe it was Theodora's or Mary's . . . telling them about the etiquette of eating dinner with murderers. She saw the story going down the generations . . . great-nieces and great-great-nephews turning their wondering eyes to the photograph of Denney Montgomery over the mantelshelf and saying . . .

'Once she had dinner with a murderer. And served it up to him as if he'd been a gentleman too.'

She was busy, in her imagination, busy looking down from that photograph at a table full of posterity, when she heard the whistle.

Oddly enough, considering her vapours of the day, she was utterly calm as she got up and went into the passage. She turned on the hall light and went to the front door. When she opened it he was standing there on the edge of the verandah, just as he had stood on the previous night. He was holding the gun pointed at Denney.

'Oh, put that damn thing down,' said Denney, suddenly fed up. 'Come on. I've got the dinner ready.'

She might have been speaking to a child who had irritated her to the point of outbreak.

She turned and walked back along the passage. She heard him wipe his boots . . . McMullens's boots . . . on the doormat. *That*, Denney thought, would make a good story when the time came for telling it. *And he wiped his feet on the mat . . .* He was a polite murderer.

Once again she was another of her several selves. Now she was someone quietly and cautiously holding her Irish temper in rein, entertaining a difficult person. She would have her time cut out keeping him on an even keel. (Thinking about yachts again: she must remember to find out how David, Vicky's husband, had sailed in the deep-sea race last week.)

At the kitchen door she looked back over her shoulder.

'It's a roast dinner,' she said. Then she went in and walked straight across to the stove, and bending down began to take the dishes from the oven.

When she straightened up and turned round he was standing inside the door. He was still holding the gun levelled in her direction.

'I told you to put that thing down,' she said. 'I'm not going to eat you, I'm not going to run away. And I can't fire a gun decently myself. Now stick it in the corner and let's get on with dinner.'

He moved round the edge of the door, exactly as he had done on the previous evening, and kicked the door shut with his boot. He sat on the chair against the wall behind the door and rested the gun on his knee. His eyes were watching her steadily, craftily.

Denney, from the other side of the room, returned his look. She stood, a dish of beans in one hand and the serving dish with the roast lamb on it in the other hand.

So that was what he looked like! She had nearly forgotten. The edge had somehow got blurred. He was very young. Delicate looking . . . in a way. But there were those fingers. Nothing so very delicate about them, Denney remembered. He was too small for McMullens's coat; it enfolded him. He had thin shoulders. His mouth was full and soft, like a woman's. His eyes sad. He had done something to his hair. For Heaven's sake, it was *wet*! He had plastered it down and probably combed his fingers through it. He had actually dressed and cleaned himself up to come to dinner.

The wet combed hair did something to Denney's heart. Pity was an insidious thing.

'You look nice,' she said, but did not alter her expression.

'I've been waiting for you.'

'Oh yeah?'

Those were the first words he said. They were caustic and his mouth twisted into a bitter smile. It brought Denney back to the realities of the situation. She shook her head as if thrusting aside some veil which for a moment had obscured her vision. She put the plates down on the table and turned back to the stove.

'What have you been doing all day?' she asked. 'Did you sleep?'

'I'm not telling you when and how and if I sleep. I been watching you all day. Like I said. What were you doing with those baskets? Down on that log? What they for?'

'Fern baskets,' said Denney, pouring the gravy from an old cup into a small jug. 'I grow ferns in them. And I sell them in the market.'

'You get much for that twaddle?'

'At Christmas time, yes. Bumper prices. But you've got to look after them all the year round. The plants, I mean. It takes about two seasons for a plant to grow to market size . . . and you've got to watch it. Water it . . . feed it . . . catch grubs and insects . . . keep it out of the wind. Put it in the sun on windless days in winter.'

'Christ . . . you must like work.'

'That kind of work,' said Denney.

She brought the gravy and serving dishes to the table and, still standing, she picked up the big knife and fork and began to cut the joint.

'Pull your chair up,' she said as she worked. 'We might as well eat in comfort.'

'Anyone been around?' he asked cautiously yet sharply.

'You've been watching,' said Denney. 'You know.'

He pulled his chair slowly towards the table. With care he put the gun on the table across the near right-hand corner. It was within lightning touch of his hand.

Denney knew it was there, but she took no notice.

'Are you hungry?' she asked. 'Do you want a big helping?'

'You bet. You damn well bet.'

'So am I,' said Denney.

Astonishingly enough she was hungry. Very hungry.

He had picked up his knife and fork and held them in a crude ungainly way. He held them both close near the head, the handles pointed to the outer edges of the table. He crouched over the table and began to eat like an untutored workman. Two minutes later he changed. He straightened and he let both the knife and fork slide forward in the palm of his hands so that he held them correctly. He began to eat and this manner sat easily and naturally on him, much more so, in fact, than his pretentious crudity a moment earlier.

As with his speech, it was easy to see that the second larrikin self had been cultivated. He had, at some time, deliberately sought to identify himself with the corner gangs. To measure up he had had to eat and speak and carry himself as they did. It was all an elaborate camouflage, and with Jack Smith it didn't work. His appearance was soft and nature wouldn't let him look like a tough.

After years of practice in this mode of life the gilt edge of his former better-bred self was tarnished now. Except in flashes he was neither one thing nor another. He didn't ring quite true.

Yet there was that gun on the table, and there was the woman he had killed!

God knows they were fact enough.

Denney did not eat with any delicacy. She was hungry. In some curious way he was influencing her. As his table manners improved hers declined. She held her fork badly. Between bites she put her elbows on the table. She lifted a piece of gristle from her plate with her fingers and held it in her fingers, elbows on table, while she picked it clean. She declined towards his uneasy standards as he inclined towards what should have been hers.

An alienist would have found them absorbing study.

'Well, go on,' said Denney. 'What did you do all day? You saw what I did.'

'Like I said. I watched. I went all round the back, an' the front. An' both sides. Say, you live pretty lonely up here, don't you? Don't you go crackers . . . all by yourself all day? Don't the loneliness get you down?'

'No,' said Denney, chewing coarsely, her mouth open. 'There's too much work to do. You saw. You might have come and helped.'

He grinned. In an older person it might have been sardonic. In Jack Smith the expression on his face was a pathetic farce.

Yet he wasn't altogether pathetic. There was that gun, and the dead woman. Denney nearly told him that the McMullens were usually here, but she decided against telling him that.

Watching Court cases for the newspaper, she had learned that witnesses talked too much. They gave themselves away. If only they'd keep quiet, she used to think. If only they'd play dumb. They didn't have to tell that . . .

'What you think I'm made of?' he asked, also speaking with his mouth full. 'Get so bloody interested in the horse bin I don't hear the cops come?'

'I thought they'd gone to some other district,' said Denney. Jack Smith tapped the pocket that held the transistor set.

'Yeah. I ain't at York any more now. I'm down Mundijong way. Early this morning I broke in a store there and got some more clothes. Only they didn't say what I had this time. An' I took five hundred cigarettes and some biscuits.'

'No?' said Denney indignantly. 'Mundijong is forty miles away. You couldn't have done it.'

'I done it all right,' said Jack Smith, putting food in his mouth from a laden fork. 'I done it 'cause they said so. I done everything. It all come over the air.' He laughed bitterly. 'Get those old fowls down Mundijong way squawking for their old men to come an' hold their hands 'cause Jack Smith's round the place.'

'I'm not squawking and you're round my place,' said Denney.

'Yeah,' said Jack Smith. 'Yeah. Why ain't you squawking?'

'I don't know,' said Denney thoughtfully. 'Maybe we just get on all right. Me and you. Maybe I'm a bit like you myself . . .'

'Yeah? What way?'

'I don't know,' said Denney. 'I'm not any good at riddles. Maybe I'm a bit lonely after all. Maybe I like talking to you.'

This might have been a diplomatic, even a cunning thing, to say, but oddly enough Denney believed it. It had the overtones of truth in her own mind as the words also had for Jack Smith's ears. He would have known instantly, instinctively, if she had lied. Too many people had used those words when they were lying to him before.

'What am I supposed to talk about now?' he asked.

'Your twin brother,' said Denney. 'Do you want a cigarette now, or have you got some of that packet left?'

They had finished the roast lamb, the beans and the golden roast potatoes. Denney never had dessert, because of her figure, and she hadn't made any tonight for Jack Smith. She had put bread on the table and they had each wiped the gravy from their plates with the bread in their fingers. They had polished the plates clean.

'I got one left. How many you got cached away?'

'Three packets in the dresser drawer. What about those five hundred you took at Mundijong last night?' She said this with utter seriousness. Her face as deadpan as his.

'Yeah, what about 'em? I'll ask me girl friend.' He pulled the transistor set out of his pocket and put it on the table.

'For God's sake don't turn it on,' said Denney. 'I couldn't stand it. Let's have some tea instead.'

'Don't you like the radio?'

'No. Never could. I always wanted to go and do something when something was on. It was like trying to live in two places at one time. You can have another packet of cigarettes. I'll get some at the market tomorrow.'

Denney stood up and went to the dresser drawer. She wasn't looking at Jack Smith, but she knew his right hand had dropped to the gun: that his hand was fondling, with menace, the barrel of that gun.

'What's this about the market tomorrow?' he said slowly, evenly.

Denney threw the cigarettes down the table to him and crossed the room to the stove. She took down the tea caddy from the mantelshelf and lifted the lid off the teapot which had been standing at the side of the stove.

'Monday, Wednesday, Friday,' she said. 'I take my stuff to market. How else do you think I live?'

She didn't usually go to market on Wednesdays. The prices were always lower. She didn't have to tell him this.

'Well, you ain't goin' tomorrow,' he said.

When Denney turned round and brought the teapot to the table, he had the gun resting on the table but its barrel angled up towards her. She began to pour the tea.

'All right,' she said calmly. 'If that's how you feel.'

As she put his cup and saucer in the middle of the table where he could reach it she lifted up her violet-blue eyes and looked directly, almost insolently at him. 'What are we going to do for cigarettes?'

'I been without cigarettes before.'

'Well, I haven't. We'd better go carefully tonight.'

She sat down in front of her own cup and saucer, lit a cigarette and put her elbows on the table.

'Go on about your twin brother,' she said.

'What do you want to know about my twin brother?' he

74

asked suspiciously.

'Does he look like you? Did they kick him out of one school after another the same as you?'

He lowered the gun, and letting it rest across the corner of the table he stood up and reached for the cup and saucer of tea.

'You bet,' he said. 'They did the same to him as they did to me. Only he was worse than me. He did bad things. I was always covering up for him. A fair stinker was my twin brother.'

'Was? Is he dead then?'

'No. He's alive all right.' Jack Smith looked up suddenly and stared challengingly into her eyes. 'I'm covering up for him now,' he said. He searched her eyes to see if she believed him. Denney wasn't sure that she did, but she made her eyes say she did. That's what he'd tell the police if they did catch him. But what about that scar on the chin?

She still couldn't see that scar. It must be under the bone structure. Not once had he raised his chin so that the light fell on it. The way he held it was probably what made him look weak. Or maybe he just did have a weak receding chin. Maybe there wasn't a scar on Jack Smith's chin. Maybe anything at all. Denney hoped she'd live to find out. She had become very curious about Jack Smith, *and his twin brother*.

'Go on,' said Denney, sipping her tea and taking another draw on her cigarette.

'He spent his whole life mostly in the delinquent jug. And in the can too. In and outa the can, that feller, all the time.'

'The can?'

'Gaol. You ain't so soft you ain't heard what the can is?'

'Yes, now that I come to think of it,' said Denney. 'What did he do he was always in and out of gaol? Was he really bad? Or did they just frame him? The same way they're trying to frame that Mundijong business. And the stolen car at Chittering . . .'

'He done things all right. He done plenty. He's a real bad 'un. Still I always covered for him. He's my twin brother, ain't he?'

Denney nodded. Jack Smith, in his speech, was back in the corner gangster role.

'What was the worst thing he ever did?' Denney asked. The second the question was out she felt her heartbeats racing madly. She shouldn't have asked that. That was leading him to the subject that should have been avoided at all costs. That was bringing murder . . . real murder, and not theoretical newspaper murder in a back bedroom of a seaside cottage . . . right into the room and right on to the table in front of them.

But Jack Smith was quite bland. He dragged on his cigarette and a long shaft of smoke drove through the air towards the overhead light.

'That murder the other day. That murder over there on West Coast. He done that.'

'Good God!' said Denney. 'Whatever drove him to such a thing?'

'She did. She did it herself. She'd got it coming. She let him down. She was a dirty, lying, lowdown . . .'

A stream of filth Denney had never heard on any lips described Jack Smith's opinion of Beryl Seaton. With each adjective his voice gained in intensity. He crushed the still-lighted cigarette in one hand and the other hand, clenched, beat a rhythm on the table. The knuckles of both hands were white. Jack Smith's eyes had changed colour. They were black and stone hard.

A sense of fatalism came again to Denney's rescue. She wished she hadn't asked the key question, but her heart now beat normally and her feet, crossed at the ankles under the table, did not beat a tattoo on the floor.

Suddenly Jack Smith changed the tempo of his manner. He relaxed against the chair back. He unclenched his hands and threw the broken stub of the cigarette into the saucer beside him. He took out another cigarette from the packet lying on the table and lit it. He began to talk, and as he talked his free right hand made those curious, pantomime gestures in the air. He held his cigarette in his left hand.

Even in his eloquence he was leaving that right hand free for a gun snatch.

Beryl Seaton, Jack Smith said, was a lovely girl. Oh yeah, she was lovely all right. Some dish. She was round and soft and her eyes were blue. Her hair curled round the top of her face, and she didn't have to go to any hairdresser. Her hair was like that. It just curled. She was always having a bath, was Beryl. Every morning and every night. She washed her hair every time she got in the bath and it came out all curled, when it was dry. It was like that, too bloody true, it was.

She washed her clothes all the time too. She was that clean you couldn't stop looking at her. And she smiled a lot too, and her eyes smiled. She didn't have to put any lipstick much on her mouth. Just a bit. But she could have done without it.

She was pretty. God, she was pretty. It was being so clean and her fair hair . . . all clean in the scalp . . . that made her pretty too.

She didn't smell of anything . . . only of being clean. You could only smell her and her clean clothes. Least that's what his twin brother said.

Jack Smith's twin brother hadn't got any friends. Soon as he got friends they quit. Or he quit. Or their fathers came up to the house and said if Jack Smith and his twin brother didn't keep away there'd be trouble. The magistrates in the Courts, they'd say . . . 'This Court rules those boys are to keep out of Smith's company. If they get seen in Smith's company they get the jug too. See?'

So he didn't have any friends. Jack Smith and his twin brother too.

The dames weren't any good either. They'd say 'Go home to yer Ma' when they'd finished. Sometimes if they had a rush on in business they wouldn't bother anyway. They wouldn't even start, let alone finish. If they were busy and the dough was plenty they didn't even take any money. 'Go on out an' play,' they'd say. 'We got some big fellers here we got to see.'

Then one day there was this Beryl Seaton. She was walking across the Domain . . . you know, in Sydney, where the big fig trees are, where the dames usually walk. Only she wasn't a dame. You could tell by the look of her. She was that pretty and clean and sort of fresh looking. She just didn't know the sort of people that walked round that part of Sydney.

Yes, he was in Sydney when he met Beryl! . . . So was his twin brother. They only came over here to the West recently, with Beryl Seaton. It was like this.

Jack Smith's twin brother was sitting on a seat near the big fig trees on the Domain and this pretty girl came walking along. And she sat right down on that seat beside him.

After a while she starts looking up in the trees, and when one of them figs . . . you know, little brown things they are . . . fell down near her she said . . . 'Oh!' Just like that, only pretty. Then she sort of smiled as if she'd made a bad break, and she looked at Jack Smith's brother kind of sadly because she'd made a bad break. And she pulled down her skirt over her knees, and looked sad. Her face went all rosy because she was ashamed she'd made a bad break by saying 'Oh!' like that when the fig fell down and give her a fright.

So Jack Smith's brother said . . .

'That's okay. They give me a fright when they fall down like that all sudden.'

So she smiled a bit and looked better. Then they got talking a bit about the park, and this and that. And about coming from Melbourne, and that he didn't live in Sydney but his people lived in Melbourne. And Sydney was a pretty big lonely place to live when your people were in Melbourne.

He didn't tell her he'd quit his people and changed his name and everything.

Denney interrupted the story here.

'Then Jack Smith's not your real name?' she said.

'Come off it,' he said. 'There's more Jack Smiths in Australia than anything else. I'm always meeting up with chaps and when you say "What's your name?" they say, "Jack Smith," and you say, "So's mine." '

'What's your twin brother's name?'

'His name's John Smith. That's why we get muddled. See?'

'Yes,' said Denney. She wondered if she really did see.

She needed more hot water for another cup of tea, but she didn't like to interrupt his story. He mightn't go on if he was stopped. Jack Smith saw what she wanted and he said . . .

'I'd like another cup of tea too.'

While she got up and put more boiling water in the teapot and brought it back to the table, he went on. He only pushed his cup and saucer a little way in front of him and he didn't notice, or didn't care, that Denney came down round the side of the table to get it.

She wanted to look up and see if there was a scar under his chin, but she didn't dare. He would have known what she was doing and that would have blown everything sky high.

She took his cup and filled it up with hot tea and took it back to him without looking at him. Then she went back to her own place and sat down and began to drink her own tea. They both lit cigarettes again.

Denney thought he had perhaps forgotten about the gun.

So he, Jack Smith's twin brother, told this girl Beryl about being lonely in Sydney and she said that's how she was. Only it was such a beautiful place. It was lovely to have this beautiful park for a walk.

Then he told her what kind of people sometimes walked around this park and she was shocked. At least he thought

78

she was shocked, but he wasn't sure that she didn't know what he meant. She was like that. As innocent as a daisy.

So, after a while, they took a little walk and when she said she was going home he said he'd go along too, just for the exercise. She said all right, and he could tell she didn't think anything of it. She was just that kind of a girl.

They walked all the way to her place in Kynemore. She had a little flat in a cheap kind of a place. But her flat was clean . . . just like her. She had a queer kind of a room in a way. There were little ribbon bows everywhere. She had 'em all along the bottom of the lace curtain over her window and pinned on top of her mirror. It was on the wall, that mirror. And there was a big wide divan with a big blue satin bow lying across the middle of it.

There was a little cane chair in one corner and in the chair was a doll. A big china doll with a whole lot of fair hair. This doll was dressed in net and frills and bows and things. You never saw anything like it.

But the place was clean. Just like her. Like this Beryl.

Well, they got talking, her sitting on that divan with her skirt pulled down over her knees and him sitting in a chair in another corner, opposite the doll. It was like three people being in the room all the time. The doll too.

Then, when he said he'd go, she said she'd make him some tea. So they had that.

All the time he was getting a wonderful feeling. She liked him, this girl. She even wanted him to stay. He could tell that, and he couldn't get over it because always before everyone wanted him to go. If he didn't quit they told him to quit. Or they threw him out.

He wanted to stay with this girl because she liked him. And that hadn't ever happened before. And she was that pretty and clean she could have liked anybody. But she liked Jack Smith's twin brother. See?

After tea they went for a walk again, and after that she said to come back because she was that lonely she couldn't bear to go home alone. She said that was why she had the doll. To keep her company.

So he went back and they both sat on the divan. Then she got a bit sleepy, and after a while Jack Smith's twin brother put his arm around her and she put her head on his shoulder and went to sleep.

It was just like that. That's how it happened.

Jack Smith's twin brother hadn't ever been happy before. He was darn near crazy. Didn't matter what he did or said, she smiled and said how lucky she was to have found him.

Every second day she met him and took him home and had tea. And nobody'd ever done this before. Everyone had always kicked him out, before. See? He was talking about his twin brother, of course. Well, this twin brother, he had to go at ten o'clock, she said, because of her landlady. Jack liked that. He liked her having that kind of a landlady. The other night she had to work back where she worked. She worked as a dressmaker for some place the other side of Sydney. She said it was a fashionable place and actresses and people like that lived in apartments there. And she was a dressmaker when they had to alter their clothes quickly.

One day there was some trouble.

As soon as he met Beryl this day she said . . . 'Go away quickly and don't come back. I'll meet you on that seat in the Domain on Saturday. The one where we met.'

He said . . . 'What's the trouble?'

She told him one of the girls she made dresses for had got into trouble with a man she had been engaged to and she had asked if she could come and stay a night or two with Beryl. Beryl was terribly sorry for her and said 'Yes.' But Beryl couldn't have any friends that week because this girl was hiding from this man who had been bothering her. And she'd be frightened if there was another man around. She had made Beryl promise . . .

He was terribly disappointed, because he had come to stake everything on this friendship with Beryl. He'd even got a job . . . in a box factory. And he'd bought some more clothes so he could look clean and neat like Beryl. And he had a bath every day, he couldn't come at two baths like Beryl, and he cleaned his teeth and fingernails and plastered down his hair with water instead of hair oil.

They were real lovers now and she was everything to him. He could tell he'd been the first because she didn't know anything about it. Every time they sat on that divan she made him teach her about love all over again. She was real dumb about that in some ways. But he didn't care because nobody else had cared about him making love, and anyway he liked Beryl because she liked him. Nobody else had ever liked him before. It made him feel that crazy. He couldn't believe it. And her a nice clean person too.

All that week she had that other girl staying he was nearly mad he was that lonely. Then, when Saturday came, there was Beryl sitting on a seat in the park. She told him to go home and pack his case and meet her that night to catch the Albury express. She'd got tickets and they were coming over here to the West. That night.

Well, he thought she was crazy. But she cried and said this girl she had befriended had done something wrong that Beryl hadn't known about and now the police were after her too for letting her hide in her flat. Beryl couldn't bear to live in a place any more where the police would know her. And think the worst of her. They'd come and questioned her at her place of work. And she'd had to go down to the police station and answer more questions. It nearly killed her.

She thought she'd die of the shame and disgrace and she wanted to go away. Western Australia was the farthest place she could think of.

Well, Jack Smith, and his twin brother, knew all about that feeling. It was a terrible feeling when everyone in a town is looking for you or telling you to 'move on' or stopping to ask questions about who are your friends now, and where you're working. They understood about Beryl and as she'd got the tickets and some money they said they'd come too, all right.

'Both of you?' interrupted Denney.

'Where my twin brother goes I go,' said Jack Smith.

'I see,' said Denney.

So they came here to Western Australia and Beryl had got a letter to somebody who knew about that little house over by the West Coast. It only cost as much as the flat in Sydney, so Beryl took it and she got another doll and more ribbon bows and she did it up all pretty . . . except there wasn't any furniture much in the living-room or the kitchen. And only a bit of linoleum down the passage. But the other room, the back room, was all done up with lace and bows of ribbon too. That's how Beryl liked bedrooms to be.

The bathroom had to be nice too. She wouldn't take a house if the bathroom wasn't nice. All tiles and hot water and a white bath. This woman who knew about the house and got it for Beryl had the bathroom done up for her.

Beryl got the same kind of job in Perth right away. Dressmaker in some place where dames with a lot of money stay. They have a dressmaker and a hairdresser right in the place, like a flashy hotel.

Jack and his twin brother, they got a job too. In a factory out Midland way. The only catch was, Beryl wouldn't let them live in the house too, and it was a long way to travel every second night. Specially as you had to go at ten o'clock. She hadn't any landlady now, but there was neighbours. She wouldn't have anyone say she wasn't respectable.

Well, Jack Smith's twin brother agreed and anyway he couldn't live without Beryl any more. She was everything to him. She was the only person who had ever liked him. She'd never nagged at him or gone against him. Everything he did was okay by Beryl. She always smiled when she saw him. Even if he was tired and snarled a bit himself, she didn't care. She just smiled . . . and her skin was all shiny where it was clean, and her hair was washed and curled round her head. Her clothes smelt like they were just washed and ironed.

He never snarled at her, but sometimes he snarled about his job, and the fellers in it. They went on cutting him and sneering at him the same way they did the other side.

But he stuck it out because of Beryl. Every second night he'd see her. He got to feeling he'd have to marry her to stay with her all the time. The night he didn't go to Beryl nearly drove him crazy. And it drove him crazy going at ten o'clock too.

Then last Friday the lid blew off.

When Jack Smith reached this point he stopped talking. Denney could see the muscles working in his throat.

'Look . . . don't tell me, Jack, if it upsets you too much,' she said.

All the time he had been talking about Beryl she thought she could see the kind of person Beryl was going to turn out to be. As his story had gone on she had wanted to warn him, as if he was still living that time and the end of the time had not yet come.

She had wanted to say, 'Jack, don't be a fool. You're riding for a terrible fall.'

It would be a terrible fall because Jack Smith, and his twin brother, or his twin brother – whichever it was – had never had anyone to like them before.

Denney still didn't quite believe in the twin brother. He was someone Jack Smith projected himself into as an escape, or a rationalization. Perhaps he just had a twin brother for company, the way Beryl had a doll with flaxen hair and frilly dresses for company. And Denney had a farm.

'I'll tell you,' said Jack Smith. 'You asked, so I'm goin' to tell. I'm not saying I did it. My twin brother did it. But I feel the same as him. See? When you're twins it gets that way. You feel what he feels.'

His eyes were black again and those long steel fingers on the end of frail hands and arms were working as if they would crush one another because they had nothing between them to crush.

'My twin brother got paid at the factory and there was a feller there. Black hair and those grey kind of eyes that sneer at you all the time. He said. "What you want dough for, mate? Don't that harlot out at the beach keep you?" Well, my twin brother went all dizzy, because he didn't know anyone knew about him and Beryl. And he didn't like hearing her called a harlot. Somehow he felt all sick like. It made him see red too.'

'What you mean?' he asked. This feller laughed, sneering like. "That girl," he said. "She likes the odd bods, I hear. They're queers that go out there . . ." '

Jack Smith's voice was coming in a strangled way now as he went on with his story. All the agony of that moment when the factory worker had said this, was in his voice, the agitation of his hands, the distorted face muscles.

'I didn't hit him. I couldn't. He was bigger than me . . .'

At last Jack Smith had forgotten his identity with his twin brother. Now it was he himself he was speaking of.

'It's always like that. I can't hit 'em. They do me over. They're bigger'n I am. If I hit 'em they'd kill me.

'I went out there to her house. I went out there. I walked all the way. Sometimes I ran. I couldn't wait for a bus. I couldn't think where to catch a bus once I'd started to walk by the crossroads out to the coast. I was hot and dirty. And I was that thirsty my throat cracked. But I couldn't think of anything but get there an' see her there all clean and with her skin shining, and her hair where she'd washed it all clean in the scalp. Fair hair like a baby's hair it was . . .'

Jack Smith was sobbing as he spoke. He leaned across the table, his breast pressed against it. His eyes measured to Denney's, holding them in a desperate will to find himself seen naked, pitiable but truthful in her eyes.

He began to dribble at one corner of his mouth.

'I got there. She said I stank. She said I was all dirty and I smelt of sweat. I asked her what that feller had said . . . and she said . . . she said . . . "Yes. Well, you had to find out some time. What did you think I liked you for? Because you were big and strong and handsome?" She laughed. I tell you, she laughed right in my face. And she wasn't pretty any more. She wasn't a nice clean kid any more. She was the dirtiest . . .'

His voice died and broke. He leaned across the table, panting as he talked. His hands worked together now, pressed between his chest and the table board.

'I know,' Denney said quietly. 'Don't tell me any more, Jack. I understand.'

All the pity of the years was heavy in Denney's voice. She understood, even more than Jack Smith understood himself.

One person had loved him, once, in a world of people who hated and tormented him. In that one person that love had been a perversion. She had loved him because she loathed him.

She had told him, and he had killed her.

Denney looked down with unseeing eyes at the empty tea-cup in front of her.

She had thought, in those years on the newspaper, that she had heard all the sad stories that could be told. She had heard of wickedness, vice, cruelty; of avarice, graft, the assassination of characters and of the bringing down of old grey heads in sorrow to the grave.

Jack Smith's story was the most pitiable of all, for he was the least lovable of all. For him, the day he was born, there was no hope. Those words he had said when he had come in last night: *I haven't had no one to talk to for three days. I get mad on my own. I just get plain crazy for someone to talk to.*

In Beryl he had found release from the hell of loneliness; in him Beryl had found the under-developed, specious, petty criminal who was physically odd enough to satisfy her own perversity.

And she'd told him.

He had seen red, and those long fingers that could bend a bottletop between forefinger and thumb had dug a knife into a breast that had been white and smooth and clean and sweet smelling.

Jack Smith was past telling Denney any more. He was leaning forward, his chest against the table, breathing stertorously. Denney half heard this breathing as, her eyes downcast, she looked at the glowing tip of her cigarette. A second before she had been on the bullet edge of danger, but she hadn't known it, nor ever would know it. A second before Jack Smith had nearly killed her, a hostage for all women who had despised him.

Jack Smith's eyes, suffused with a red light, had seen in front of him the taunting Beryl with the small white even teeth, like a doll's teeth. Or like the teeth of a little child.

This breathing had half strangled him, a mist had crept through his brain. His eyes turned up and a thin thread of foam flecked his lips.

Denney, looking down at her cigarette, remembered her first year as a cadet reporter on the newspaper.

They had sent her down to the Children's Court. There had been a case of a young girl.

She was fifteen, Denney remembered. She had fair curling hair and a skin like snow with roses spilt on the cheekbones. She had been very clean and neat. From her appearance she might have been acquainted with angels, yet the story of her pursuit of love shocked a case-hardened Court.

It was true that fact was not only stranger than fiction, it was worse, for few people would believe the facts of life if they were reproduced in print.

That fair pretty girl in the Court — her story had been unprintable just as the motivating facts of Jack Smith's murderous act would be unprintable.

This night, sitting here at the other end of the table from Jack Smith, Denney knew that what Jack Smith said was true. She had seen, with her own eyes, the counterpart of Beryl Seaton years ago in the Children's Court.

The beating of Jack Smith's feet on the floor suddenly brought Denney back to life.

The cigarette burnt her fingers and she dropped it in the saucer.

'My God!' she said. 'What's the matter now?'

The fact that Jack Smith was leaning forward, his chest against the table edge, prevented him from falling from his chair.

His eyes were sightless. The hand that had been holding the cigarette knocked intermittently on the table. His feet rattled against the floor. His mouth, partly open, had a foam of saliva falling over his lower lip like a lace curtain.

'My God!' said Denney again.

As she half rose in her chair, the sight came back into his eyes, his hand on the table, and his boots . . . McMullens's boots . . . under the table ceased their racketing.

He sighed, took in a deep breath and then slowly raised his hand, as if it was weighted, and wiped his mouth with his cuff.

'What is the matter?' said Denney sharply.

'Nothing,' he said. He sounded exhausted. 'Nothing. I wanta sleep. God, I wanta sleep. I wanta go to sleep.'

He looked down at the floor beside him as if searching for something. He made a convulsive effort, like a person in the last extremes of exhaustion, as he got up from the chair. It fell backwards behind him.

He reached for the gun with his right hand and took hold of it clumsily.

'Gotta have this . . .' he said thickly.

He took a few paces and then knelt down on the floor. He stayed like that, fixed as a statue. Denney too was transfixed in an awful quandary.

Then slowly, laboriously, Jack Smith completed the business of lying down. He put the gun beside him, his right hand on the barrel.

'Just gotta sleep,' he said. 'Just gotta sleep.'

It occurred to Denney that he was asleep even as he said the words. It also occurred to her that he had had some kind of a fit. She hadn't been looking when it started. But something had happened to him that he could not control.

Denney sat at the table for five minutes before she got up and walked round it to where Jack Smith lay on the floor.

It seemed now as if all her troubles were over. She only had to open that back door and run for it.

In a minute, when she was sure he was sound enough asleep, she had only to bend over him and take that gun.

He was helpless, now and for ever.

She would have to take the gun when she ran. Otherwise she, and whoever she brought as help, might have to face him barricaded up in the house defending himself with that gun, if he came out of that deep, unnatural sleep.

Of course a shotgun wouldn't be much good in the face of a good-sized police battery, Denney thought.

He might leave the house, though, and lurk somewhere in the orchard. She had no right to endanger someone else's life. One could wait until daylight to return, of course, but how would she safely get the watering and feeding done if he'd escaped outside and they didn't find him straight away?

He could pot her off . . . a bottle on a fence, as Ben would say.

No, the watering and feeding must not be endangered. She would as soon commit murder herself as leave that scorching morning sun to destroy her years of love and work.

She stood looking down at Jack Smith. His hand grasped the gun and his right forefinger was wound in the trigger bolt.

She couldn't pick up the gun and run for it now, could she? The way he held the gun meant his finger would be caught in the trigger hold. It would wake him.

Denney wasn't going to run, and she was thinking up excuses why she was not going to run.

He lay there on the floor, his eyes closed, the pulse in his neck beating remorselessly and strongly, asleep like a dead-drunk, yet she was not going to run away.

When he had slowly and laboriously laid himself down on the floor, she had involuntarily and with finality said to herself: 'He is lost, finished. *Doomed*.'

If Denney ran now, Jack Smith was a dead man. If she ran he was a man hanging by a rope round his neck.

So Denney was not going to run away. That was all there was to it. Someone else could put a noose round a man's neck. Not Denney Montgomery.

She had faced this situation so far, she had to face it to the end. She didn't know what the end would be, but it had to be as logical as it was final. She wanted to cry because she knew she was in her own trap – not Jack Smith's – but the tears wouldn't come.

She picked up the fallen chair and set it right and then sat down on it, looking at him.

He opened his eyes and looked back at her. He was not cheating, he had been asleep. In a minute he would close his eyes and go to sleep again.

She would sit here and think what to do.

'Have the telephone line put through here next week, that's for sure,' she said.

She reached for the packet of cigarettes Jack Smith had been using and extracted a cigarette and lit it and began to smoke it.

'This is where I am a bird-brain . . . a zany,' she said. 'Ben would know what to do. He wouldn't even wait. The girls would flutter and squeal and tie him up with ropes, or something. Why can't I move? Why can't I do anything?'

Boiled down, why did she feel a certain fellowship with him? Why did she feel . . . 'There, but for the grace of God, go I'?

Something had happened to her thought processes and she couldn't judge. She thought, as she sat there, that none of her sisters had ever been in a situation like this. Theoretically they would give a lot of advice. There would be a family conference about it. What Mama maddeningly called 'a round table conference' so they would all put their teeth on edge. There would be a good deal of ringing up and not so much consulting of one another as a telling of one another what ought to be done.

It happened every Christmas over who was to give the family Christmas party, what each one was to bring, and who was to be invited.

It happened when there were weddings or christenings in the family. Each one knew best and not one had ever convinced the others as to her point of view. Though, Denney had to admit, there was sometimes a ganging up between two, even three, and the fourth or fifth was then defeated by weight of numbers. Of course, Gerry always took the line of withdrawing from discussions and merely turning up to the party, or wedding, or christening . . . in this case it would be a murder . . . as if it was a duty which she performed for peace's sake only.

Gerry was the youngest Montgomery and Denney was only just beginning to discover that this line of action on Gerry's part was merely a shrewd way of getting out of any of the work as well as avoiding the nerve strain of family conclaves.

Vicky, Theodora and Mary were different. They were all weighed down with conscience and didn't avoid any family duty. They grasped the end of a telephone and dialled a family number at the drop of a hat.

'Thank God,' thought Denney, reversing her earlier opinion that in cases like this . . . a murderer lying sleeping on her kitchen floor . . . she would have the telephone connected, 'Thank God, I haven't got a telephone.'

Jack Smith opened his eyes again. By the spasmodic movement of his right hand Denney knew he was feeling for and reassuring himself about the gun.

'What you doin' there?' he said.

'Watching you sleeping,' said Denney. 'Want another cup of tea?'

He hadn't been asleep more than five or six minutes. She chose to think she hadn't run away because instinct had warned her he wasn't really asleep, or at least not deeply asleep, and she would have collected that spate of lead pellets in her back after all. Denney was quite satisfied with this rationalization.

It all went to show that a woman did have a special instinct and it should be obeyed. This excellent piece of judgment on her part would serve as a good story next time she had an audience. She could see in advance the spellbound eyes of that audience as it listened to her. *If she lived to tell the story.*

It occurred to Denney that, if she lived, she had a good chance of appearing in the light of a heroine before her friends and acquaintances.

The thought gave Denney pleasure, for so far all her sisters had been able to achieve something notable in the public eye . . . married money, or written a book, or gone to war . . . or something. It just might happen that Denney would line up with them, eventually. *Woman brave in the face of certain death.* Denney, the erstwhile reporter, felt that would make a good headline.

'Yeah, I wanta cuppa tea,' Jack Smith said, beginning to get up, slowly and laboriously.

Denney went to the stove and began to push the coals together. The second kettle, always on the hob, was not far off the boil. As soon as Denney put it over the coals it began to sing.

She emptied the teapot into a bucket under the sink and brought clean cups and saucers from the dresser. She took the used plates and cups from the table and piled them up in the sink. By this time Jack Smith was back in his seat at the end of the table and the kettle was boiling.

All the time the operations of moving plates and making tea were going on nothing was said in the kitchen.

When Denney looked up she noticed that Jack Smith's face was an unhealthy grey colour and he looked sleepy, but that otherwise he was normal. She was sure now he had had some kind of a fit. He was an epileptic perhaps. Again pity stirred deeply in her. The gun was back across the corner of the table near his right hand. Denney had the extraordinary feeling that he didn't know what had passed during the last quarter of an hour. He acted as if he had never been on the floor: had not left his seat.

'Yeah, so that's what happened,' he said dully, pulling the cup of tea towards him after Denney had poured it out. 'My twin brother killed her. He didn't mean to, but she had it comin'. He wasn't sorry . . . he told me. She done the worst dirty thing to him any cat ever done. She wouldn't ever do it to no one else now.'

'So he ran away and you're covering up for him,' said Denney, admitting by these words they were back to the twin brother theme again. She sat down in front of her own tea. How many cups of tea was this she had made for Jack Smith?

He fumbled for a cigarette from the packet which Denney had left lying on the edge of the table. His gestures were all clumsy now, as if his touch, his unconscious measurement of distances, was not sure. He felt for the things like a blind man. He kept yawning.

'Yeah, that's right. I'm covering up for him.' He spoke in a flat monotonous voice.

'You love your twin brother? Nothing's going to happen to him?'

'Nothing's going to happen to him. By God, I gotta see nothing happens to him.'

'It won't,' said Denney flatly. 'I won't let anything happen to him either. Not after those things they say about the car stolen, and being at Chittering and York. And the cigarettes stolen at Mundijong.'

He looked at her with expressionless eyes. It occurred to Denney that he was too tired to care very much. He was too tired to understand clearly what he next would do.

They were silent a long time, and when he had finished his tea he stood up, holding the gun. He put the remnants of a packet of cigarettes in his pocket.

'I guess you'd better go to market and get some cigarettes in the morning,' he said. 'I guess you'd better.'

'It's not a bad idea,' said Denney also without expression.

'I might stay here quite a while,' he said. 'We might need quite a stock. You and me.'

'Okay,' said Denney, then added, 'I'll look after you, Jack, for a while. You need looking after.'

He walked over to the door carelessly, his back turned to Denney. He opened the door slowly as if it was a weight, and nearly too much trouble.

'You got to promise one thing,' he said, turning round. 'You got to promise you don't tell no one I'm here. You got to give me God's honour on that. If they find me they might find my twin brother.'

'I promise,' said Denney, nodding her head. 'I won't tell anyone about you, Jack. And I'll never tell anyone about your twin brother.'

'You better not,' he said. A touch of the old menace came back into his voice. 'I'm tired tonight, but I won't be tired to-morrow. I'll be watching. Don't you bring no one back, 'cause I got this gun, see . . .' He paused. 'Don't you forget this gun. An' I can set fire to this crazy ol' house. It's all wood. An' that bush out there, she'd go up like a blaze of brown paper. I thought about that today, but I reckon I had to have someone to talk to. I get that crazy with no one to talk to. But don't you bring no one back. I don't want to talk to anyone but you.'

'I won't, Jack,' said Denney. 'You needn't worry. I've never broken a promise in my life. I'm not going to start now. I'll bring you back plenty of cigarettes. And the newspapers. You can keep a watch on the place for me.'

'Yeah,' he said, rubbing his right hand up and down the barrel of the gun. 'I can do that. I can keep a watch. I got this gun.'

'I go early,' said Denney. 'I have to do the feeding and some of the watering first.'

'Okay,' he said. 'You can do that. I'll let you.'

The wind that sometimes came in late in the afternoon had died down and all the time the two had been in the kitchen there had been utter stillness outside. Denney had heard that stillness through the open window, behind its blind, all the time she had been sitting there. Unconsciously one ear had been cocked for a sound to break that stillness. Unconsciously she had prayed the sound that might break that stillness would not be a whistle.

'Not Ben . . . Not Ben . . .' had been the quiet refrain in her heart. Strange that it was a whistle that would herald him, as Jack Smith too had chosen a whistle to announce his presence.

Now, as Jack Smith stood in the doorway, the east wind could be heard rising, a faint purr on the eastern skyline. One could hear it quietly travelling over the tree-tops beyond the range, up the valley to the top of the ridge and, louder now, down through the tree-tops of Denney's bush.

The windmill clanged and the vanes spun round in a new zest.

Jack Smith raised the gun with a jerk.

'What's that?'

'The windmill,' said Denney. 'I forgot to turn it off. Come on, you can help me. You can hold the hurricane lamp for me.'

She got up and went to the door leading to the back verandah. As she went she had her back to Jack Smith and his gun. She opened the door and walked out on the back verandah and lifted the lamp down from the nail where it hung on the verandah post. She went back into the kitchen for matches. He was still at the inside door, the gun up. He was swaying as if half asleep.

'Come on,' she said again, picking up the matches. 'You can hold the lamp.'

She went back to the verandah and, lifting the glass shade of the lamp, lit it. As she bent her head she saw his shadow, with the gun, thrown across the verandah floor as he came out. He slid round the corner of the door and pulled it shut behind him. He wasn't taking any chances of being seen against the lighted doorway of the kitchen. He had that much sense left in him.

Denney handed him the lamp and he took it. He followed her down the three steps to the gravel square, the lamp in one hand and the gun in the other.

'Light your own way,' said Denney 'I don't have to see, because I know the way. It's just across here.'

It was a moonless night, not quite black because of the brilliance of the stars. But dark enough. It would be another hour before the moon rose in the east.

Why didn't she run now? There were saviour shadows everywhere.

Psychologically Denney was incapable of that kind of run. In imagination she saw herself running, panting, breathless, pursued: every stick and burned gum leaf cracking out her whereabouts. Denney didn't have water in her knees now, but she knew it would be there if she ran. And it would betray her. She would fall, a hunted animal, to the ground. Besides, she was suddenly terribly sorry for him. He was a child lost in the dark, and needed her hand. She forgot everything else.

She walked calmly, her arm swinging, and shoulder thrust back, across the gravel square to the windmill.

'Hold the lantern so,' she said. 'I'll show you how I turn off the windmill. Release this lever, see? Let it slide and hold under that hook. Maybe you could do that for me some time, Jack?'

Was she mad? She'd think about that later.

She gave him an old rug, kept on the cane chair on the verandah, because that east wind could sometimes turn chilly in the night.

He took it, saying nothing, and went away, carrying his gun under his arm, into the shadows of the sheds beyond the gravel square.

Denney went inside and locked all her doors.

She washed up, clattering her dishes, defying the need to think.

She knew now, in the desolation of her fatigue and the problem of her pity for Jack Smith, that she had been playing a game of histrionics with herself. While she had entertained Jack Smith, murderer, she had seen and appraised the drama in the situation. She had seen herself a heroine. She had been reading admiration in Ben's eyes instead of that affectionate rixture of exasperation and patience. She had heard the chorus of her sisters silenced by the fact they had been out-witted, out-publicized and outdone by Denney, the not-so-good sheep of the family.

Now she knew, because the thought crossed her mind, un-invited, that she had not made a run for it when the oppor-tunity had offered because she hadn't the courage to do it.

When he had lain, only semi-conscious, on the floor . . .

Out there in the shadows of the tankstand . . .

She was not intrepid, dare-devil, fleet, resourceful; she was not a heroine. She had let pity be a substitute for courage. It was easier that way.

'Denney's the slow-witted one,' her father used to say. 'Hasn't enough nous to get herself out of the rain.'

She hadn't had enough nous to run for her life.

These sombre self-seeing thoughts prevented Denney going over in her mind Jack Smith's story of degradation, despair, and final frenzy. She began to forget the pity she had felt for him in the pity she now felt for herself.

She locked all the doors and windows as she had done on the previous evening and, still dressed in her housecoat and underclothes, she lay down on the sofa and pulled the rug up over her. She lay staring at the stars through the window of the sitting-room, waiting for those stars to fade and the grey light that heralded dawn in the bush to creep through the hills. Then she could get up and pick the apricots and the tomatoes, water and feed her birds and animals, pack her fruit cases and eggs in the back of the station wagon . . . and go to market.

If that 'turn' Jack Smith had had was really an epileptic fit he would sleep long and deep. Denney knew that much about epilepsy.

Why didn't she take a chance now?

'God only knows,' she groaned.

The sun was actually up when Denney awoke. Such a thing had never happened before on market day.

CHAPTER FOUR

Denney, that morning, did not have time to worry as to whether Jack Smith was awake and if he would let her go to market. The sunlight streaming between the trees in the orchard had been more compelling than a fire alarm.

She flung the rug away and ran to the bathroom, unlocking doors on the way.

'The damn things,' Denney said, furiously turning keys. 'What the hell did I lock the place up for?' She had had a period when she had decided swearing was degrading in women. As she needed emphasis in all moments of stress she had adopted 'damn' and 'hell' as the farthermost limits to which she would let her tongue slip. She used these expressions with a nice viciousness. Minor blasphemies had, however, crept back unnoticed into Denney's daily vocabulary, so that she often adopted both forms of swearing in a slightly incongrous marriage of which she was quite unaware.

The 'damn' and the 'hell' furiously assaulted the morning air, and the Almighty was called upon at regular intervals while Denney flew through the processes of showering, dressing, slashing on that lipstick, then racing about the business of feeding the fowls and letting them into the patch of elephant grass; feeding and milking Rona; feeding and watering the horses; turning the sprinklers on the vegetable patch and giving the tomatoes no more than a lick and a dash of water. The ferns were heavily dampened from yesterday's over-watering and Denney let them stay at that.

She remembered to padlock the tanks because she couldn't afford to have Jack Smith run amok with the storage water. If he wanted a drink he could get it from the sprinklers.

As he didn't come out of his hiding place to help her lift the cases of apricots and tomatoes into the station wagon she decided to lock up the house too.

If he was hungry he could suck raw eggs and eat green vegetables. And serve him right. There was something uncouth in a man . . . man or boy, whichever he was . . . that he let a woman lift heavy boxes and didn't come to her assistance.

'And he knows damn well I'm only going to market to get cigarettes for him!' she said furiously.

She had almost forgotten the identity hiding behind the name of 'Jack Smith' in her fury and grievance against him.

She had slept beyond sunrise. That was his fault. Now he let her lift cases unaided.

She hoped he'd starve, or die of thirst, or something.

Of course he wouldn't do any of those things with all that water pouring for hours from her sprinklers, and the tomatoes and apricots and eggs. Not to mention a chicken or two that might have its neck wrung before nightfall.

Such was her mood on this hot summer Wednesday morning. Anger had banished fear and self-pity too. Denney had a grievance and knew it. She revelled in it.

Tired, sweat-stained, her anger petering slowly away, Denney drove the station wagon down the track to the gate. She drove over the cowcatcher without once looking back.

She accelerated down the track to the open road that followed the old railway line towards Kalamunda. She swung right to cross to the lower road to stop at the Gooseberry Hill store.

Barnes, the man who ran it, was sprinkling water to flatten the dust beyond the shadeless doorstep.

'No need to go up to the house with anything,' Denney called out. 'I'll pick up stores on my way home. Leave the order on the footpath, will you?'

'Okay, Denney. You're late this morning, aren't you? You don't usually go to market Wednesday.'

'Something special today,' said Denney, letting out the clutch and moving the gear from neutral to one.

'I was gonna come up an' bring the stores. See if you're orl right. The Macs still away?'

'They'll be back next week. I'm all right. Thanks all the same.'

She moved off and waved her right arm backwards through the window.

In the rear vision mirror she could see Barnes, sprinkling the footpath and looking after her.

'No man ought to hold a hose that way,' thought Denney. 'Why doesn't someone tell them? They're always doing it.'

As she moved into top gear she added . . .

'I've just saved your life, Barnsey, only you'll never know it.'

The truth inherent in that thought suddenly sobered her.

'My God!' she thought. 'What am I doing? Am I mad?'

She could have stopped. She could have told Barnes. She could have used his telephone.

Why didn't she do any of these things?

She had raised her speed to fifty, but now she slowed down. The station wagon was reduced almost to a crawl. She would be in Kalamunda in a minute. She would pick up the mail with the newspapers. There was a police station there too.

Doubtless those horse-riding cops had moved their headquarters in rank order from Chittering, to York and then to Mundijong on the hot trail of stolen cars and broken-in stores. Not to mention the five hundred cigarettes!

She must remember to pick up some cigarettes.

At the memory of the Chittering, York and Mundijong incidents Denney's Irish jaw stiffened.

'He wasn't even there,' she said. Denney did not like injustice. Injustice made her blood boil. It made her do things like pester Members of Parliament and City Councillors. It made her write letters under nom-de-plumes to the Sunday papers.

Jack Smith might have committed a murder, but he never stole a car or broke into stores. Not in Chittering, York or Mundijong, anyway.

She was passing along the Kalamunda end of the road now, and her speed had somehow accelerated. It was with a decidedly dangerous swerve that she rounded the corner and came to a stop outside the main store.

The day's newspaper billboard was outside.

MPs TAKE ALL-NIGHT SITTING ON
BETTING BILLS

Denney sat in her stationary car and read it.

That, she thought, was all they had to do while she fought for her life in a lonely hills homestead.

She agreed with herself now that, though she had not had to fight a physical battle, it had been a psychological battle. She had defeated Smith by control and patience. She was sure it had left her half a stone lighter in weight. That was all to the good anyway.

On some other day . . . when she could bear to do it . . . she would remember and think again of those awful moments of terror. There had been that sickening end-of-the-world feeling when she had opened the front door and seen him standing on the edge of her verandah, covering her with the gun. There had been those long hours near the shelter of the bush yesterday, when she had been afraid to run for it.

She would think about it some other time. Not now. It made her just a little sick to think about it now and she had a long run down the Kalamunda Hill, across the sandplain, across the Causeway, and she couldn't afford to be sick.

There was no point, Denney thought, in dying under an overturned car when one had survived two nights and a day in the near company of Jack Smith.

Denney began now, sitting in that car looking vacantly at the newspaper billboard, to comprehend fully the fact she had escaped.

Her spirits rose in spurts and starts as if her brain would not fully take in and appraise the momentous fact that she was free and alive. Even this knowledge was still vested with the aura of unreality. The events of the past forty-eight hours had no reality surely.

She hadn't stopped at the Gooseberry Hill store and raised the alarm simply because she had been caught in a sequence of actions that had had so much pace about them since she had woken this morning that she had not been able to think properly.

Ben had said once, when they were out shooting . . . 'You don't stop and think, Denney. You pull away at that trigger as if you haven't got a mind behind your finger. You've got to use your brains if you're going to be a marksman. You've got to figure out what the game's going to do next. You've got to judge its pace . . . You've got to anticipate . . .'

What he had really meant was that Denney's actions were impulsive and spontaneous. If she thought about them afterwards it was to rationalize them.

She was going to think very carefully what she would do next. She was not going to rush into any action now that might have disastrous consequences.

There was her farm to begin with. She wasn't going to have Jack Smith set fire to it. He could very easily, if he was cornered. The east wind had not died down yet and her farm lay in a cross gully that was a funnel for a hot wind.

No one going after Jack Smith could stop a fire there before it had razed everything to the ground.

She'd padlocked the tanks.

Denney's heart dropped. What on earth had she done that for? The only water supply was from the half-inch pipes from the well that fed the sprinklers on the vegetable patch.

Police going out there to capture Jack Smith weren't likely to take the volunteer fire brigade from Kalamunda with them. And only a negligible supply of water when they got there anyway. They wouldn't know that Jack Smith had already thought up that one about burning the place down either.

Farmers in cross gullies would know the terror and anxiety of bush fire, but the police would never know it. It wasn't their job.

Only people like Ben Darcy would know that a person would rather die in a fire himself than see his place burned to the ground.

Once, on her newspaper rounds, Denney had had to go to the scene of a house that had been on fire.

Most of the furniture had been piled in heaps on the outer edges of the lawns. Huge fire hoses had been run across the road and had watered down what hadn't been burnt of the house. It was a smoking, sizzling ruin.

The owner, a middle-aged man, had been standing in a group of friends, silent, watching.

'Anyone injured?' Denney had asked, nicely professional with her notebook out and her pencil poised.

One of the men in the group had turned round.

'No,' he replied. 'Everyone got out, including the cat.'

This was pleasant news and Denney, always soft-hearted, had had a feeling of shared relief.

'I suppose he's insured?' she had asked, nodding her head

in the direction of the silent owner.

'Oh yes, I think that's okay. Still, nobody likes to see his home burn down.'

'Of course not,' said Denney, but still feeling there wasn't much of a human interest angle to this story as far as the newspaper was concerned. All the same, newspaper or no newspaper, she was pleased for the owner's sake that no harm had been done. No one was killed or injured. Even the cat was safe. There were possibilities of a headline in that.

She had gone away in search of other news and in the morning had not been surprised that the newspaper had given only an inch notice on a back page to the matter of the burnt house.

Years afterwards, when Denney had faced her first fire-hazard summer in her newly cleared, newly planted acres she remembered that silent man, his implacable back when she had announced the Press. Half a lifetime of love for cherished things had died in anguish on that hose-strewn lawn that night. She hadn't known. She hadn't even guessed.

After a mere three years she would have put that young orchard, those rows of beans and summer lettuces, her two horses and the fowl run, before her own life. They were her life. They were more than her life, they were the evidences of her immortal soul. They were rarer and more treasured than life. They were her dreams.

Ben knew all about that.

Once bushfire had run through his gully of the Hills. Again and again he had run through blazing falling trees to free his horses, drive out his cows and his sheep, release the penned birds. With shovel and beating branches he had fought fire off his fences, his outhouses, his stables.

Ben, slow moving, slow talking, had been a whipcord of speed and strength that day . . . and not once had he paused to calculate personal danger. He had to save his property, his livestock. That was all.

All these thoughts and memories flashed in a minute through Denney's mind as she sat in her station wagon outside the main store in Kalamunda.

She had to sit here and think calmly and clearly now.

Was there any likelihood of Jack Smith doing a thing like that today? He had threatened it last night.

He had decided against it, because he was lonely. He had to have someone to talk to. He had to have Denney.

No, Denney thought. He would wait. He would wait till she came home with cigarettes, and they could talk.

But if someone came? If he saw the police?

Evening would be a better time to capture Jack Smith, Denney thought. The wind had always dropped then. A fire could easily be controlled.

She certainly wasn't going to risk someone like the store-keeper and the local policeman going out there. To begin with they stood a good chance of being shot by Jack Smith from ambush.

Denney wouldn't do that to anyone. Not even the local policeman.

No. She had to play this hand very carefully.

Denney got out of her car and crossed the road and the footpath and went into the store. Annie Sheedy, the young assistant, was the only person in the shop. She looked up and smiled when Denney came in.

'Hallo,' she said. 'We were wondering about you. Out there on your own . . . You know about the police through here the day before yesterday?'

Denney nodded.

'I know,' she said. 'Have you got my papers for me?'

'Yes, and the mail,' said Annie Sheedy, diving under the counter and bringing out a roll of newspapers. 'Yesterday's and today's,' she said. 'Evening paper too. The mail's inside 'em.'

'Thank you,' said Denney, taking the parcel. 'Thank you very much.' She stood hesitant, her eyes large and a very dark blue this morning, looking intently yet with diffidence at Annie Sheedy. 'Mr Ross not in?'

Mr Ross was the proprietor of the store and Annie Sheedy said he was not in. He wouldn't be in until after midday. He'd taken the mail and stores to the homesteads over Piesse's Gully way. Was there a message?

'No . . .' said Denney slowly. She shook her head. 'No, there isn't any message.'

She did not move and Annie Sheedy, a slight twenty-year-old girl with straight yellow hair and a freckled skin, looked at her, puzzled.

Denney took in a breath, then turned abruptly away. She was half-way to the door when she turned round again.

'Oh, I forgot,' she said hastily. 'I want some cigarettes. A carton of Specials. A whole carton. Have you got one?'

Annie Sheedy looked relieved, as if this matter of the carton of cigarettes was the thing that had caused that thoughtful hesitation on Denney's part a few minutes earlier. She must have been trying to remember what it was she wanted to buy. Denney was like that. Annie Sheedy wouldn't like to say how many times Denney had been half-way to Gooseberry Hill when she had come posting back, swinging that station wagon of hers round the curve at a dangerous pace, and herself dashing across the road regardless of any other traffic, because she had forgotten something.

'My head will never save my tyres,' Denney had said more than once. Mr Ross, the proprietor, agreed. 'Your tyres or your life either, if you come round that corner like that, Denney,' Mr Ross, elderly, stout and bespectacled, had said more than once.

Mr Ross drove a nineteen-thirty-six jalopy at a sedate pace around the Hills district on his business. He drove it with dignity and his movement over the gravel roads and dirt tracks to the orchard homesteads was a progress, not a journey.

'Won't ever do it again,' Denney would say. 'Cross my heart.'

But she did, and she still gave the same answer to the same warning.

'Is that the lot this time?' said Annie Sheedy, handing the carton of cigarettes over the counter. 'If there's anything else . . . a real order . . . Mr Ross 'ud take it out for you.'

'Oh no,' said Denney quickly. 'Don't let him do that. I mean, nothing would be worth that, would it? Unless it's the monthly order.' She floundered a little as she recovered. She was sometimes amused and sometimes a little tired of Mr Ross's admonitions, but she didn't want to see him shot down by Jack Smith inside her own boundary fence.

'I'll call in tonight if I want anything,' she added, turning away. 'I've got to fly. I'm awfully late . . .'

'Mind your speed down that hill, Denney,' said Annie Sheedy, leaning over the counter to be sure her warning was heard.

'I will,' said Denney, as she always said it.

Annie Sheedy shook her head as she heard Denney slam her car door and rev up the engine.

'She'll come to a sudden end one day, that girl will. That's for sure,' thought Annie Sheedy. And she wasn't thinking of Jack Smith and his gun, because she didn't know anything about them. She was thinking of the curve round the breast of

Gooseberry Hill, where the road was now bitumen but which had once been a gravel track, and where Denney and her four sisters had picked orchids and leschenaultia by the creek that ran under a wooden culvert and over white polished stones between wild goose bushes, ti tree and swamp gum down into the rocky gully below. That was twenty years ago, and Annie Sheedy was only just being born.

Denney did not speed as she went down the long curving steep hill on the bitumen road this morning.

She was trying to think.

She wished the thought of bushfire hadn't crossed her mind. If she hadn't thought of it she wouldn't be worrying about it. At the bottom of Davies Crescent she nearly made a U-turn up the Hill and went home by the crescent instead of the long way round through Kalamunda.

She wanted to have a look at her farm. She needn't go right to it. From the lower road near Barnes's store she would see if smoke was curling up from the bushlands beyond the old railway line.

Even as she thought of it she banished the idea. She couldn't sit there at Barnes's store all day . . . just *looking*.

When she did go back she would have to have a reason for going back. He wouldn't be expecting her until sundown. No reason *she could think of* would sound right to a man on the run for his life. He would be a fool if he wasn't suspicious. Even Denney could see that.

She continued on her way slowly, for Denney was oddly and incomprehensibly reluctant to arrive at her destination, the markets, now. Once there she would have to make a decision. Her feet on the brake and accelerator were acting for her. They were involuntarily postponing arrival. She drove slowly.

She tried to banish the bushfire anxiety from her mind as she drove. She finally succeeded in doing so by thinking of Jack Smith's story.

In her imagination she could see all those incidents in Sydney that led up to Jack Smith's attachment to Beryl Seaton. Lonely, spurned, sickening of a persecution complex, he had met with someone who was pretty, charming, innocent . . . and, my God! she'd liked him. Later she had loved him. At least that was what Jack Smith had thought. No one else had ever liked Jack Smith before.

How did anyone as tough as Jack Smith come to believe Beryl Seaton? He must be tough after a life in the 'delinquent jug' and the 'can'.

He didn't look tough. He looked a boy. They said he was twenty-three. Denney would have guessed sixteen or seventeen. What was wrong with him, anyway? Why did he look the way he looked? Like a mother's darling, only in the wrong clothes? And those curious agate hard eyes. Very old eyes in a very young face.

My God, he'd looked pathetic in that coat, and those boots of McMullens's! He had looked like a thin, wanted, pale-faced child with a lock of hair that wouldn't stay in place.

With a sudden spasm of pity Denney remembered how he had wet and plastered down his hair before he had come to dinner last night. She forgot, temporarily, he had come with a loaded gun. She remembered the stupid doting mother and the stepfather with a stick in his voice, but she forgot the fingers that could bend a bottletop and the teeth that could bend a threepence.

'He's had a rotten deal all his life,' thought Denney as she ran her car under the subway and into the main stream of traffic turning into the Metropolitan Markets. She had crossed the sandplain and the river without knowing it.

Wednesday wasn't such a busy market day and in any event it was late. Ten-thirty by the clock on Denney's dashboard.

She swung her station wagon alongside the kerb inside the market driveway and from force of habit looked around for one of her Galahads. She sat, both hands on the steering wheel, peering through the windscreen.

She was there less than five minutes when Toni Manigani swung himself down from the top of several crates of vegetables and came to her aid. He had seen the bonnet end of her car and knew she was there. He pretended not to know that she was waiting for someone to help her.

Denney couldn't remember Toni's other name. Two years ago Denney and Toni, sitting together on top of bags of beans, had watched their stuff being auctioned for the price it cost to cart it across the alleyway to the Treaty stores.

Toni had had tears in his eyes and Denney had been using the kind of language that did not include 'damn' and 'hell'. She had not used it aloud. Even in such moments of her distress Denney did not use strong language in front of men, let alone the Market Galahads. Denney liked to keep up the illusion that she was a cut above that sort of thing. She liked to believe that the Tonis and the Benitos and the Alphonsos of the Metropolitan Market thought she was a 'lady'.

To that end she always wore the kind of clothes and the kind of make-up that did not go with unloading station wagons of heavy fruit cases and bags of beans.

That day of shared sorrow had bound Denney and Toni together as friends. When she had learned he had a sick wife she had visited the sick wife . . . an Italian woman who had lived in the community for twenty years and could not speak a word of English. A little black-haired girl with blackcurrant eyes and gold rings in her ears had been in bed suffering from earache. Denney had packed her up, taken her to the doctor, got the ear drop prescription, and when she returned the child to her home had administered the ear drops herself.

This simple solution of the problem of a child in pain seemed, on the surface, to be quite miraculous to Toni and his wife. They had had tears in their eyes when they had thanked Denney for her kindness. Toni's wife, having no English, had thanked her by giving her a bunch of arum lilies. Denney did not say that arum lilies might be dead right for St Margaret's, Westminster, but in Australia they were a noxious weed. She took the gesture for the meaning that lay behind it and ever after she and Toni were the best of friends in the market : even though she couldn't remember his Italian surname.

This was not the first time Toni had come to her aid.

'You wanta unload, Miss Denney?' he said, smiling with his black eyes in a way that moved his face to kindness and tenderness. Denney had often noticed, in the market, how frightening black eyes could be in anger but how lovely they were when they were kind. She always kept on the kind side of black-eyed people.

'Oh, Toni!' said Denney, getting out of the car. 'Yes, please. Will you be a darling? Look, there's hardly anything and you might as well take it over to Ellison's. It's not worth auction-ing today. I only brought the stuff down because I had to come to town.'

'Okay,' said Toni cheerfully. 'What'll I do with this car, Miss Denney? You gonna take it away? You wanta ta leave it here?'

'Would you run it over the road for me, Toni? There's room to park there today. Toni, how's your wife?'

'She's pretty gooda today. She's all ri'.'

'And Mary? She got all her second teeth yet?'

Toni laughed, showing his own beautiful even white teeth.

'She gotta mouth fulla teeth,' he said. 'You oughta see, Miss Denney. You come out one day. My wife she'll cook da ravioli, da spaghetti . . . You know how . . .'

'I'll be there,' said Denney with enthusiasm. 'Thank you so much, Toni . . .'

Cars and trucks were rolling past them and as they talked Denney had to keep pressing herself against the bodywork of her own car so as not to be mowed down by the traffic. Toni eased himself through a half-open door into the driver's seat.

'I'll be seeing you, Toni . . .' Denney said, putting her head inside the window to speak to him. She withdrew it to turn away, then she remembered something. 'Toni, if you see Ben, tell him I won't be at Luigi's this morning, will you? I've got business. On second thoughts, Toni, don't tell him I'm here at all, will you? He won't be expecting me on Wednesday.'

'All right, Miss Denney. Only he might seea da car over there . . .'

'Then hide it behind some other cars, like a darling. What the cat doesn't see the mouse doesn't care . . .'

Toni laughed, his dark eyes kind and full of jet lights, his white teeth flashing.

'You are a one, Miss Denney. I thinka you gotta 'nother boy friend.'

'Lots,' said Denney airily. She waved her hand and went off down the market alleyway, her shoulders back and her right arm swinging.

Denney walked as if she owned all the Metropolitan Market, and when that right arm wasn't swinging it was raised in a gesture of greeting. Denney, like Mr Ross of the Kalamunda store in his jalopy, made a progress when she moved from one point of distance to another.

She did not use unladylike language in the presence of the Market Galahads, but 'Hiya!' with that right hand lifted in a gay salute was not only habitual, it was right and proper for the market, just as some years ago it had been right and proper for the Terrace when she had worked on a newspaper.

Denney was very alive to the fact one had differing personalities for different places. She wouldn't have dreamed of saying 'Hiya!' as she met the older generation of Montgomery friends in Pepper Tree Bay. In these latter cases she courteously offered 'Good morning' or 'Good afternoon.' She always agreed with opinions in the Bay on the state of the Nation, abhorred left-wingers, deplored modern methods and was horrified when young matrons went about their shopping these days without hats and gloves.

Except in the blazing heat of summer, there on her farm, Denney did not wear a hat or gloves, but if she was going a-visiting in Pepper Tree Bay down on the plain she put them in the back of her car ready. If she was hatless and gloveless and saw one of the Old Brigade – the 'Establishment' as Theodora called it – swimming up in the distance, she dodged into a shop or across the road and was happily convinced she had not been seen. She was unaware, all her life, that that tall slender figure, with the unmistakable walk . . . shoulders back and right arm swinging . . . would have proclaimed a Montgomery even at the ends of the earth.

Denney now walked through the alleyways of the Metropolitan Market quickly and gaily as she always did. The business of making that progress, seeing everyone and greeting everyone, was all-absorbing, and as her mind could deal with only one thing at a time, the business of Jack Smith and the things she was about to do, or not to do, were banished.

She had gathered a certain momentum as she went through the market and emerged into Wellington Street, so that she still walked quickly, her mind preoccupied with Toni and Benito and Alphonso. It wasn't till she reached the lights at the William Street crossing that she began to slow down and, alas! think of other things.

She had to think about where she was going right now, for at William Street crossing she had to make up her mind whether she turned left over the Horseshoe Bridge and so to Roe Street and the police station, or proceeded straight on into the heart of the city.

This matter of direction was really, at the heart of it, the case of whether she delivered up Jack Smith to authority now, or after she had had a cup of tea.

She was not going to drink coffee, that was for sure. This business of having coffee at Luigi's was a mere pandering to fashion. Ever since the war more and more people had been getting up espresso coffee bars. Never before, in the economic history of Australia, had a beverage been so systematically and forcibly pressed on the population. Australians were tea drinkers and the Montgomerys were super-tea drinkers.

The espresso bars with their gleaming chromium and black frontages, their Continental furnishings and their frightful prices had put the stamp of fashion on the matter of what one drank when one dropped in off the pavements for a quiet cigarette and a thirst quencher.

Now it was the toughest proposition in the world to find a tea-room that served good, old-fashioned tea, preferably out of an earthenware pot. The espresso bars had banished the tea-rooms off the streets of Australia. If one wanted a good cup of tea these days one had to be in the 'know' about certain small premises lurking discreetly out of notice, almost like sly-grog shops, in the corners of arcades or in obscure backwaters of the shopping areas.

Denney had meant to thrash out this business of drinking coffee with Ben before. So far she had forgotten to do so. It was so much easier to say . . . 'I'll meet you at Luigi's' and, alas! so much easier to find your way there. And so elegant to be there.

This morning, however, she was going to drink tea. All she had had before leaving home had been a glass of Rona's milk and a thick doorstep of bread and butter and marmalade.

Now she was going to have tea. She needed time and tea in order to think over her next move. And to hell with coffee!

Loitering there on the corner of William Street so that she lost the lights and had to wait another round of reds and yellows, Denney was busy ferreting in her mind for a decision as to which of the one or two obscure tea-rooms she knew of she would now visit.

This was entirely a waste of time, for the tea-room Denney knew best was the one in an arcade off Beaufort Street, just opposite the openings from Roe and James Streets. Here she had repaired often in search of news in the newspaper days, for here there gathered the flotsam and jetsam that always drifted in and around the police courts. News hawks, genuine journalists, junior lawyers despatched by their legal firms to look after the smallfry cases in the police courts; detectives and Court officials themselves.

A hundred yards away was the State Library, and from there that cloistered tea-room also garnered the ubiquitous re-search worker and literary dilettante.

The Court Tea Room was, in short, an inexpensive club for those who had professional business on the north side of the Railway Bridge.

Here, without direction from her motor nerves, Denney's feet would naturally take her.

Its very proximity to the Police Court, its certainty of providing her with old acquaintances whose presence might help her in this matter of the Jack Smith dilemma, was an added magnet.

There were, of course, one or two tea-rooms in the safer areas of the city shopping area . . . that is if Denney was going to decide for Jack Smith and against the police . . . but her legs were already carrying her along William Street to the Beaufort Street Bridge.

By going thus, the long way round, past the Police Court and police station, to the Court Tea Room she was deluding herself, quite happily, that she was not going to the police station *yet*.

She was going to think it all over first.

Having arrived at this decision, and like a long-running foal scenting water, feeling the nerves of her stomach crying out for tea, Denney's walk once again gained momentum and she went forward, her shoulders back and her arm swinging, her eyes snapping with purposefulness.

To get there, and drink tea, that was the thing! After that, she would decide.

For the first time in her life Denney was not making decisions impulsively. She was, she thought with pride, acting with caution. If she was aware of anything, other than the necessity for tea, it was that at this moment she held Jack Smith's life in the hollow of her hand; not to mention fire danger on her farm.

She must act wisely. Very, very wisely.

Denney crossed the railway bridge, looking down for a passing moment on what Theodora called 'Perth's toy trains'. That had been a piece of snobbery, Denney had thought, because Theodora had got big ideas after her trip abroad. Denney had never been abroad and for that she was thankful if it left her to admire everything about Australia without making invidious comparisons. For the life of her Denney couldn't see how there could be that much difference between a three foot six gauge and a five foot gauge.

Her father had said, when he came back from Ireland, that the Swan River from the Mount was the most beautiful thing in the world. That was the only piece of real wisdom Denney had ever known her father to express, and she gave him full marks for it. In everything else he ever said or did, he was wrong. This attitude to her father, on Denney's part, had been tattooed on her soul with each recurring lash from the strap . . . or walking stick . . . whichever her hot-tempered father had been able to lay his hand on first.

Yes, Denney had very decided sympathies for Jack Smith in the matter of fathers, step or natural, who had sticks in their voice or in their hands.

The process of recollecting certain incidents in her childhood relationships with her father caused Denney to arrive at the Court Tea Room and select a small table for herself in the corner against the back wall, without realizing the passage of time or the fact she had walked past the police headquarters without noticing its existence.

She was still saying something to her father's ghost when she ordered the longed-for pot of tea with a slice of toasted currant bread.

When Denney was a child she had longed to grow up in order to be able to answer her father back. She had looked forward with impatience to his old age . . . when he would be bedridden and unable to exercise his stick or his six foot two of height. Then, *then* she would be able to tell him what she really thought of him.

He had outwitted her and died long since. This had deferred her stored recriminations until Judgment Day and, sadly, Denney hoped she wouldn't meet him even then.

Banishing the thought of her father with the first comforting taste of her tea, Denney braced back her shoulders and looked around.

The tea-room was, as yet, sparsely filled. There were two lawyers she knew by sight who had probably finished early on the ten o'clock court lists. There was a young untidy man who, even down the full length of the tea-room, smelt of newsprint and wore the special blasé air of the cub reporter.

There were two girls with brief cases by the legs of their chairs who were probably students taking a half hour off from their final swot at the State Library.

Looming shadows in the doorway warned her of the arrival of two older newspaper reporters whom she did know but, because she wanted to think, did not want to join her. She bent her head down over her teacup until she knew they had seated themselves.

She lifted her head, but they were engrossed in themselves, their nicotine-stained fingers fumbling with packets of cigarettes and their appetites turning already more to thoughts of the hair-of-the-dog than pots of tea.

Denney knew them well. They were good reporters but they were better drinkers. Journalism was a hazardous profession and the chief hazards loomed, two-storeyed and plush-lounged, on every major street corner.

Two plain-clothes policemen came in. Denney did not know them but she knew they were policemen because they were tall, handsome as all policemen in Ireland and Australia are, and yes, they had big well-shod feet. This business of policemen having big feet was not a legend. Denney had once had a bet on a well conducted eye-quiz on the subject in this very tea-room. In a three-day observation contest not one policeman coming in or passing along the street had had anything less than notably large-sized feet.

Denney looked round the tea-room. It was clean but bare. It was utilitarian and lacked ornamentation. There were no flowers and the walls were bare of pictures. The small square tables carried spotless tablecloths, but there was nothing on them. The establishment waited for patrons before they put anything on the tables, and then it was only what was ordered with the china and cutlery to carry out that order.

As her longing for tea was assuaged she began to be sorry she had come here. It got her nowhere. She wasn't thinking. For some reason she couldn't think. There were too many distractions in watching the people coming in, and guessing or knowing who they were. If she did know who they were she was too busy remembering things about them.

Though she no longer wanted to stay here she couldn't make up her mind where now to go.

Perhaps if she went to the State Library it would be quiet and she could think.

You just can't go into a State Library and sit down at a reading table and think, she told herself. You had to have a reason for going there. One good reason would be to look up that word 'zany' Ben was always using. If there was such a word in a dictionary it mightn't be a bad idea to find out just what she, Denney, really was. A zany. It didn't sound very inviting. She didn't want to be depressed by finding out what Ben really thought of her.

Denney tried to remember what was the other thing she had wanted to find out in a State Library. It had been at the back of her mind for a long time. Now what was it? Like a shopping list, it was useless if you couldn't remember it . . .

the list or what was in it.

These thoughts had, for some reason, begun to depress Denney. She looked down at the tip of her lighted cigarette and if any of her acquaintances there had looked in her direction they would have wondered what was worrying Denney.

She sat, her head inclined downwards, her thoughts bringing out sad lines that were always there yet which were continually camouflaged behind a bright and sometimes superficial smile. Denney's mobile face easily looked gay and easily was sad. The moments when Denney felt lonely, when she sensed desolation, were those moments in crowded places where she knew most people.

A long shadow loomed up across her table and a large strong hand gripped the back of the chair on the other side of the table.

Denney looked up.

'Oh!' she said. 'You!'

'Well, it is a long time,' said Detective-Inspector Riley. 'I haven't seen you down this way for a long time, Denney. Where you been? Can I sit down here?'

He sat down while he was talking. He had taken off his wide-brimmed felt hat and put it on the rungs under his chair. When he straightened up from performing this chore his face was a little flushed but he was smiling in a friendly way.

Denney's heart had jolted as if it had been she who was on the run, not Jack Smith. Also she feared she had not only looked surprised when she had seen him standing there, she had looked anxious.

She recovered herself.

'I was daydreaming,' she said.

'Yes, so I noticed. I wondered why you were so preoccupied. And so alone. If I remember right, you used to be in the thick of things here.' He nodded his head backwards indicating a group of reporters and lawyers who had just arrived and who were sitting at the one large round table in the room.

Denney had a feeling she had to think quickly and make quick replies. She mustn't let Detective-Inspector Riley catch her out. She had to remember it was the little things, the little mistakes that people made that delivered them up into the hands of the righteous. She had seen it happen lots of times when she had covered the Police Court for the newspaper.

It didn't occur to Denney that she, being an innocent person, had nothing to hide. She had all the guilt feelings of one who had committed an offence herself, merely because she had not yet made up her mind how, or when, she was going to do something about Jack Smith.

For a few moments she stared vacantly at the handsome face of the detective sitting in front of her.

He was tall, like the rest of his profession. His good looks were of the Irish-Australian type; higher cheekbones than the average, widely-spaced blue innocent eyes. He had a square forehead and a good thatch of dark brown hair. His teeth were even, strong and white and his chin square and firm. He was well dressed in a tropical weight charcoal-grey suit and his large strong hands on the table before him were very well kept.

Denney had known him for a good many years and the things she had known about him were the things she had liked but which now created this sense of anxiety in herself.

On duty he gave an impression of restful quietness. His blue eyes had never held anger or venom yet in Court she had seen him both angry and venomous. Because of these contradictory aspects of his personality she had decided he was a very good detective. He always made his victim feel he was his friend. She had seen him take a licking from the magistrate as well as from the defence, and turn away unruffled, unperturbed. She had seen him tumble the defence with deft unexpected evidence and be equally unperturbed and unruffled.

He had a terrific reputation in the police precincts for personal courage and resourcefulness. The stories of his feats in the outback of the north-west with the mounted police had become legendary.

If any other member of the police force had sat down at that table, opposite Denney, she would have been less afraid.

The fact that she was afraid now was an emotional reaction. She knew that the whole course of her actions during the last twenty-four hours was contrary to what a person like Ben would have followed and Inspector Riley would have demanded.

Ben was always right. Denney knew that as she knew that she was so often apparently wrong. She wasn't like Ben . . . like Mary, her sister; like the ordinary man in the street. Her actions were always dictated by a strong feeling for or against her fellow human beings, according to their particular relationship with her at the moment.

She could rationalize every thought, deed and word of the last forty-eight hours and would even admit they were motivated by 'feelings' and not by laws of reasonable behaviour.

Inspector Riley, like Ben, if he knew the story of these last two days, would have said . . . 'But you should have run for it when you had the chance. You should have disarmed him when he lay on the floor. You should not have promised that you would tell no one of his whereabouts. You certainly shouldn't have given him a hot roast dinner and provided him with cigarettes and the entertainment of your gullible ears. You should have had the courage of moral right and told him to give himself up. Even if you hadn't done any of the foregoing you should have telephoned information from the store at Gooseberry Hill at nine fifteen this morning. Failing that you should deliver yourself of all information now. *This very minute.*'

Denney knew all these things, yet she sat silent, looking at Detective-Inspector Riley and wondering with a touch of panic why he had come to sit there, opposite her. He had never done such a thing before.

He lit a cigarette and took no apparent notice of the fact Denney made no answer to his comment. He also looked carefully at his match and the tip of his cigarette and not at Denney's stricken eyes.

He had often looked into eyes with that expression in them, but they had been the eyes of guilty people.

'Worrying about something?' he said easily, looking up suddenly and catching her eyes and holding them.

For a second time Denney made an effort to gather her wits together.

'As I said, I was daydreaming,' said Denney. Then she added brightly, getting nearer to the self that Inspector Riley formerly knew, 'You don't snap out of a dream at the snap of a finger, you know.'

He smiled.

'Not even a bad dream?'

Denney looked indignant.

'Why should I have a bad dream?' she asked.

'Thought you might be worrying about that fellow we were hunting up your way three or four days ago. Jack Smith.'

'Oh,' said Denney. She moved her empty cup and saucer two inches away. She was trying to think what to say next.

She had a reputation for quick repartee and Inspector Riley would know it. Why had quick replies failed her now?

She grasped at a straw.

'But he's gone to Chittering Brook, hasn't he? Or is it York, or Mundijong now?'

'You've been reading the papers,' he said. He looked pointedly at the bundle of tied papers she had brought with her when she got out of her station wagon. They were too obviously unread.

'I haven't,' said Denney. 'There's always the radio, you know.' This wasn't grasping a straw, it was grabbing a tree trunk.

'I suppose you heard in the early morning news they'd picked up clues to his whereabouts?' he said.

He did not look at her but turned to give his order to the waitress.

'A pot of tea, and sandwiches. For two, please.' He turned back to Denney quickly. 'You will have another cup of tea with me, won't you?'

'Yes, thank you,' said Denney, her voice not quite under control.

'Careful', she was saying to herself. 'Don't ask him where or how. It's the little things they ask and say, that give them away. It is always the question that is a lie in itself that catches them. There probably wasn't anything on the morning news.'

'So you've found him?' she said, swallowing and then tensing all her muscles to gain control of herself. She had to be calm. She hadn't the slightest idea as to why she now identified herself with the one who had erred; why automatically it was she who was on the defensive, she who was on the run.

'Not found him, but we soon will. You heard all about it on the air?'

Denney nodded. Too late she saw she had fallen into the trap. She had committed herself to saying she had listened in to the early morning session. How on earth had she come to do that? She hadn't listened in. She need only have said that she hadn't done that. She was too busy. It was yesterday . . .

What time yesterday had Jack Smith listened in to his transistor set and learned about the Mundijong business?

She must get off the subject of the air somehow. She must pull herself together, and think clearly.

'What will you do with him when you find him?' she asked.

There was a brittle brightness in her voice.

'Try him, then hang him,' said Detective-Inspector Riley without expression. He held out his packet of cigarettes to Denney. 'Do you smoke these?'

'Yes, thank you.'

Denney put out her hand to take a cigarette and once again, too late, she knew she had fallen into the next trap. Her fingers were blue, as if they were cold, and there was a perceptible tremble of her hand as clumsily she extracted a cigarette from the proffered packet.

As she leaned forward while he put a match to her cigarette she had respite from those friendly quizzical disarming eyes.

He doesn't know I'm guilty of anything, she thought. He couldn't possibly know. I'm making a mountain out of a cup of tea.

The thought calmed her and she looked up as she drew in the smoke from her cigarette and quietly exhaled it.

'I thought the law courts stood for Justice,' she said. 'Why do you think you'll hang him, before he's even found guilty.'

'Because he committed a crime for which the penalty is death. He did it and we know it. The law courts do indeed stand for Justice. That will be their finding, and hanging will be the result.'

'How do you know he did it? It could have been someone else. Someone like him. He might have a twin brother for all you know.'

Inspector Riley's eyes snapped off all expression. His face went deadpan.

Denney's heart dropped. Had she fallen into another trap?

The waitress brought respite with the tea. Some minutes passed while she set the cups and saucers about and deliberated as to where she would put the teapot and hot water jug.

'In front of me,' Inspector Riley suggested. 'I'll pour for a change.' He paused and then said without looking up, 'Denney wants time to gather her wits, and rally the defence.'

Denney did not have the courage to ask him what he meant. She didn't want him to develop this theme. She couldn't think of a way of changing the conversation because sheer nervousness had contrived an emotional blockage in her thinking powers.

'Medium strong. How's that?' he asked, looking up. He wasn't smiling.

'Yes, thank you,' said Denney. 'No sugar.'

'What's brought you to town today?' he asked quietly. 'The market?'

Denney nodded.

'Monday, Wednesday, Friday.'

'Not always on Wednesdays,' Denney said. Her spirits rose. She was telling the truth now and was on safer ground. She had very nearly nodded as she had done when he put that question about listening in. That had committed her to a lie. Denney was not naturally a liar and she had seen at once that if you tell one lie you are committed to a dozen more to support it.

'The fruit ripens quickly in this hot weather,' she added by way of explanation.

'How many cases of fruit did you bring down this morning?' His question was friendly, yet once again it trapped Denney. She had actually brought two cases of apricots, two cases of tomatoes, and ten dozen eggs. If she exaggerated this he had the simplest of all ways of discovering. Her account slips in the market.

'Four cases,' she said. Fruit could include tomatoes for Inspector Riley's benefit. She could distinctly remember being taught in school that any part of the plant that contained seeds was the 'fruit'. That meant cucumbers and peas and beans as well as tomatoes. Botanically speaking, she was quite correct and if Inspector Riley queried her she would give him a lesson in Nature Study. The thought helped bring Denney nearer to her old, her true self.

'Don't tell me that was a long run for a small profit,' she said pertly.

He laughed.

'I don't think you'd make the petrol on those profits,' he said.

He let a silence hang on the air while he sipped his tea, and Denney did likewise.

'What other business brought you down out of the clouds on to the coastal strip?' he asked. 'Not such slim profits surely?'

Denney could have said, 'Mind your own business,' but she wouldn't do that to a friend. To a friend or an acquaintance she could have said, 'See the Bank,' or 'Go to the dentist.' She could say none of these things because she was talking to a police inspector who could check these things. He might want to check these things if he suspected her of aiding Jack Smith. But why should he suspect? Why couldn't she treat him the same way she had treated him dozens of times when she had been on the newspaper?

Was it that she did indeed have a guilt sense? Was it that she knew she should already have divulged the whereabouts of Jack Smith? In the eyes of the police every minute lost was a mile lost. He could have got away by now.

If only he would have done just that, groaned Denney to herself.

'I wanted to go to the State Library,' she said. She glanced at her watch. It was eleven forty-five. It had been nine-fifteen when she had reached the Gooseberry Hill store. Two and a half hours ago. Two and a half hours lost in a police search.

'Back to your student days?' he asked in a noncommittal way.

'Yes, we never stop learning,' said Denney a trifle sententiously. It sounded silly in her own ears.

'When you were on the newspaper rounds did you ever look up old case histories?' he asked.

'Heavens no,' said Denney. 'As if we didn't have enough "cases" as it was . . .'

'I did. I learned a lot about my business of detection from old cases,' he said.

Denney was caught in the web of her own curiosity.

'What kind of cases?' she asked.

'Murder cases.'

'Murder cases? Why murder cases? We don't have enough of them in Western Australia to matter that much, do we?'

'Don't you think they matter? Don't you think that a murderer at large, or a murderer let off is a danger to other people?'

'Well . . . I suppose so. In some cases. Snowy Rowles for instance. He killed people to get their possessions. But most murderers don't do that. They kill someone in passion. It's generally a love affair, or something. They're not killers. They don't want to kill anyone else.'

'For a newspaper woman you're very limited in your knowledge,' said Inspector Riley dryly as he poured himself another cup of tea. He looked inquiringly at Denney as he held the teapot poised over her cup. She shook her head.

'Well, I learned all I want ever to learn of crime, in those days,' said Denney defensively. 'I wish we didn't have to talk about it now.'

'A great many people feel like that unfortunately. They don't feel inclined to help the police with their investigations, for instance. They have a reluctance to touching pitch, as it were. They don't want to appear in Court. They don't want to give evidence that might help put a fellow human being behind bars. They don't want to be *involved* . . .'

Denney nodded thoughtfully.

'I suppose that would be the case with some.'

'Not with all?'

'Well, there would be those who would be uncertain. They might think they had made a mistake. It was the wrong person . . .'

'Still no harm in informing the police, you know. These things are investigated and not divulged to the Press until they are certainties. You ought to know that.'

'Some people are not able to defend themselves properly,' said Denney. 'They are stupid, or ignorant . . . or something has happened in their lives to warp them. They don't have the same chance of freedom and justice as an *intelligent* person.'

'What sort of a person would you give as an example?'

'Oh, I don't know. There are lots. I used to see them in Court.'

'But you were thinking of one particular case?'

'I can't think of one at the moment,' said Denney. 'I remember getting that impression.'

'Would it make much difference to you if you were murdered by an intelligent person, or a moron?'

'I wouldn't be there to know,' said Denney shortly.

'Exactly. That would also be the case of Jack Smith's victim.'

'She . . .' began Denney. She stopped dead. 'She was probably a not very nice person to have known someone like Jack Smith.'

Detective-Inspector Riley looked at Denney speculatively. She began to feel a hot flush stealing over her bosom and throat. In a minute it would suffuse her face.

She coughed, took out her handkerchief and dabbed at her nose. These were furtive movements which were a daily commonplace to Inspector Riley, but he gave no sign that he noticed anything about Denney except that she was a young woman having a cup of tea with him.

'Do you think anyone who knew Jack Smith . . . anyone at all . . . would be a *not* very nice person?'

Denney took this as directly personal and she hit back at once.

'Certainly not. He could meet some quite nice people, by accident of course. One could easily get caught up in having a cup of tea with him, or something. It wouldn't necessarily mean one wasn't a nice person.'

'Quite.'

He fished for another cigarette and offered Denney another. She took it and there was silence while he went through the process of lighting them.

'Tell me,' he said quietly, his voice very friendly. 'Why do you feel so defensive about Jack Smith?'

'I?' said Denney. 'Why I . . .' She had been going to say, 'Why, I don't even know him.' Yet these words she could not utter. It was a blasphemy to think of Peter near the Garden of Gethsemane who denied Someone thrice; yet somehow there was that in her relationship with Jack Smith that she could not deny him. All his life he had been spurned. He had been turned away from and denied, even by his own mother. He had been rejected by his fellow men. If there was a tragedy in Jack Smith, that was it. He had needed help and had not received it.

Insomuch as ye did it not to one of the least of these, ye did it not to me .

Denney didn't go to church *now*, but her father, for all his quick temper and mastery over a walking stick, had been a clergyman. Three services every Sunday throughout childhood had given Denney a slick and unforgettable acquaintance with the Bible. It was the unconscious source of all her apt allusions. It took no prompting to create the allusion between Christ enhungered and Jack Smith who was the least of these His brethren.

All of this was on the surface of Denney's mind. To have denied Jack Smith would have been the last pathetic treachery in a whole history of treachery.

'Why . . . I feel sorry for him,' said Denney slowly.

Having accepted Jack Smith, she was now stuck with him. Like taking poison, she had taken it, and now she had it. It was too late to reconsider.

'You are not alone, thinking that way,' said Inspector Riley.

There was a hint of sympathy in his voice. It disarmed Denney for a minute.

'A lot of people feel that way,' he said. 'Not that they know anything about Jack Smith in particular. It's a general feeling people have for the hunted. It's a perfectly natural feeling in decent, kindly, Christian people.'

'Then why did you say you would catch him, try him and hang him? Aren't you a decent, kindly, Christian person?'

'Yes. But if I were hunting for Jack Smith I would also know that he killed and he would probably kill again. I would weigh my duty to the community against my duty to feel kindly towards a malefactor. The way of duty is the hardest path to take, you know.'

'You're paid for it,' said Denney with unexpected bitterness. 'You take an oath. After that it is always your duty to carry out your oath. It lets you out of everything else . . .'

'Let's me out of what else, for instance?'

'If you met a criminal for whom you had sympathy, or pity . . . you don't have to struggle about what is the right thing to do. You have taken an oath. It binds you. You have no choice.'

'And you think ordinary citizens have the right to a choice?'

'Whether they have a right or not I don't know. But if the choice is there they have to make it . . .'

Inspector Riley tapped his cigarette ash into the ashtray.

'Come come, Denney,' he said. 'We are talking about a murderer. A man who has killed a woman. A man who, while he is at large, is a threat to the lives of other people. There would be no choice about whether one did or did not divulge his whereabouts surely?'

The bland blue eyes were covering Denney like a gun.

'I don't know,' she said lamely. She had to have an excuse to drag her own dark blue eyes away from those speciously interrogating lighter blue eyes of the Detective-Inspector.

'The law would very smartly deal with such a person,' he said softly. 'There is such a thing as being an accessory after the fact.'

'An accessory after the fact,' repeated Denney. 'What is that exactly? I seem to remember . . .'

'Someone who has aided or helped the offender after he has committed the offence. That someone has committed a felony.'

There was a long silence and again Denney tried to cover it by a cough and a sniff and the using of her handkerchief.

'And what happens to such a person . . . in the case of a

murder, for instance?' She pretended it was the cigarette smoke in her throat that had caused the uneasy waver in her voice. She coughed again.

'They hang too,' Inspector Riley said blandly.

'What? But they couldn't do that . . .'

'Couldn't they? When you have time in the State Library you should read some of those case histories, Denney. There was the case of Poulson and David for instance. Do you know about that?'

Denney, her handkerchief over her mouth, shook her head.

'David was seventeen. A minor. Got it? He shot a man while in the act of burglary. Poulson, a man of nineteen, an adult, accompanied David on the burglary. He didn't carry a gun and he was the other side of the house when David shot the man. He was the one who got hanged. David couldn't be hanged because he was a minor.'

'But they couldn't,' said Denney, 'hang this man Poulson. He didn't even do it. He probably didn't even know this other one, this David, was going to shoot a man?'

'Both their defences were that there was no intention to shoot or kill. But a gun was carried. That was enough to prove intention. Poulson knew David carried a gun, and he accompanied him. The fact that he wasn't immediately present was beside the point. He was an accessory before and after the fact. He was hanged.'

'And David got off?'

'Oh no. He went to gaol for life. He died there.'

There was a minute's silence.

'What did you say about Jack Smith . . . and . . . and an accessory after the fact?'

'Anyone who aided or abetted him after the fact of the murder is an accessory.'

'Not if they just found him? Knew where he was . . .? That wouldn't have anything to do with the *murder*.'

'Would they be able to maintain innocence in such a case? For instance, Jack Smith could have said to this person, "I'm going to kill that woman." This person could have replied, "Okay, and come back here afterwards and I'll hide you." An accessory after the fact, and due for hanging.'

'But if it wasn't true?'

'A suspect must establish innocence by evidence. On the word of a murderer? Not very easy.'

There was a long silence, then suddenly Denney recovered

herself. What was he trying to do to her? Trap her? But he couldn't know she had anything to do with Jack Smith? He couldn't possibly know. He couldn't even guess. It was her own sense of guilt that made her afraid of him. And she did have a sense of guilt.

She must get away somewhere and think. That was why she had come here. To think. She hadn't had a chance. She was confused . . .

There was no chance in Heaven of her saying . . . 'Look, I'll tell you where Jack Smith is.'

There had been too much talk of hanging. How could she live through the rest of her life if she had hanged a man? Never a day would go past when she would not say to herself . . . 'I gave Jack Smith up. I hanged him.' People would point to her as she walked down the street and say . . . 'That is the woman who gave the evidence that helped to hang Jack Smith.'

The cigarette had almost burnt itself out and now it burnt Denney's fingers. She dropped it in the ashtray.

'Look,' she said. 'I've got to get to that State Library. That's why I came here, you know. It's later than I thought.'

She started hastily to gather together her handbag, her roll of unread newspapers.

'What was it you were going to look up in the State Library, Denney?'

'Passionfruit,' said Denney. With an awe-inspiring flash of memory Denney remembered that that was the other thing, beside the word 'zany' that she had wanted to read about in the State Library. Passionfruit, it had been said, grew riotously well in the Hills district. Denney had bought two vines two years ago as an experiment. Riotous was a mild word to describe their growth and fruiting. She wanted to find out more about passionfruit, their types, their life span . . . the proper aspects for crop growth. Earlier this morning, sitting here and racking her brains, she hadn't been able to remember what it was she wanted to look up in the State Library. Now, miraculously, as quick as a genius for repartee, her memory had come to her aid.

'Passionfruit,' she repeated with relief. 'In the horticultural section. They'll get a book for me if I ask for it. If they haven't got it, they'll get it. Wonderful, isn't it? Then they'll lend it to me through the Kalamunda Library.'

She was standing up now. Inspector Riley drew in his long legs and stood up too. He had already reached for his hat under his chair. He swung it round, pivoting it, on the tips of his fingers.

'Why didn't you get the Kalamunda Library to borrow it for you, Denney? It would have saved you all the trouble.'

'I . . . Well, I just never thought of it.'

'Look up a few of those case histories while you're about it,' he said with a smile.

'Won't have time,' said Denney, shaking her head. 'Anyhow, I don't like them. Thank you so much for the tea. Next time it'll be my shout.'

She contrived her brilliant smile and went past him, walking quickly to the door, saying 'Hiya!' here and there as heads turned and a surprised look followed Denney who had been drinking tea with Detective-Inspector Riley. Riley was supposed to be out on that murder hunt. And Denney had once been in the reporting business. Was she getting a scoop? Back in her old game?

Speculation followed in Denney's train as she went through the door and out into the fierce burning heat of the hot summer's day. Her shoulders were back and her right arm was swinging, but with not quite the same bravado that was so typically Denney.

Detective-Inspector Riley thoughtfully watched her go as he paid the bill. He noticed that Denney had not remembered that the bill for her first pot of tea had not been paid and the chit still lay on the table by her plate. He now was paying for it, together with the tea he had ordered himself.

CHAPTER FIVE

Denney walked along Beaufort Street, crossed James Street and went into the precincts of the Library. It stood grey-stoned and monumental. Denney remembered that it fronted what had once, in the early days of the Colony, been the gaol. At least the section to the right of the main entrance had once been the gaol.

After the first quick thought that the early pioneers had

been better architects than Denney's own contemporaries, she remembered the rather frightful history of some of the early gaol convicts.

Denney, like a great many Australians, had come to love and even revere the memory of the early convicts. Though the transported men who had come to the Swan River Colony at a period when the transportation of convicts to New South Wales had ceased, were never treated with the callous viciousness of those on the Eastern seaboard, yet, in the sense that they deserved pity, Denney and her countrymen identified them all with one another.

Authority had proved a contemptible thing and the convicts were piteous marytrs, victims of a sustained cruelty that still made the blood of latter-day Australians curdle in anguish.

Convictism was not a scar of shame so much as a cause of burning indignation a hundred and eighty years after the events.

Denney, walking across the grass between the James Street footpath and the main door, remembered her duty to feel anguish for those long dead convicts and shame and disgrace for their keepers. Her own parents had come to Australia in the year 1899, long after the death of convictism, but Denney often proclaimed, and meant it, that she would feel prouder to have descended from a transported man than from a member of the Forces that brought them and the Regiment that guarded them.

These sentiments assailed Denney as she looked up at the fluted stone columns supporting the rounded dome of the Museum next to the Library. They brought her to a standstill with a jolt. Not even for ten minutes, this hot November morning, could she escape the reminder of police, gaols and hangings.

They had hanged convicts there behind the dignified walls of the State Library, and for crimes remotely less than that of murder.

All its stacked walls of books, its reference libraries, its proud archives, its erudite attendants could not give all the splendour that is the natural due of a State Library to that building.

Denney sat down on the stone ledge that ran along the south wall of the building. She was in the shade there. She felt cooler.

She had her bundle of newspapers and her bag in her lap

and she folded her arms over them as she leaned her head back against the wall and closed her eyes.

Maybe I look like a tramp, thought Denney. *I couldn't care less!*

She was weary in her heart as well as in her body. She had to think. That was what she had come for. She had to think. By this she meant she had to think out a course of action that was right.

If she could find someone . . . some person in power . . . who would help Jack Smith it might balance out the perfidy of delivering a man up to be hanged. He might get off on the grounds of being mad. Insane, they called it.

How could she go about finding such a person? How could she convince anyone that Jack Smith was mad?

The trouble was, he wasn't mad. He was just twisted and pathetic. She'd seen him have a fit. That might help.

What would a sensible rational person like Ben do? He would, of course, give Jack Smith up. But then Ben had not made a promise. How much would Ben have worried afterwards, if having given Jack Smith up, he had to live through those minutes when a certain clock in a certain place tolled eight in the morning?

Denney remembered a blood-curdling newspaper picture of a woman who was being carried on a litter to her hanging. That happened in Melbourne only a few years ago. They had said she was not drugged, she had merely collapsed. Her legs hadn't had it in them to carry her to her own execution.

In spite of the heat of the day, Denney shivered.

She thought of Jack Smith lying on the floor of her kitchen; a slight thin-faced boy with a lock of hair fallen across his forehead. He had been almost shrouded in the hot coat that was too big for him.

He had fallen there in some kind of a fit.

Denney as she stood over him had had one clear uncluttered emotion. It had been . . . 'There but for the grace of God go I.'

Who had arranged that Jack Smith should be born of the parents who had conceived him? Who had arranged that she . . . and all the other law-abiding people of the world . . . should have a life so free from the hate of their fellow human beings? In spite of her paternal relative and his swashbuckling walking stick Denney had had a life of love and companionship. Who had arranged that? And produced a dill of a woman and a stepfather with a stick in his voice for Jack Smith?

'I can't do it,' she said. 'I can't do it.' Her hands pressed hotly down on the handbag and parcel of newspapers in her lap. They were clenched.

Then a second afterwards, opening frightened violet-blue eyes on the traffic passing rapidly and noisily along James Street, she added . . . 'But I'll be an accessory after the fact.'

She got up. Her legs were heavy as she walked up the three stone steps into the main entrance, then up the staircase into the main library.

She stood just inside the door, blinking in its dark coolness after the brilliant light outside.

Why had she come here for help? Why did she think she would find help between these high walls and amongst those laden bookshelves.

'Can we be of assistance to you?'

A young man, tall, fair and just a little æsthetic looking, was standing beside her.

'Oh. You're the librarian?' Denney said, gathering her wits.

He smiled a trifle self-consciously. He was a very junior member of the staff, but Denney's address nevertheless pleased him. It added years to his dignity and his manner.

In the old days, Denney thought, you could go and hunt around the shelves yourself. Now, apparently, it was necessary to ask someone for what you wanted.

'I want a law book,' she said. She assumed a slightly important air herself. 'A dictionary of terms.'

The young man looked pained. He regretted ignorance. It was quite clear the young lady required *a* book and not *the* book. It was left to the librarian to know intuitively what she wanted.

'I think you might like to consult *Stroud*,' he said firmly but pleasantly. 'He is the authority on English Common Law, you know.'

Denney didn't know, but the confidence of this soft-footed, soft-voiced young man convinced her that *Stroud* was indeed the man she must consult, and at once.

They went up the wide staircase and across the small, square cool hall into the long room of the main reference library.

How lovely and peaceful and safe it was in this high-domed galleried sanctuary! Half a dozen people were sitting about consulting not one book but stacks of them.

'Fancy spending one's life reading,' Denney thought, and for a moment her old self popped up its head. She wanted to make a joke about the solemn-faced brigade behind spectacles and books at the side tables. She also wanted to make a joke about this earnest young man hastening her, decorously, down the full length of the vast room to the bookshelves at the very end. It was the kind of scene of which she could make a funny tale to regale the family when next they met. But she couldn't quite make it. The events of the last eighteen hours had dampened the spirit of that inward Denney.

Deft handed as he was deft footed, the librarian slipped a large tome from an upper shelf and placed it carefully on a ledge.

'I will bring one or two other references I have in mind in case this does not quite meet your requirements,' he said and vanished, silently, behind bookshelves at the side.

Denney opened *Stroud* with the reverence she felt she was expected to feel when handling anyone so recommended by the hushed tones of the young man.

She ran her finger down the index. There it was. Accessory, listed under the subdivision Felony. That was what Detective-Inspector Riley had said it was. A Felony.

And what exactly, wondered Denney, was a Felony. She knew broadly what a felony was, but now she wanted to know specifically. She would look that up too.

A pale slim hand slid two other tomes on to the reading ledge beside her.

'Would you care to use a table?'

Denney shook her head.

'I'll only be a few minutes. I want to look up an *Accessory After the Fact.*'

She expected the young man to look pained, surprised or even suspicious of a person looking up such a definition in Law, but he was not impressed. He had, in his day's work, to find far stranger and more salacious references for itinerant inquirer. Denney felt slightly dashed. After all, if she was an accessory after the fact, she wasn't a very nice person to be wandering loose about the Library. It was disappointing not to provoke some reaction here.

He slid silently away and Denney turned over the leaves of the book until she found her point.

ACCESSORY.

She noticed it got headlines too. As a sometime newspaper woman Denney knew just what headlines meant. This wasn't trivial. This was commanding.

Everyone is an accessory after the fact to felony who, knowing a felony to have been committed by another, receives, comforts or assists him, in order to enable him to escape from punishment; or rescues him from an arrest for felony; or having him in custody for felony, intentionally and voluntarily suffers him to escape; or opposes his apprehension.

She closed the book slowly and put it back into the gap left when the librarian had removed Stroud from his resting place between other solemn pronouncements on the principles of British Justice.

Mr Stroud, whoever he might have been, was quite clear. Very final too.

Denney knew that what Detective-Inspector Riley had said was true. She was an accessory after the fact. According to how the Judge might care to look at it, she was as guilty as Jack Smith.

She felt a little bit sick, but that didn't interfere with her swift retreat from the Library. Her mind was completely absorbed and she did not see another tall figure behind that side bookcase idly lifting down one book after another, leafing idly through the pages and returning them, also one after the other, to their resting places. The librarian, pained, might have been justified in thinking this man, this tall alert man who had failed to remove his hat in the presence of the Arts, didn't seem to have any clue as to what he was looking for in books. Until Denney left the library.

She had to go and see Mary. Mary was a lawyer. Mary would put the position clearly. She would have to be just as careful of Mary as of Detective-Inspector Riley. Mary had that kind of mind that she always knew when you were up to something. Mama said Mary could always see your convolutions convoluting . . . so you couldn't put anything over her.

There wasn't any need for Denney to walk the long distance back over the railway bridge, down Barrack Street, past the Town Hall . . . the convicts had built that too, and put the windows in in the shape of broad arrows as a gesture of architectural defiance to authority. Denney could have caught a tram or taken a taxi to Mary's office in the Terrace, but today she knew she would have an attack of claustrophobia if she got into anything closed up. Denney did, on occasions, have attacks of claustrophobia. She would walk up eight floors of a high building rather than go in an automatic lift. She didn't mind an attended lift.

There were times, in trams or cars, when she wanted air so badly that if she were not near a window she had to get out.

Today was one of those days. If Mary's office had been twice the distance from the Library, and if the midday temperature had been 110° instead of the mere 100° that it was, Denney would have walked that distance.

If her shoulders were a little slack, her walk less confident, her right hand stilled by the fact it now carried the newspapers (*Why don't I throw these damn things away?*), an on-looker might have put this slight change in Denney's usual walk down to the heat of the day. No one could, of course, ever guess the weight of the heart that was in her. Even the fact that all colour, except the blue of her eyes, had left her face might legitimately be put down to that same heat.

She passed stout sweating women laden with shopping bags, men with their hats on the backs of their heads and carrying their coats instead of wearing them, young girls on their stilted heels with wobbling behinds. Their attempt at glamour did not quite make up for the fact that their hair hung damp to their foreheads.

Even the cars, big American tourers, neat compact English sedans, light zipping Australian Holdens, seemed to have lost something of their haste in this still sultry middle hour of the day.

Denney turned west at the junction of Barrack Street and the Terrace, crossed with the lights, and somehow felt better in the wider spaced tree-lined street. At the top of the hill she could see the old red brick Barracks with their mock battlements.

A town planner from abroad had advised West Australians to remove that old historical building in order to allow a finer vista down the length of the Terrace from Parliament House. The Barracks were not architecturally beautiful, he had informed the citizens.

This advice had been received in a courteous silence. West Australians could not explain to a man from abroad that the

Barracks held a beauty for them he would never be able to see with foreign eyes. That building stood for their history, their birth pangs. As a nation they had not come trailing clouds of glory from some other world. Their primordial memory was one of discovery ships, pioneer ships, convict ships, immigrant ships. The Barracks, relic of the birth of a nation, reminded the citizens they were not born of privilege but of hardship, endurance and the will to survive.

Denney walking up the Terrace in the direction of Mary's office, thought again of soldiers and convicts.

'Over my dead body!' she thought, remembering the advice to destroy the Barracks. 'They stay there.'

They made her think of Jack Smith again, instead of the fact she felt ill and that her head was swimming so that she felt as if she walked keeled over a little like a ship that had had a shift in ballast.

The building where Mary had her offices had an attendant, so Denney went up in the lift.

She turned right down the corridor, past other legal offices and came to Mary's door. She went into the reception room and wondered why it and the secretary's room beyond was empty. Then she remembered it was lunch time. Through the pebbled glass of the door into Mary's room she could see the shadow of her sister's head as she bent over her table.

With a sigh of relief Denney opened the door and went in. It was lunch time. Mary was in, and alone. This was the first break in luck Denney had had today.

Mary looked up and said 'Hullo!' in a surprised way. Denney never came to see her sister in professional hours. The surprise was tempered with pleasure, for Mary liked to be turned to by her sisters. She liked them to know she was at hand with all the business know-how of living in a modern world. She couldn't of course possibly tell them that they were naïve babes in the jungle of modern life. But she thought it. She felt they needed protection but she could never tell them so. They were completely confident in their collective innocence. Mary had a sense of relief when one or other did turn to her for some advice. Now she could get her finger on their affairs and look after them.

Mary, not as tall, but as slender, was four years Denney's senior by the birth register but a hundred years the wiser by experience. She would have died rather than admit this fact to her sister and Denney would have thrown herself in the river rather than accept it.

As Denney walked in, shut the door behind her and sat down in the leather chair which stood against the wall behind the door, Mary put down the cup from which she was drinking thermos tea and looked at her sister over the top of her glasses.

Denney stretched her feet out in front of her in an inelegant fashion and let her handbag sink to the floor on one side of her and the parcel of newspapers fall to the floor on the other.

'Why don't you go to an optician and get your glasses fixed?' she said.

'I will some time,' said Mary, and with the hand that held a sandwich she pushed her glasses back on the bridge of her nose. The glasses had nice frames and Mary was rather pleased with them. They managed to combine both the professional and the glamorous. When she wanted to look learned she could somehow achieve it behind those frames. When she wanted to look like a very attractive young woman she could manage that too. It was all a matter of how she looked through them, and what hat she was wearing at the time. Sometimes, of course, the hat was a wig.

'Some time,' repeated Denney with exasperation. 'By that time you'll have bunged up your sight for good and all.'

'I'm awfully glad to see you,' said Mary. 'What brings you in?'

Denney could see Mary putting on her welcoming smile. Denney knew it was genuine and Mary was glad to see her because Denney wouldn't be here if she wasn't looking for help. Denney knew very well Mary liked to help. However, Mary was a very busy woman and most people had to have an appointment to see her. Mary's gladness was, therefore, dutiful as well as genuine.

'I wanted to ask you something. What's an *accessory after the fact*?'

'Good heavens!' said Mary, immediately anxious. 'You haven't been getting yourself mixed up with something silly, have you?'

Denney was righteously indignant.

'What a thing to think!' she said. 'Of course I haven't. I'm asking for a friend. We had an argument about it.'

For the purposes of this conversation Detective-Inspector Riley could be the 'friend'. Denney did not like telling lies but she was very happy to rationalize any statement so that she could make it balance out with the truth in her own mind.

She felt a spasm of hot indignation that Mary should immediately jump to such conclusions. That was Mary all over. Suspicions. That's what came of being mixed up with the Law. One was always suspicious, or on guard, or something. As if she, Denney, would get herself 'mixed up with something silly'!

It was this sort of thing from the family that had made her go out and get that block of land and carve a farm out of it for herself. She had to show the family something about herself that was equal in achievement to their own successes.

Denney was so clearly indignant that Mary apologized, though behind those attractive spectacle frames her eyes were compassionate and wary.

'You've got an awful mind,' said Denney truculently. 'You always think the worst.'

'Sorry,' said Mary again. 'Anyhow, who is your friend and how on earth do you come to be talking about an *accessory after the fact*?'

'It was a detective I used to know when I worked on the paper. He told me that if a murderer was helped by someone . . . after he had committed the murder . . . that someone was an accessory and could be hanged for it.'

'It all depends what was the nature of the help,' said Mary, puzzled. 'But what a subject to talk about! Why murderers only? There are other crimes where an accessory can be taken into account.'

'Well, murderers are in the air, just at present. So I suppose people talk about murderers.'

'What murderer in particular?' said Mary. Her glasses had slipped down her nose a little and she was looking over the top of them again. 'Jack Smith?'

'Look, Mary, you're a lawyer and you know jolly well that's slander, or libel, or something. I never did know the difference between slander and libel. Anyhow, even the newspaper and the radio only refer to him as "the man wanted for questioning".'

'All right,' said Mary, her eyes closed a moment in acceptance of the rebuke. 'Who were you talking about then?'

'Well, it was Jack Smith,' said Denney uneasily. 'And we got into an argument.'

'Does he think there is someone else in this business, besides Jack Smith?'

'Oh no. We were just talking. They can't find him, you see. Someone might be hiding him. We were just arguing about what would happen to that person.'

'And you've come up here to settle the point?'

Denney was aware that Mary's eyes were watching her. There was something of the mother watching the reactions of her difficult child in the expression in Mary's eyes but Denney was not able to interpret it. She preferred to look beyond Mary, through the window that gave a glorious view over the still peaceful river.

'I thought I might as well find out,' said Denney irritably. 'How does one get educated if one doesn't ask questions? And what's wrong with getting a lawyer's opinion, specially when you can get it for free?'

'Have you got a ten pound bet on this argument?' asked Mary, the irritated mother becoming a little more apparent and the sister-anxious-to-help receding somewhat. She reached across the table for a cigarette case and took a cigarette and then passed it across the table to Denney.

'I don't bet any more,' said Denney and then lit her cigarette. 'I gave it up years ago. I don't even go to the races any more.'

'Anyhow he's a detective, he should know the answer. Why didn't you accept his opinion?'

'Because I wanted to know what would happen to a person who hid a murderer and I didn't want to go into details with him. He might think I had something to do with it.'

There was a long silence in the room while Mary slowly, eyes half-closed as if to protect them from cigarette smoke, exhaled a long breath laden with that smoke.

'Nobody would be such a damn fool as to hide him,' Mary said at length with the kind of emphasis that brooked no questioning.

Denney's eyes came away from the window and its view of the river and fixed themselves on Mary.

Mary, looked up, saw the sudden childish alarm in Denney's eyes. She was struck by two things. Denney, wearing a blue dress and facing the light and the river beyond, had the bluest eyes she had ever seen; and that Denney had something on her mind more worrying that the definition of a legal term.

'Look, Denney,' she said with the kind of patience that usually exasperated her sisters and took an extra toll of her own nervous strength. 'You've got this business of Jack Smith on your mind. Now come clean. Are you nervous being up there in the Hills on your own? I know he was supposed to have been traced up there several days ago, but he's well away from there now.'

'Of course I'm not,' said Denney in a voice which, for once, did not carry conviction. 'If I was nervous I'd come down and stay with one of you, wouldn't I?'

'I'm not sure. You're scatterbrained enough to think your vegetables and animals are more important than your own well-being.'

'Scatterbrained?' said Denney with umbrage. 'That's a new one. Generally I'm a "zany" or a "nitwit". Now it's "scatterbrained". Anybody would think I couldn't get myself in out of the rain. And look what I've done. I got that land. Nobody gave me any advice about that. I just went and got it without telling anybody. Then everyone thought I'd lose my money, and I'd make a botch of it. And what have I done?'

'I know,' Mary interrupted softly. 'I'm sorry. I apologize. As a matter of fact what you've done up there in the Hills is a wonderful feat. And every one of us knows it, Denney . . .'

'I can tell by the tone of your voice you're giving me a pat on the back,' said Denney haughtily. 'For all the family's brains I'd like to see any of them pitching in with a hoe round a patch of vegetables . . .' Her voice unexpectedly broke. What did her patch of vegetables matter if Jack Smith set fire to them? Or if she hanged at the local Tyburn at Fremantle?

'Why, Denney, what's the matter?' said Mary with sudden compunction. Denney's eyes had filled with tears, she fumbled for the handbag on the floor to get her handkerchief and when she had found it she sat there quietly but bitterly crying.

In a minute, when she could speak, she would tell Mary all. The ball, if Mary had only known, was in her court.

The telephone on Mary's desk rang and she picked up the receiver.

There was a fellow lawyer on the other end and the conversation meant a long and involved interchange about legal procedures on a forthcoming case.

It was seven full minutes before Mary put the receiver down, and as she did so her two young typists could be heard coming through the outer door.

Denney's moment was past. She could not talk with an office full of people, she told herself. She would go and see Vicky. Vicky would give her some tea, and she would be able to *think*.

She stooped for her bag and newspapers again, and stood up.

'Look, Denney,' said Mary kindly. 'Go into the typists' room and have a wash and brush up. After that you'll feel better. If something's worrying you, I'd like to help you. You know that, don't you?'

'Nothing's worrying me. I'm hot and tired and crabby, that's all. I'll do my face up when I get to Vicky's.' She was standing up now and turned away to open the door. 'And I don't care a damn what is an accessory after the fact!'

'Don't worry about that argument, for Heaven's sake,' said Mary. 'It's too involved. Inspector Riley is bound to be right. After all, it's his business to know. You can't win every argument you get into, you know, Denney.'

'It wasn't the argument altogether,' said Denney, going through the door. 'That was only half of it. Oh well, I'll see you next time I come to town. If I ever come.'

She went across the typists' room and through the door into the corridor. Mary, standing behind her table, heard Denney's footsteps dying away to silence as they neared the lift.

There was something nearly tragic in Denney's retreating back and fading footsteps.

Those last words of hers . . . 'If I ever come!' They were the sort of silly melodramatic words that the Montgomerys were fond of using when they felt defeated, or misunderstood. They probably wouldn't mean anything at all, coming from Denney.

Mary's secretary came into the room.

'There's a Mrs Kilmore to see you. She has an appointment.' Mary nodded.

'Ann,' she said, 'remind me to ring my sister Vicky, will you? I'll put the call through after Mrs Kilmore.'

She sat down. As far as Mary could remember she had never seen Denney cry before. If she wept when John died she wept in private.

Vicky's house round on the east side of Pepper Tree Bay was a beautiful two-storeyed home with white outer walls and a heavenly tiled green roof. Young eucalyptus trees grew tall here and there on the large billiard table lawn, and creepers were long and shade-giving over the pagoda sheltering the side door. At the side and back of the house there were shrubberies of hibiscus, oleanders and bougainvillæas.

It was a lovely house and in this respect the only subject upon which Vicky's entire family was unanimous. They hastened there on any pretext whatever, not only because Vicky's house was lovely to look at and lovely to be in, but the larder was always well stocked and the refrigerator and deep freeze full of entrancing food. Vicky was a wonderful cook, and the appearance of anyone at all was enough to set teacups moving on the green shelves of the modern streamlined kitchen, and newly tried recipes emerging from refrigerator shelves and cake tins.

Denney had gone back to the markets from Mary's office and retrieved her station wagon from the car park. There was still a little business being done in the market, but mostly with the treaty stores and the retailers on the fringe. The car park was all but empty and Toni Manigani and Denney's other Galahads had long since gone about their business back on their blocks at Wanneroo, Spearwood or the Hills.

There was no occasion to call 'Hiya!" to anyone, and in any case Denney hadn't the heart for it just now. She was an accessory after the fact and due for gaol, if not hanging.

Toni had wound up the windows of the station wagon against possible car thieves. Denney unlocked the driver's door with her second key and the hot imprisoned air smote her with a blasting hand as she got in. She quickly wound down all the windows back and front, then closed the door. She stretched her feet forward and leaned against the cloth-covered back rest. She opened her bag and took out her cigarettes and matches. To do this she had to move the parcel of newspapers.

'Why don't I open you and read you?' she said, addressing the newspapers. She thought she would do that in a minute .... when she could be bothered.

She sat smoking her cigarette, her eyes half closed against the spiral of smoke and looking through the front window of her car at nothing.

She hadn't been to see the police and she hadn't told anybody where Jack Smith was hiding. Why?

'How crazy can I be?' she said to herself, yet even as she said this she knew, deep within herself, she was incapable of going to the police. She tried to rationalize her silence. She had given a promise. How did anyone break a promise? The Bible was against it. The school she went to was against it. There wasn't anybody who wouldn't be against it. Now was there?

For instance. The priest in the Confessional doesn't have, in practice, to tell what he hears through that grille. The doctor doesn't have to tell what he hears in the consulting room, all because what he is told is confidential and under the oath of silence.

Well, her promise had been an oath, hadn't it? So what was she worrying about?

What she was worrying about was why did she not want to tell, promise or no promise, oath or no oath. Denney didn't know the reason.

Though born in Australia she came from a race of people who despised an 'informer'. In Ireland they shot an informer dead, against a stone wall. He was the lowest of the low, the last bottom end of the muck that came through the sluice gates. Denney's folk-lore had not been of the Australian bush, since her parents had come from Ireland in their adult years. The fable stories of Denney's family had been tales out of Meath and Down. Leprechauns, and fairies in the glens, bewitched stones on the peasants' mantelshelves, had figured largely in that folk-lore; but looming black and evil in the real political stories out of the Montgomery past was the worst badman of all, the *informer*.

Denney's grandfather had been killed by another man in the Troubles in the eighties. This, when retold to the grandchildren, was a tale of differing religions, differing politics and ignorant peasants. Theodora, when she had gone to Ireland, had come back with the outrageous story that it had all been over a cow sold by a man named Riley who had punched Grandfather because Grandfather had thought it was a nice cow but the price was too high.

This version was rejected by the family at once. A man named Riley had stood a wilful murder trial for the death of Grandfather! It had to be political, and momentous, to suit the Montgomerys' sense of melodrama.

Riley!

Denney stubbed out her cigarette and lit another.

Of course there must be millions of Rileys in Ireland just as there were a couple of dozen Montgomerys. But what if he, Detective-Inspector Riley, happens to be a descendant? You only had to look at him to know that he, or his father, had come out of Ireland.

That man Riley who had killed Grandfather was acquitted. In those days there was only Wilful Murder, or nothing, in Ireland. There were no degrees of killing. Nobody could prove that Riley wilfully murdered Grandfather. So he was acquitted.

Well, maybe Detective-Inspector Riley, all on account of his name, might let Denney off that charge of accessory after the fact. An eye for an eye and a life for a life. That was fair enough. Another Montgomery didn't have to die because the Rileys of this world became too officious. A Riley got let off back there in Ireland, why not a Montgomery down here in Australia and cry quits to the whole business of inter-family relationships.

Already, in her mind, Denney had accepted Detective-Inspector Riley as the descendant of a family foe. It suited her line of reasoning.

Denney's spirits revived. Her thoughts had come full cycle from worrying about Jack Smith's survival to worrying about her own. Once again her mind had dodged the issue by escaping down tributary channels.

Denney straightened up ready to proceed on her way to Vicky's house. She felt better, a lot better. What a godsend that was! She had remembered about a man called Riley. Her own father always felt he'd got the wood on anyone called Riley. When he was Rector of Pepper Tree Bay he had always quarrelled with the Archbishop on a point of principle. The Archbishop was a man called Riley.

Denney threw the stub of her cigarette out of the window and turned the key in the ignition. Then she remembered there was a fifty pound fine for throwing lighted cigarettes out of windows in the fire hazard season. She got out, picked up the cigarette, then getting back into her car stubbed it out in the ashtray.

'I'd take an axe to anyone who did that up my way,' she said, then thought of Jack Smith threatening to set fire to her farm. Her spirits sank again.

'Dear God, why doesn't someone catch him?'

When she swung the car out of the car park it managed to turn itself in the direction of the river and the four mile run around its blue and golden fringes to Vicky's house, and not in the direction of the police station.

If the threat of a fire-razed farm would not make Denney

give Jack Smith up, then she should have saved herself the bother of further thought, for nothing would bring her to that conclusion. Her hands, her feet, the drive wheels of her car acted for her. They controlled her. They took her in the opposite direction from the police headquarters.

It was nice to arrive at Vicky's house. The white pallisaded walls, the green Italian roof, the trees and shrubs about the velvet lawn promised cool shade and well-being. A whisper of the south-wester coming in over the river, ruffling its serene surface like catspaws over the glass, touched the topmost leaves of the young eucalyptus trees.

The very coming of Denney to Vicky's house made her feel better.

Vicky's car was in the car port south of the side door, but so were the children's bicycles. Denney liked her nephews and niece very much, but she was sorry they were home just now. Would Providence never give her a chance to speak to a sister alone? It would be lunch time. Maybe they would be off back to school in half an hour.

When Denney went through the side door into the kitchen she knew there would be no such luck.

'Hallo, Denney!' was chorused all round. Nobody used the word 'Aunt' in Denney's family on the sole ground that it was an ugly word. It sounded ugly and looked ugly when written down, therefore it was *out*.

Vicky, through the open door of the workroom, was packing swimsuits and towels into a basket. In the kitchen, the children were helping themselves to large quantities of apple and passionfruit pie, heavily burdened with ice-cream from the refrigerator. There was general bedlam.

'We're going to the beach!'

'We've got a holiday!'

'There are visiting teachers at our school and they're having meetings. We're going swimming.'

Vicky came to the dividing doorway and said, 'Oh, hallo, Denney!' in a welcoming voice.

Vicky did not look like a busy housewife. She was always groomed, lipsticked, and wore the prettiest floral cotton frocks, even while getting breakfast. Right now she looked as if she had barely stepped out of the hairdresser's and the manicurist's. She was a pretty woman by natural endowment anyway.

'Had something to eat?' Vicky went on. 'Help yourself.

Come for a swim with us? We won't be long. You've got time.'

'Yes, come on, Denney,' said one nephew.

'Of course she's coming,' said the niece.

'Do you want vanilla ice-cream or chocolate?' asked the second nephew, already having put an enormous slice of fruit pie on one of Vicky's pretty floral china plates.

'Hallo, everybody!' said Denney. 'Hell's bells, you kids will have figures like elephants if you eat that much in the middle of the day. All right, put another dab of the chocolate on, please, Mark, but don't blame me if I get so fat you'll refuse to know me when we meet in Hay Street.'

She sat on the high stool by the corner table and let her nephews and niece present her with a laden plate, a spoon to eat with, and a wafer biscuit to help the spoon.

'What goes on?' she asked.

Everyone told her again, and Denney smiled and nodded her head and agreed it was a good day upon which to be given a holiday. Yes, of course she'd come for a swim. Who wouldn't come for a swim on a blistering hot day like this?

'Maybe I'll drown,' she thought in a hollow way. That would be a way out. They say drowning is a pleasant way to die. You see the whole of your life passing before your inward eye. Does an inward eye die? She must ask a psychologist that some day, if she ever met one.

Anyhow, if she drowned she wouldn't have to worry any more, would she? Hah! Cheated the hangman's noose, and another Riley to boot.

In spite of these thoughts arranging themselves uninvited in a minor key at the back of her head, she smiled and nodded and answered back her nephews and niece. Vicky produced another swimsuit which she knew from past experience fitted Denney and told her to go into the upstairs bathroom to change. The kids would fill up the downstairs change room.

'And if you don't all come this minute,' said Vicky with sudden impatience, 'it will be too late to go at all. The south-wester is already coming in.'

The south-wester would whip up big waves down there at the ocean beach. This was great fun for diving and mastering the dumpers; but sent sand whipping on the beach if it got too strong.

Within twenty minutes everyone was piled into Vicky's car

and she backed it out into the side street with a zip and swerve that matched Denney's way of handling her station wagon.

'Why don't you get a new car?' said Vicky, seeing Denney's shabby station wagon parked on the verge of her own precious mother-coddled lawn.

'Can't afford it,' said Denney from under her youngest nephew.

'Don't breathe down my neck, Denney,' said the nephew.

'If you don't like it get off my knee and get on to Mark's knee.'

'Mum, there's room in the front if you squeeze up, can't I come there?'

'All right. Get over the back of the seat and don't knock my hat in my eye while you're doing it.'

During the ensuing operation Vicky did not reduce her speed below fifty and she took two corners while the youngest member of her family transferred from the back seat to the front.

Denney could see the point about not taking corners at a pace. She must remember to mend her own habits when she took that Kalamunda corner in future. *If there was any future.*

After that sad thought Denney was silent, and as everyone else in the car was talking at once her silence went unnoticed.

Even at the beach, after they had all taken their turn at being tossed and turned in the breakers, for the south-wester was moderately in, and were sunbaking on the sand, Denney remained silent.

She lay on her back, her head pillowed on her two hands, and looked out across the ocean to the islands and the reef on the edge of the world.

That reef was indeed the edge of Denney's world; she had never been beyond the islands which she could see, blue and hazed, against the western sky. The sun, still fierce, shone brazenly on the water, so that looking at it too long, without shading her eyes, made Denney's eyes water.

When Vicky, lying on her stomach full length in the sand, lifted her head and said, 'What's the matter, Denney?' Denney replied, 'It's the sun in my eyes. I'm not crying.'

'Then for Heaven's sake turn over. Anyhow, you have to tan your back as well as your front, you know.'

Denney rolled over, and like Vicky rested her forehead on

her folded arms.

Strangely, the tears still came and she had to sniff, then reach for her handkerchief in the beach coat Vicky had lent her.

Vicky sat up with a jerk.

'Denney,' she said in a voice that was imperious and staccato. 'Are you, or are you not, crying?'

If Denney was in trouble then Vicky, as the eldest of the family, was going to get to the bottom of it. This, because she was the eldest in the family, was very much Vicky's business. Love, as far as Vicky was concerned, was the only thing that ever made a woman cry when sunbathing on a hot summer's day by the Indian Ocean.

'No,' said Denney. 'I've got sand in my eyes.'

Vicky was exasperated.

'First the sun, then the sand,' she said impatiently. 'Come off it, Denney! Something's bothering you. You might as well tell me now and be done with it. You know I'll find out sooner or later. It's much better I should deal with your troubles than Mary or Theodora.' She refrained from mentioning the youngest of them all . . . Gerry. Gerry was young and inexperienced. She must be spared.

Denney, head bowed on her arms, did not answer.

'Is it that Ben person up in the Hills? Don't tell me you're in love with *him*. Really, Denney, there must be something wrong to make you cry. And you are crying.'

'It's not Ben. And don't call him "that person in the Hills". And if I wanted to be in love with him I'd be in love with him. He happens to be rather a nice person, only not very chivalrous.'

Vicky felt she was coming to the root of the matter now. Love was the cause of all the tear-shedding in the world.

Denney turned over and sat up. She blew her nose and then brushed back her wet hair from her face. She looked out to sea again as she wrapped her arms round her knees, but she narrowed her eyes to a slit against the inquisitive gaze of Vicky and the burning rays of the sun.

'He left me alone up there on that farm,' said Denney, now becoming indignant. 'How was he to know that Jack Smith, that man they're hunting for, wouldn't break in and . . . well, wouldn't break in?'

'Look, Denney. We all asked you to stay down here till they caught him. You're the one that's as stubborn as a mule. And why should Ben be responsible for keeping you company? He lives the other side of the range, doesn't he? And he has cows to milk morning and night.'

'He came over to see me on Sunday and after dark he rode away. Just rode away. Like that. Left me stone cold flat in an empty house. Why, I might have been murdered in my sleep!'

'In that case I think he is unchivalrous,' said Vicky with asperity. 'I'd wipe him. Just wipe him. But for goodness' sake don't cry over him. He's not worth it.'

'No, I won't,' said Denney, but the tears welled in her eyes all the same.

'Look, Vicky,' she said and there was an unmistakable catch in her voice. 'It isn't that. It's something more. Perhaps David could help me.'

David was Vicky's husband and she was quite sure David could help Denney. He was very wonderful about helping all the girls when they were in trouble.

In explaining this Vicky's voice had softened to something warm and human and motherly. Denney was in trouble, but there were warm arms and kind hearts waiting for her behind those white walls and beneath that green roof round there on the Bay. The solicitude in Vicky's voice was almost Denney's undoing. It did more than threats from Detective-Inspector Riley and flat definitions of law from Mr Stroud.

'Well, look . . . You'll think I'm mad. I know Ben does, and I sometimes think it myself . . .'

There was a spatter of small feet kicking up sand.

'Mum, can we go home now? I've got to pull my yacht up out of the water before sundown. Jimmy Rowsell's lending me his jinker and the Club said I could use the slips for two days only. Mum, I've got to paint it . . .'

It was the youngest nephew.

'Look, darling . . .'

There was more spatter of sand from more feet.

'Come on, Mum. We've had enough. Can I keep my swimmers on in the car? I'll put the towel under me so I don't wet the seat.'

Denney swallowed her sob and blinked back her tears. She scrambled to her feet and stood tall and slender in the sun, tossing her hair back and shaking out her towel.

'Gee, Denney, you look nice in a swimsuit,' said the niece. 'Better than Mum.'

'What nonsense,' said Vicky, getting up. 'My figure has always been better than Denney's.'

For once Denney did not debate. She turned away, and ploughing her feet steadily, walked through the sand to the bank above which the car was parked.

'We'll talk about it later,' Vicky called after her. 'Wait till David comes home and I'll tell him.'

'What's the matter with Denney, Mum?' the little girl asked.

'Something to do with someone called Ben,' Vicky said, gathering up towels, thongs and rubber caps. 'Denney never knows her own mind. She's half in love with him and half out of love with him.'

This was the gist of what she later told Mary over the telephone, and behind closed doors. Mary telephoned because she wanted to know if Vicky thought there was anything wrong with Denney.

'A lovers' tiff, if you ask me,' said Vicky. 'She's hipped because Ben didn't stay with her the other night, you know, the night when that murder man, the wanted fellow, was wandering about up there in that district. Oh *no*. She's not scared now. The fellow's gone away somewhere. I read it in the paper. She's just upset about Ben.'

'Maybe someone could put a flea in Ben's ear, anyway,' said Mary. 'I'll give him a ring some time. If we can't persuade Denney to stay down here till they catch that fellow, at least Ben might have the grace to do something about it himself. If he's fond of her, he ought to appear to be fond of her.'

'That's the question,' said Vicky. 'Is he in love with her?'

'I wouldn't know,' replied Mary, and hung up.

Mary was imbued with the principle that not only 'must justice be done, but it must appear to be done.' Mary was probably the only person in the family who confounded Justice with Love.

CHAPTER SIX

Denney swung her car away from Vicky's house and sped round the Bay to the northern end of it. She turned west into a side street leading from the Bay but within sight of the water. Again her car, her hands on the wheel, brought her somewhere she had not intended going. It had not even crossed her mind to call on Theodora today.

Theodora had been a school teacher and she wore glasses. It was rumoured in the family she could do algebra, geometry and the Calculus, which were things Denney had not attempted to master. These facts gave Denney an inferiority complex which was not Theodora's fault.

Denney knew this was not Theodora's fault and she guessed that her older sister would be soft-hearted and understanding about any of her sisters' troubles. Denney herself, as a schoolgirl, had felt worse about the teachers who were kind than about those who raised their voices and were severely unjust.

Denney, if she had analyzed it, would have realized that teachers being unjust gave her something of a sense of triumph. It put her in the right instead of in the wrong. It dissipated the sense of guilt that vaguely haunted her because she had not been a streamlined pupil eagerly studying and occasionally succeeding. The schoolroom had either been a prison or a comedy-making vaudeville stage, according to Denney's mood or the strength of command of the instructor up there on the platform.

Vaguely, Denney was nostalgic for lost opportunity and regretful because it had been her own perverseness that had made a parody of school life. Therefore she loved Theodora, who had been a teacher; but loved her more greatly at a distance. It was a matter of association.

The drive wheels of her car and her hands on the steering wheel obeyed the crying child that was within her and brought her seeking succour in this side street leading away from the Bay.

Theodora was in the front garden watering her shrubs. Andy, her brown-skinned, blue-eyed, water-dreaming nephew, was painting his canoe, upside-down on blocks, a dreadful shade of red.

Andy saw Denney first.

'Wow! Here's Denney!' he said. He took his paint brush with him as he climbed on the step of Denney's out-dated station wagon and addressed his favourite aunt with his most seraphic and welcoming smile.

'Andy, I love you,' said Denney, 'but put red paint on my car at the peril of your life!'

'I won't,' said Andy. 'Don't fuss.' But he didn't remove the dripping brush from the vicinity, nor his paint-spattered self.

Theodora, tall like all her sisters, had a wisp of dark hair streaking her forehead under the ancient leghorn garden hat. This hat, decorated with equally ancient roses, had many years before been Mary's bridesmaid's hat when Theodora married.

The older sister looked up at Denney with a welcoming smile and, with a characteristic gesture, removed her glasses with the hand that held the hose. This operation caused the water to spray uncontrolled over her feet, over the fence and over the bonnet of Denney's car.

'I've had one swim today,' said Denney in a meaningful voice.

'I'm so sorry,' said Theodora. 'Are you coming in, Denney? Sam's bound to have a bottle of beer in the fridge.' Sam was Theodora's husband, and Andy's uncle.

Denney looked at Andy and the red paint. She stayed behind the wheel of her car.

'I was only passing,' she said. 'I've been swimming with Vicky and the kids.'

'Do come in,' begged Theodora again, advancing to the fence. She leaned over it and permitted her hose to water the shrubs on the street lawn beyond the fence while she looked at her sister. 'You look pale. Is it hot up there in the Hills?'

'Like blazes,' said Denney, still not moving. If only Andy would go away!

She loved Andy as if he were her own, but right now he, and his paint brush, were in the way of private talks with Theodora.

And she hadn't that much time. Sooner than later she would have to go home and feed those fowls and milk Rona. Rona in pain from a distended udder was a subject she could not bear to think upon.

It was only mid-afternoon. She just might have time. Perhaps if she went inside with Theodora, Andy would prefer to stay outside and continue plastering that diabolical red on the sides of his canoe.

'Yes, come on,' said Andy. 'I can pour the beer. You know, tip the glass on its side so it doesn't froth. And pour me a passionfruit drink. Then I'll show you the dredge and crane I built out of the Meccano set . . .'

'Is passionfruit drink all the go with the kids?' Denney asked him.

'Too right! Everything else is *out*.'

'That's good. I'm putting in two hundred passion vines in

the autumn. I'll share the profits with you, Andy, if you keep those kids drinking passionfruit instead of fizzy stuff.'

'Right!' said Andy with emphasis. He was finding that collecting bottletops was a slow way of arriving at a fortune. 'Come on, I'll pour the drinks . . .'

With a paint-stained hand he struggled to turn the handle of the car door.

'Denney, are you all right?' asked Theodora, putting her glasses back on her nose in order to inspect her sister the better.

Again water from the hose shot everywhere, for Theodora was using her left hand to support herself against the fence as she leaned across the flower bed. Her flowered faded cotton frock had caught on a picket and she had been busily changing hands, or was it the spectacles and the hose that changed hands while she released the fragment of a dress that had once been pretty but was still a favourite, like all Theodora's ancient possessions?

'I'm perfectly all right,' said Denney with asperity. If only the family would stop asking her if she was all right! All of them seemed to think she wasn't capable of looking after herself. Probably wanted to put her to bed and feed her up on steak juices because they were certain she'd never make a go of that place up there in the Hills. Probably thought she was starving herself, or something. When she did call on them they tried to fill her up with gargantuan meals on the thesis that when one lived alone one never bothered to cook proper meals. Denney, they said, would be careless about her food.

As if she could afford to be anything else, with a figure that had to be watched!

And she wasn't careless, anyway. She always cooked dinner for herself at night. What did a scrap breakfast and a scant lunch matter when one cooked a good dinner at night?

'Look, Theodora,' Denney said. 'I've got to go. Just called in to see if you were all right. Andy darling, get off my car, and for crying out loud take that flaming red paint away, will you?'

Denney revved up the engine and swung the car widely away from Theodora's driveway. The bumper touched the box tree growing in the street lawn. Denney reversed and bent the bumper bar as engine pressure removed the car from the vicinity of the tree.

'Look what you've done!' said Andy.

'Oh, Denney!' reproached Theodora from under the ancient rose-begarlanded straw hat. 'Do you have to drive like that?'

Denney stalled the engine, then threw the gear into neutral. She sat, white-faced, and looked with unseeing eyes at the wound in the side of the tree.

Nothing goes right today, she thought bitterly. Then with a set mouth, without farewell, she started up and drove away.

Theodora and Andy looked at one another.

'Something's wrong with Denney,' said Andy sagaciously.

'Very wrong,' said Theodora. She put down the hose so the water could run freely on to the roots of the red hibiscus by the gate. She pushed her glasses farther on her nose and her leghorn hat on to the back of her head.

'What will you do?' asked Andy, protective and anxious for Denney.

'I don't know,' said Theodora. 'Perhaps I'd better go and ring up Vicky. Vicky might know. Or Mary . . .'

'Yes,' said Andy. He ran across the wide chair-strewn verandah and pushed open the screen door of the house. He left paint marks over the cream painted woodwork for which he did not apologize and which Theodora, in any case, did not notice. 'Hurry up. Come and ring them up now. Denney might be sick, or something. You'd better ring Vicky up first and Mary last. Mary always knows best so it's best to leave her till last so you can tell her what Vicky said.'

'Alas,' thought Theodora. 'Even the next generation has got this habit of ringing up the family about everything that happens. There's no escape from the family in our family!'

This was precisely what Denney was thinking as she drove away. She thought Vicky's children were a charming riot and wished that Sam's nephew was her own, but on this day there had been no escape from them.

There was no privacy in the Montgomery family. That was the trouble with it. One just couldn't sit down and *talk*. Well, not when one wanted to, anyway. Nobody in the family would dream of sending their kids outside. The modern way of bringing up children: something to do with psychology.

All the same, Denney had to admit, they were charming children. If only they didn't want to go home and attend to yachts that had to be lifted on jinkers or, as in Andy's case, didn't want to act the host with red paint flying about like wounded snow in a drift of the wind!

Denney drove slowly back into Perth, along the tree-ed and

portico-ed Adelaide Terrace over the Causeway – which crossed the lovely blue wind-stirred river – then across the flat sandplain to the lower slopes of the Darling Ranges.

She drove slowly because her car took her homeward but she was reluctant to arrive.

She hadn't thought anything out. She hadn't had time to *think*. All day she had been struggling for time to think and so far not one single coherent thought had settled down to be properly considered.

She drove so slowly up the first steep rises that she had to change to second gear. Her thoughts drifted about like sombre moths beating at lights that should have served as a warning of death instead of fallaciously directing the way to life.

If only she could drive on for ever. If only she could arrive. She wouldn't then have to decide what she should do!

All the time she evaded the fact she had already made a decision of sorts. She had not delivered up Jack Smith to justice. Her involuntary actions, not her thoughts, had made that decision for her.

Curiously enough she was not afraid of Jack Smith now. The dilemma of remaining or escaping had given ground to the dilemma of giving up Jack Smith or harbouring him. Even this ambivalence was now retreating before her anxiety as to how she was to continue living with herself, now and for evermore.

She had to face the prospects of her own company, knowing of her act against the community; knowing also that the price, as Jack Smith went his way, being misled by occasional people who beguiled him into believing they liked or loved him, was perhaps more corpses.

If no one liked, let alone loved, Jack Smith, why couldn't they pity him?

Why was *she*, Denney, chosen of the ten million inhabitants of her country to pity him?

The day had been hot and the south-wester had dropped altogether, leaving the air still, humid and hot on a land that waited for the softening touch of cool night and the rising of the east wind in the late hours or early morning.

The sandplain oaks stood still with their grey untidy heads drooping. The prickly undergrowth was as moveless as a petrified forest. The occasional clumps of stunted eucalyptus saplings stood, their leaves down-pointing, waiting another five hundred years before they gained the mighty pretensions of being jarrah trees.

Through the car window, as it steadily climbed the Kalamunda hill, the laden scent of the Australian bush touched Denney's nostrils and in spite of her troubles she registered the old warming sense of coming home to the Hills. There was comfort in that.

She swung left off the Kalamunda road before she reached the town. She would take the by-pass to Gooseberry Hill over the Crescent. The track was bushy all the way with bigger trees, less thirsty undergrowth. She could hear the sound of the creek sliding down into the gully behind her.

The sun was behind Denney now, and the trees threw chequerboard shadows over the road.

It was cool here, and scent-haunted from gum leaves fallen long ago, dying and drying, on the gravelled earth.

Denney was physically aware of it all, for it fed her arterial system with its life's blood, yet what she was actually thinking was:

'There are a hundred and forty-eight million people in Indonesia, for instance. And about six hundred and fifty million people in China. With all those people around, why was it given to me to be visited by Jack Smith? Dear God, why *me*?'

Down across the plain where the river carved its bays there was a great ringing-up amongst the Montgomery sisters.

Theodora rang Vicky and Vicky rang Mary. Then Mary rang Theodora. Nobody intended to bother Gerry with the business of being worried about Denney, but Gerry brought herself into the mêlée by ringing up Vicky on the subject of a piece of antique furniture she had discovered on the pavement of a second-hand store in East Perth.

'Must have come out with Stirling,' she said. 'Believe it or not, darling, it's Queen Anne.'

'Denney's got four of them,' said Vicky, speaking of the chairs. 'Picked them up in a sale. By the way, Denney was down today. There must be something wrong with her love life. Mary and Theodora think so too. She looked positively unhappy.'

'Why blame her love life? It could be she's going broke on that place up in the Hills. I always said she would.'

'She's not. David did her accounts for her last taxation year.

It must be her love life. It couldn't be anything else.[1]

'That *Ben*.'

'Well, just how well do you know him, Gerry? The rest of us only had distant glimpses. Denney keeps the whole affair extremely discreet, if it is an affair. Is it? How much do you know about it?'

'Oh . . . he's tall, and rangy. Talks with a drawl when he talks at all. He's got something though. Don't ask me what. Just something makes you look twice. Then think again. You know the kind. Quickens the old pulses. Leave it to me. I'll fish it out if there's something wrong.'

'Well, look, Gerry, Mary and Theodora think we oughtn't to interfere in a love affair. They say it's absolutely disastrous and that Denney would be murderous about it if she found out.'

'Poof! I know Ben myself. I'll ring him up about the price of eggs, or something. I'm very good at *hearing* nuances on the telephone.'

'Is he on the telephone?'

'He'd better be. If he's not I'll call and see him. By helicopter, if there's no other way. He's about thirty miles out, isn't he?'

'But . . .'

'Don't worry. I won't give Denney away. For crying out loud, don't you think I know enough about love affairs to keep quiet about them? Just leave it to me.'

That, thought Vicky, putting down the telephone receiver, was quite the most satisfactory way to interfere in Denney's affairs. Leave it to Gerry. Gerry, tall, dark-haired, fun-making, would know just exactly how to do that and get away with it. And she certainly did know about love affairs. Too much, if you asked Vicky.

Of course if Mary and Theodora had had any sense at all they would have thought of Gerry before.

As the eldest of the family she had had the sense to think of it herself. Or so Vicky thought.

Chief-Inspector Riley stood above his work-laden table and looked thoughtfully at the book in his hand. The routine thing to do was list this book, *Stroud's Judicial Dictionary*, as impounded as material evidence and note the fact in his twelve-hourly report to his superior officer.

He could, on his own authority, pass it on for dusting.

There would be fingerprints on it. Supporting evidence.

With a faint ironical smile he reflected he had not been able to find any reference book on passionfruit in the Library that had been used for reference that day.

Denney had lied.

He dropped the law book into his drawer, and closed it. He turned away to his window and looked out on the gravel yard of the nearby Police Court. He put his hands in his pockets and stood looking thoughtfully at nothing. If he moved his head the fraction of an inch he knew he would see the main police buildings and beyond them, out of sight, was the monument to Pitman and Walsh, two policemen killed by murderers Coulter and Treffene while in the line of duty.

He turned round and took one pace to reach his desk. He turned the key in the drawer which held *Stroud's Judicial Dictionary* and dropped the key in his pocket. He leaned over his table as he reached for his table telephone.

'Give me the Chief, Bob, will you?' he said into the mouth-piece.

Without conscious notice Denney knew that Jack Smith had not, this day, burned down her farm.

The skyline was clear. No bushfires anywhere on the range today. No cloud of smoke sat cushioned on the hilltops nor in the gullies; no smoke haze shadowed the innocently clear water-blue sky above the Darling Ranges. Jack Smith had not burned down her farm.

She swung the station wagon off the road on to the track running west along her boundary fence towards the opening track to her farm.

'First things first and right things in their right place,' said Denney to herself, relieved that her farm would still be standing. The mental effort of relegating Jack Smith to his proper pigeon-hole of nasty criminals was beyond her now, and in any event there were too many ramifications to this particular kind of ethical and moral problem. Someone had once told Denney that philosophy was like mathematics, and it was as hard to work out a piece of philosophical reasoning as to solve a problem in the realms of higher mathematics. Well, Denney, who knew nothing of philosophy or mathematics, would take their word for it. She could prove they were right now, from her own experience. Thinking wasn't getting her anywhere. It was too hard. There was too many ifs and buts.

Her farm still stood, that was the great thing. Jack Smith had not razed it to the ground.

'Then to hell with thinking at all,' said Denney, swinging over the cowcatcher. 'I'm stuck with Jack Smith and that's that. Of course I can put him to work on the place . . . but for how long? Just how long would it last? And wouldn't I then be stuck with the problem that had I, or had I not, done the right thing?'

She swung the station wagon into the shed and got out and slammed the door. She leaned through the window and took the bundle of newspapers and carton of cigarettes from the seat.

'Why am I still stuck with you?' she said, looking at the newspapers in her hands. 'Anybody 'ud think the way I've carted you round all day there was ever anything interesting to read in you. Oh, well, there's always the For Sale column. Funny how people want to sell grand pianos and mink furs and wedding dresses – Worn Only Once.'

Her quick professional eye took in the wellbeing of her farm. The tomatoes and greens were wilting badly from the day's heat, but there was nothing unusual in that for the time of the year. The apricots, very young trees, looked as if there might be only one more picking. The horses were in the paddock corner near the feed chute. Rona was baa-ing, and the fowls were cluttering and fluttering.

Everything in the flat, hot, still air was normal.

Denney stood below the steps and threw the bundle of newspapers and the carton of cigarettes on to the back verandah. Her hat was still on her head and she hadn't time to take it off.

She went across the yard to the windmill and turned it on. There was no movement from the vanes, they were as still as if locked for ever in the moveless air. There was no hint yet that the east wind would ever rise again. Denney sighed. There would be a heavy water loss from evaporation in this heat and the lower tank was still too hot for her to keep her hand on it. She removed the padlocks from the tank taps and hung them behind a post in the nearby shed.

She instinctively looked at the ground under the garden tap, though she knew that if Jack Smith had come into the garden to wash and drink he couldn't have used that tap. There was no flow into the pipes from the windmill.

She supposed she would never pass that tap without looking at the ground, seeing in imagination the footprint that had frightened and haunted her imagination all day yesterday.

Was it only yesterday? In her mind she had lived ten years of her life since then.

Denney, her hat still on her head, fed, watered, picked and packed. She milked Rona, using a bucket she had left standing under McMullens's lean-to verandah yesterday.

Sometime or other in the last twenty-four hours she had remembered the old saying that death by drowning was quite pleasant. One lived, in those last few minutes, all one's life again.

Denney couldn't remember how or when she had thought about that some time today, but she was thinking about it very hard now as she went about her outside chores.

Fleetingly she had lived again odd scenes in her life. She recalled images of McMullens and herself burning off. Ben and herself burning off. Ben and herself swimming in the deep pool of the creek. She remembered these incidents with a nostalgia as if they were things past never to be repeated. And as if they had been happy occasions. They very nearly had been happy occasions.

As she milked Rona, Denney thought about this stream of consciousness that had flowed through her in the last hour.

'I must be going to die,' she said. 'I keep thinking of everything that's gone instead of what goes on now.'

She knew, as she carried the bucket of milk up to the house, that she needn't have worried so much all day about wanting the time or the opportunity to think out what she should do.

It would all have been to no avail. Her mind had been made up last night and she had been a fool not to know it.

She was not going to give Jack Smith up. She was stuck with him, and because of that there might be no tomorrow or no next week. Each hour was therefore no more than a bonus.

She could put him to work on the place; give him a home, decent clothes, good food. Even Denney knew that that was not the end of the story. It was only a way of filling in the bonus time allotted by Fate.

What Denney did understand, as she unlocked the back door and let herself, and the bucket of milk, into the hot air of the enclosed kitchen, was that she was powerless to foresee or plan the future. Each day would have to look after itself. She could do nothing about it.

All the same, that stream of memory had made her think

154

of drowning people.

'I must be going to die,' she said simply. And accepted the fact.

Denney lit the fire, had her shower, put on a fresh cotton housecoat and did her hair and made up her face.

She went back into the kitchen and prepared vegetables for two, for cooking. She put a rich egg custard into the oven and then, on second thoughts, made a second one and placed it beside the first on the oven shelf. There was nothing like cooking two meals in one and it saved the cooking tomorrow. Who knows? She might be still alive tomorrow, and want to eat.

On this principle she added more vegetables to the pots. The left-overs could be fried the next day. That would save cooking time. She was going to be very busy tomorrow, if alive.

To hell with lining the fern baskets for Jack Smith's benefit. She was going to clear the apricot trees of all their fruit. What wouldn't sell she'd bottle. If she left the fruit on the trees much longer it would be an open invitation to the fruit fly to come in.

She would stake up the autumn-bearing tomatoes. McMullens had left the stakes neatly piled at the end of the rows for her. Without staking, the plants wouldn't bear heavily.

She would give the horses a run . . .

Where the dickens was that Jack Smith?

The least he might do was come in at a regular hour to his meals! Anybody would think this was a boarding house. On second thoughts, it wouldn't even make the grade as a boarding house, for those institutions had their strict eating hours.

Denney wondered if Ben was the kind of a man who went in punctually to his meals. She must ask him some day.

She wanted to grill chops tonight, and what was the good of grilling Jack Smith's chop if he didn't come to get it until it was no more than a frizzled cinder on the oven shelf?

'Damn and blast him!' said Denney. 'As if he hasn't caused me enough trouble already.' If she had had a son she would have boxed his ears for such lack of consideration.

She looked through the kitchen window and perceived there was no sunlight now. Sundown shadows had gone and the bush, the horse paddock and the vegetable patch were as silent as if waiting for the Crack of Doom. Come to think of it, the Crack of Doom was something that might happen any minute now!

Then gradually, upon the air, came the faint purr and throb

of an engine. It was a motor-car and, second by second, the sound grew louder.

With head bent sideways, nerves unexpectedly tensed, Denney listened to the sound of that engine and plotted its course in her mind as it moved rapidly, bumping badly over the corrugations, northward along the road below her boundary fence.

When it turned east into the track leading to her own gate Denney recognized it as the Ford utility that belonged to Albert Barnes at the store.

She ran through the house to the front and watched through the open door.

She had always thought that to 'have one's heart in one's mouth' was merely a figure of speech. She now knew that this was an exact description of what can happen to some people under certain circumstances.

What, dear God, should she do?

There was nothing she could do.

If Jack Smith was somewhere there in the bush, watching behind a loaded gun to see what would come out of Denney's day at the markets, he would think she had brought his enemies to the homestead.

What would Jack Smith do? Shoot Barnes?

Maybe shoot herself and run for it. Maybe just run for it without the shooting. She had no way of knowing or guessing the answer.

She stood and watched Barnes's utility approach the cow-catcher. Would he cross it and come right up to the homestead or would he turn it in the gravel circle worn into a turntable by usage, and park outside the gate? Either way he was wide open to be shot, a black stump in a paddock, a bottle on a fence. Denney felt very sick.

Barnes turned the utility and came to a stop outside the fence. He got out, slamming the drive door behind him and walking round the utility to the truck end. He lifted out a small wooden crate, then balancing himself with it, neatly crossed the cowcatcher and came up towards the homestead. For five seconds Denney watched his brown weather-lined humorous face above the blue-shirted shoulders and arms that held the crate. Below that crate she could see his long khaki-clad legs with the shabby army boots stirring up the dust as he came on. For those five seconds Denney loved Albert Barnes as one loves someone upon whom tragedy is about to alight with annihilating intent.

She looked at him with the 'we-who-are-about-to-die' comradeship that only those who are about to die can understand.

Then her old instinctive sense of improvisation came to her aid. It was all her fault and they had to be comrades in life and death to the very end.

She went through the front door and ran down the three steps to the gravel track and down to meet Mr Barnes.

The last red flares of the sunset sky shone in the crowns of the trees behind him. Everything in the world was very still except Mr Barnes.

He grinned at Denney as she came up to him.

'Got this load in today and thought I'd bring it up on my way round Long Road to the Harris place. How you doing, Denney?' he said.

'All right,' she said.

He looked quizzically at her pale frozen face.

'Guess I brought it at the wrong time. You in the middle of eating, I suppose?'

'No, not yet,' said Denney. 'Look, just leave it on the front verandah, will you? I'll move it later . . .'

'What? With McMullens away? What you think I am, Denney? You might be pretty rugged on that hoe and the horse bins, but no woman ought to go farming who's got to carry her own case a' drinks round the house.'

He was moving as he talked. He passed Denney on the track and went round the side of the house, Denney followed. He went up the steps of the back verandah, pushed the screen door of the kitchen open with the toe of his boot, and into the kitchen. He put the crate on the end of the table. Released from his burden he pushed his unnecessary hat on to the back of his head, and scratched his crown as he looked at the two places set at the table.

'Expectin' someone for dinner? he said. 'Golly, sorry I shoved in.'

'Yes, I am,' said Denney.

She was inside the kitchen too and she stood and looked at Albert Barnes. He caught the curious, anxious, indecisive expression in her blue eyes. Those eyes were nearly always gay and challenging. Denney was someone who always had a smile and a quick word: a piece of smart talk to give. Now she stood silent, pale-faced, and with that strange expression in her eyes, almost as if she wished to say something but found it hard to communicate.

'Anything wrong?' he asked.

'No,' Denney said, and then added, 'You'd better go, Mr Barnes. You might be late round at the Harris place.'

'Well, I can't say I haven't had the push-off, can I? Sorry I came at the wrong time. Thought you might like to know the drinks had come. Brought 'em round on my way to Harris's place, as I said.'

He sounded as if he was offended. Mr Albert Barnes was more than storekeeper to his customers, he was a friend and adviser. It was as clear as the palm of his hand to him, right now, that Denney hadn't wanted him to come round the house to the kitchen and badly wished him to go. Yet it was a reluctant wishing. Albert Barnes couldn't quite understand. Something phoney about Denney and the whole set-up. Maybe it was that Ben Darcy from over the range coming to dinner. Maybe, as it was a long way to come, Ben Darcy reckoned on staying through.

He, Mr Barnes, didn't think Denney was that sort. You never could tell about people could you? All the same he'd give her the benefit of the doubt. Maybe Ben Darcy did stay through when he came, but everything was all right and above board. Denney just, naturally-like, felt embarrassed about it.

Mr Barnes kept his eyes averted from the two places set at the table.

All the same, he thought, you'd think she'd set it up properly; best silver and a vase of flowers and that sort of thing. Considering Ben Darcy was probably courting. And Denney couldn't go far wrong on that one either. Nicely lined, was Mr Ben Darcy; and a tiger for work out there on that place of his. One of the picked lots in the Hills!

'Guess I'll be going,' Albert Barnes said again. He wondered why they were both standing there uneasily, he not really making a move to pass out easily and automatically. It was for all the world as if she had something to say and couldn't say it. As if she wanted him to go yet didn't want him to go.

Phoney, if you asked Mr Barnes.

'I see they haven't caught that feller,' he said. 'The one that was kickin' around up here. Good thing he's moved on, for peace of mind up here. Bet you a tanner he's trying for the Eastern States. Got to cross the Nullarbor Plain after he gets through the country towns this side of the border.'

Mr Barnes had eased round Denney and was in the doorway himself now. He stood sideways, half in and half out.

'I'll walk down to the gate with you,' Denney said. For that offer she deserved a Victoria Cross.

Albert Barnes tried not to look astonished. First she didn't want him to come in, then she wanted him to go as if she was in some kind of a hell of a hurry. Now she was going bush-walking with him down to the gate. He wondered if maybe she'd fallen down and given her head a crack, or something.

It was his turn to be embarrassed by this offer. His customers were his friends, but they didn't walk down to the gate with him when he left the stores.

'That's all right, Denney,' he said with a laugh. 'Don't want to spoil your dinner and all that.' Then, he didn't want to hurt Denney's feelings either. It wasn't every day in the week a nice eligible young woman offered to walk down to the gate with him. And a good-looking one too, only he'd never thought of Denney that way. Besides, she came from a different kind of set-up from what he came from. You could tell that by the way she talked.

'Not that it isn't a good night for walking,' he said with a laugh. He ran down the three verandah steps to the gravel below.

'I'm coming,' said Denney desperately. 'You don't have to run. Please don't run. Just walk naturally. I mean slowly. I mean, as if there's lots of time and nothing to worry about. We'll just walk down as if you came to deliver the stores. Nothing else . . .'

Denney was on the gravel beside him and she put out her hand and touched his arm in a gesture that meant him to turn and walk slowly and sedately round the house and down the track to the gate.

Mr Barnes was so bewildered he wondered if it was he himself who had fallen and cracked his head.

Maybe it was loneliness that was getting Denney down. There are two kinds of loneliness. Albert Barnes knew all about that.

'Well, that feller . . .' he stammered. 'I reckon if he's got his wits about him, he might just make it. Seems to have stolen more'n one car since he did that girl in. You know what, Denney, if I was on the run that's what I'd do. Pinch one car and go a bit or two in that, then change to another. Though he's making a mistake leaving 'em on the side of the road. It's like leaving a trail behind you . . .'

'I suppose they'll blame him for every stolen car,' Denney

said. 'But how do they know it was Jack Smith? Doesn't anyone else ever steal a car in this State? And please don't talk about him any more. Let's talk about the cost of living: out aloud, as if we want the birds and the bees to know there's an awful price on being a human being these days.'

They were going down the path now and Denney raised her voice appreciably.

'I suppose the last monthly bill you sent me was the size it was because they've passed the basic wage rise on to the customer. You can see my point about the birds and the bees. There's no rise in price of honey for *them* . . .'

Mr Barnes wondered why Denney had to raise her voice. Did she want the whole dratted neighbourhood to hear her? And come to think of it, the only neighbours were the birds and the bees: throw in her own livestock and a snake or two in the bush.

'Look,' he said irately. 'That bill of mine was the same as ever. Not a penny up on a tin of peas, let alone honey. If I recollect, it was a bit short on last month's account.'

Mr Barnes in his indignation had stopped and faced Denney, but for the second time she put out her hand and, catching his arm, urged him on towards the gate. Not too quickly, yet not too slowly. Just naturally.

'Oh yes it was,' she said loudly, an unnatural excitement in her voice. 'Oh yes it was, Mr Barnes. Your accounts are far too high. Of course I realize you deliver now and again. The crate of drinks today, for instance. Thank you for delivering them.'

Mr Barnes would have come to a standstill again only Denney pushed him on.

'I've never charged a tanner in my life for delivering . . .'
He was really angry now.

'Of course it's useful to have my drinks delivered today for me, though I must admit I didn't expect you. I would have ordered the cigarettes from you if I had realized you were delivering today. I would have stopped and given you an order.'

Denney's voice was louder than ever.

Mr Barnes scrambled at top speed over the cowcatcher because he was annoyed with Denney for treating him in this manner . . . shouting in his ear and questioning his accounts. She must be mad, and come to think of it, he'd been thinking that way ever since he set foot on the ruddy place. You never could tell with women when they had a boy friend in the offing. Scared he'd see Ben Darcy riding up that back track or maybe scared Ben Darcy 'ud see him, Albert Barnes, in Denney's kitchen and her all alone on the place. That's what she was.

Damn all women to hell, said Albert Barnes as he got in his truck and slammed the drive door.

'Mr Barnes,' Denney said softly, but he did not hear her as he revved up the engine. 'Good-bye, Mr Barnes, I think you are safe now. Nothing has happened. But please go quickly. Quickly. Good-bye, Mr Barnes.'

There were tears in her eyes as she watched the cloud of dust, brown against the darkling sky, left by the utility speeding round the corner post of the boundary. 'I don't suppose you'll ever know . . .'

She turned and walked slowly back up the track to the homestead. Perhaps Jack Smith had shot through during the day. Perhaps he had gone away and was not lurking behind any one of those image-still bushes that crowded along the track by her boundary fence. As she walked down to the gate with Mr Barnes she had waited for the orange spitfire from a gun, but nothing had happened. Perhaps Jack Smith had gone away.

Denney was too tired to care any more. If Mr Barnes had been about to die, then she had been about to die with him. Funny, the people you die for! Mr Barnes was just a store-keeper and something of a trade friend. That was all. Whoever would have thought that one day Denney might have willingly elected to die with him, because if he died at all it was her fault. It was the least she could have done.

'And nobody will ever know,' thought Denney sadly.

She was too tired to care any more, herself.

Near the verandah steps she turned round and looked down to her boundary fence. She stood quite still, a willing target, too tired even to dramatize herself, though, lurking at the back of her mind, was the appreciation of the fact it would make a good story, weeks, months, years hence . . . if ever she lived to tell it. Her sisters would gawp and gape, and generations later the descendants of the Montgomery family would look up from the breakfast table at the photograph of Great-aunt Denney over the mantelshelf and say – She actually walked down to the gate in the face of death with a man she didn't even know, because she thought it was a point of honour to die with him, if he had to die on her place!

In case anyone in the future generations didn't know the apt definition of *noblesse oblige*, there was Denney's story waiting on hand, ready to serve up with the porridge.

Denney turned and went slowly round the side of the house, up the three steps on to the back verandah and so into the house. She took the dozen bottles of mixed soft drinks and beer from the crate, put two in the fridge and the rest in the bottom left-hand cupboard of the dresser. She put the crate, turned on its side, outside the back door.

She wasn't thinking, but she knew it was hot and soundlessly still. If a gumnut had fallen in the bush she would have heard it like the firing of a shot from Jack Smith's gun. No stir of breeze had moved the vanes of the windmill. It was as still, silhouetted against the purple sky, afterglow of sunset, as a photograph in a newspaper. When the east wind rose in the night she would hear the windmill before she heard the wind soughing, a wave of air, over the treetops; smelling of the desert and the dried grasses of the dustlands beyond the range.

She went back into the kitchen, leaving the door open. One had to have air, whether one was about to die, or about to become an accessory after the fact, or not. One had to have air.

This dying business, from one cause or another, seemed to Denney inevitable, and as she was tired, cross and altogether fed up she couldn't figure out why her mind kept switching on to the miserable subject.

She stood in the kitchen and looked around and wondered what point of the meal preparation she had reached when Albert Barnes had chosen to drive up.

Oh yes, the vegetables! They were boiled soft, of course. She would drain them, then mash them up and fry them in oil with some bacon while her chop cooked. Like the Spartans before Thermopylæ, she would have to eat first. No, they did their hair. Well, damn and blast her own hair to hell! She was hungry. And Jack Smith, if he came, could wait for his chop. She would cook her own and Jack Smith could have his when it suited her to cook it.

She wondered if he would like two chops. Probably would.

Denney, the tip of her tongue tucked in the corner of her mouth as she worked at her meal, thought about how young Jack Smith looked.

Just a boy, when you came to think of it. He had a sort of pale face, with soft skin. Ought to have been a girl, really. Could that have been where all the trouble began? Was he one of those males with too much female in him? Denney had read that everyone had both male and female in them but one sex became predominant at the expense of the other. She must look it up next time she was in the Library.

That reminded her she had forgotten to look up about passionfruit. If Jack Smith didn't do something or other about getting out of her life, sooner than later too, her farm would go to wrack and ruin. What's more, she'd end up in a mental hospital herself.

The mashed vegetables, with a rasher of bacon, frizzled happily in the pan, and Denney put her chop on the stove top to grill in its own fat. She peppered and salted it, then turned it over and applied the pepper and salt again.

Now where was she up to?

Oh yes, about Jack Smith looking girlish. Well, what she had read said that everyone had both sexes at first and then one sex became predominant. Only *some* people had just a shade too much of the wrong sex mixed up with the right sex. What she really meant by that was that when the under sex was down and out it ought to stay out, and the predominant (she remembered that word was the right word to use) ought to stay top dog and be done with it. Only sometimes this under sex got a bit uppity. That way you got some men that were a bit effeminate. You got some women that were a bit masculine too. Hmm! Everyone knew what *they* were called.

Denney was quite ruthless about the weaknesses of her own sex. She thought with hot dislike of the women who were the you-know-whats. But when it came to Jack Smith with his pale skin and fair hair and soft full mouth with the lips that were too wet, she felt only pity. After all, he didn't elect to be born like that!

She turned the chop over again and the fat on the black iron oven top spat venomously.

'Poor devil,' she said. 'He never even had a chance before he was born.' Right in his mother's womb the cards were stacked against him. If he'd had a reasonable mother, an educated one: a mother that knew about these things the way Denney knew about them, he could have been protected. Maybe helped. Had an operation or something. Like they do in Stockholm. Instead of that he got a stepfather, with a stick in his voice. And everyone laughed at him, and kicked him out of schools. Nobody had ever loved him, or even liked him.

Well, here was she, Denney, stuck with him. She wondered again why God had picked her.

'When you think of the millions of people in the world He might have picked . . .' said Denney as she lifted the chop on the end of the grilling fork to the hot plate waiting on the oven shelf.

She scraped half the vegetables and half the bacon on to the plate beside the chop. She scrupulously readjusted this by a spoonful to make sure Jack Smith got just as much as she did, and put his share on another hot plate. She put a saucepan lid over this to keep it from drying out and put the plate back in the oven.

She was not, however, going to cook that chop until she was good and ready. When Jack Smith came, if he came at all, he could wait while it cooked.

She put her own meal in the place she had set for herself and sat looking at it. She picked up the knife and fork but did not plunge them into the longed-for meal. She sat holding them, looking with unseeing eyes at the plate.

Supposing he didn't come at all? Well, that was all right by her, but if he didn't come how was she to know he didn't go on through life slaying women in foreign places like the Eastern States? She'd be several accessories after the fact, wouldn't she? She, like Jack Smith, could only hang for one crime, but she wasn't thinking about herself. She was thinking about the people Jack Smith might kill.

When you come to think of it, they'd be the same kind of persons that Beryl Seaton had been, wouldn't they? And think how she felt herself about people who threw lighted cigarettes out of their cars in the fire hazard season. She'd murder them, herself, wouldn't she? And didn't they deserve it?

Denney plunged her knife and fork into the chop.

'There's a murderer in the heart of every one of us,' she said finally and with satisfaction. 'Now I know why I don't intend to give Jack Smith up. I didn't have to think it out after all. I'm a murderer too, *in my heart*. I'm on the run too, like everyone else. We're always running away from something we've done wrong or some wrong we know we might do . . . given the chance. Well, not given the chance exactly, but under great provocation. That's what the word is . . . provocation. *Great provocation.*'

Denney enjoyed that two worded conclusion to her long day's dilemma in exactly the same sense that she now enjoyed the grilled chop. She had cooked it exactly right. A little pink in the middle and faintly charred on the outside.

It tasted good. She felt happy, very happy.

'I'm a murderer too,' she said. 'That's why everyone feels like death when there's a hanging on. They think . . . "There but for the grace of God, go I." It all depends on the way the cards are stacked, and they know it. Those who don't hang are just lucky. The jack of clubs didn't come up when God dealt out the cards.'

CHAPTER SEVEN

WHAT was that?

Denney straightened her back and sat still, the knife and fork suspended by her two hands in the air. She could feel her heart beating in her throat and ears.

It was a stick cracking in the bush, of course, or an old tree branch breaking down from a tree. It happened all the time in summer because the temperature had a big drop at night time. Even though it was still warm, out there in the bush there would be a ten degree drop from the afternoon's temperatures.

Denney often heard the nuts falling in the bush and tree sticks and branches cracking. She often heard the timbers in her own house cracking as they expanded and contracted in the changing temperatures.

What was the matter with her that she had to jump like that?

Really, this business was terribly nerve-wracking.

It wouldn't be Jack Smith. She knew that for sure. He'd come in snakewise, as silent as the slippery reptile that he was. Just wait till he did come in . . . if he was going on frightening her like that! And keeping her waiting for his chop too.

Denney put down her knife and fork, leaned her elbow on the table, her forehead on her hand, and started to cry, something she had been talking herself out of ever since Mr

Barnes had gone safely away.

The tears rolled down her cheeks and fell into the grease left by her chop in the plate. When her nose had to be blown she had to get up and go to her handbag which she had left on the dresser.

'Damn and blast!' she said as she blew her nose. The only possible thing left to do now was smoke a cigarette. If she'd had a cigarette half an hour ago, she wouldn't have felt like this.

She went out on to the back verandah, leaving the kitchen door open so that the rectangle of yellow light threw its pattern on the verandah floor. She took a packet of cigarettes from the carton which had lain there against the wall ever since she had come home, and then sat on the top step of the verandah and lit the cigarette.

She sat there smoking, her elbows resting on her knees, her eyes looking above and beyond the rim of bush that stood at the foot of her garden, at the ink-black sky and the stars, bright as minute apricot fires, gazing down with such indifference.

There was a pale glow in the eastern sky and presently the moon would rise. On such a night, it, with all its myriad stars to help, would flood her farm with silver light in which one could read a book.

If Jack Smith didn't come early, Denney decided, she was not going to bed. There was one thing being caught in the garden or the kitchen or on the verandahs . . . front or back . . . but quite another thing being caught asleep.

There wasn't going to be any kind of that hanky panky. No thank you. Not in the bedroom, or on the sofa in the sitting-room either. Being raped, as far as Denney was concerned, was definitely *out*. Even if he could rape!

Hmm!

She sat and looked at the stars and she thought about Ben. One other thing she was sorry about. She hadn't told Ben she loved him. Well, she hadn't really known it, but the stars made her realize it this early evening. It would be too late now, like Mr Barnes ever knowing she had offered to die with him.

What a mute, inglorious heroine she, Denney, was turning out to be!

She loved Ben very much, but quite apart from the fact their farms were miles apart, and never the twain would meet, she probably would never be able to tell him. Not that he had ever asked her, but what did that matter? It's nice to be loved by anybody or anything, even if you don't want to love back in return. It was too late now. Even if she lived she would be a disgrace and so she couldn't ever tell Ben.

Such a pity.

Denney had smoked two cigarettes and in that time nothing had stirred in her garden nor in the orchard or the bush. Not even the vanes on the windmill had moved. The windmill always started working with a clank and she must remember when it did, if the east wind rose, not to jump out of her skin again. That had been really quite exhausting. She ought to take a tonic for her nerves, that was for sure.

She got up stiffly from the top step and went into the kitchen.

She pushed the coals together in the stove to keep the oven warm and then gathered her own dishes from the table and took them to the sink. When she'd finished washing up she would make a cup of tea.

She had reached the soaping-the-water stage when she remembered the new tea towels she had bought a week ago had fallen out of the back of the dresser drawer and were lying somewhere cached between the wall and the dresser.

She went over to the dresser and started to edge it carefully out from the wall. It was loaded with china and Denney was too tired to take all that china down and out, not to mention the bottles of soft drink and beer that Mr Barnes had brought. If she was careful she could edge the dresser away from the wall and probe out the tea towels, still folded in their pristine newness, with the broom handle.

One more inch and she would be right! At that moment the dresser rocked slightly and tilted forward. Denney was holding it upright with one hand, her body bent sideways and the other hand and arm lending the dresser security at the base. She wondered what to do next.

At that moment she looked up and between strands of fallen hair saw Jack Smith's gun edging its way round the corner of the kitchen door.

She stayed still, a figure in a game of statues, and watched that gun inching its way into the room. Her heart stopped functioning altogether, and so did her brain.

Seconds later Jack Smith's hand, and then Jack Smith's body, his pale face and fair hair above it, was in the doorway, the gun held before him.

Denney was caught in her dresser-saving position, her body bent down sideways, one hand holding the dresser at the base, the other hand higher up, holding it from falling forward.

'Anybody 'ud think that gun was yours instead of Ben Darcy's,' she said caustically. 'All the same, thank God you've come. One more minute of this and the whole damn dresser 'ud be down. Me under it, not to mention the china.'

'What you doing?' said Jack Smith, his face deadpan, his voice soft and flat.

'Oh, for God's sake, can't you see?' said Denney. 'Come and help me. I can't stay here for ever. Quick, grab the top.'

The dresser rocked on its bases as if to add its own warning. Jack Smith methodically put the gun down on the kitchen table and came to Denney's rescue. He put up both hands and braced the dresser back against the wall.

Denney said 'Ouch!' as she straightened up stiffly. She pushed the hair back out of her eyes. 'That was a close go. Thank Heaven you came in time.'

'What you doing?' he asked again.

'Trying to get some towels that fell down behind it. Look, now you're here you pull out the dresser while I hold it from falling forward. Then I'll get the dratted things out. Come round this end and lift it out. You're stronger than I am. I'll hold it up in front. That's right. That's enough. Six inches 'll do. Now just wait a minute till I get the kitchen broom.'

Jack Smith methodically, mechanically, had done what Denney asked, possibly astonished at himself for so doing. He didn't usually give a lending hand: let alone to women in distress. Not his line at all.

The towels were retrieved and the dresser pushed back in its place. Denney, putting one towel in the dresser drawer and shaking out the other ready to use, realized that her heart was beating after all.

She looked at Jack Smith over the shaken towel.

'Your vegetables are in the oven,' she said. 'But you'll have to wait while I cook the chop.'

Jack picked up the gun and went to the end of the table. With a foot he kicked back the chair and sat down. He put the gun precisely where he had put it on the previous evening.

'Can't you forget that thing?' said Denney, going to the stove. She had her back to him as she bent down and stirred up the coals again. She added kindling to them and blew on them until the kindling had caught. She couldn't go on waiting to be shot in the back for ever. She'd just have to put up with it – if it was coming.

'I'll have to wait till the stove heats up a bit,' she said. 'How about a cup of tea?'

Jack Smith nodded. Denney turned and looked into his eyes for the first time since he had come into the kitchen. For the rest of the time she had been pretending she was too busy to look directly at him.

He had the face of an enemy and his eyes were stone hard.

'What you been doing down there? Down in the town?' he said.

'Taking my stuff to the market,' said Denney. 'I got the cigarettes. You want a cigarette, Jack? They're on the window-sill.'

'You get them,' he said.

Denney, who had been lifting the lid of the kettle to see if it was really on the boil, looked round.

'Look,' she said. 'I've been working all day. I'm tired. What's wrong with you getting them?'

'You get them,' he said.

Denney turned to the window-sill and, retrieving the cigarettes, sent them sliding down the length of the table as she had done last night.

'I don't know why I wait on you,' she said. 'Look, I've got your vegetables cooked in the oven, and your place set. I've been waiting for you to come to grill your chop.'

She had turned back to the stove and was pouring the boiling water from the kettle into the teapot. 'What have you been doing all day?' she said.

Jack lit a cigarette. He made the packet spin like a top on the table in front of him.

'That's what I asked you. It don't take all day to sell that stuff in the market, do it?'

'No,' said Denney, bringing the teapot to the table and taking down cups and saucers from the dresser. She took a jug of milk from the bucket she had brought in when she finished milking Rona. 'I've been to the Library to find out about passionfruit.'

'Passionfruit! What's that got to do with getting cigarettes and coming straight home?'

Denney poured the tea and passed him a cup. She pushed

the sugar down the table towards him and then sat down.

'I'm going to put trellises of passionfruit along that northern slope. Least I think it's the slope. That's what I had to find out. The best breeds, the proper aspect. There's big money in passionfruit these days. The bottling companies buy up all they can get. Like sandwich bars. You can make money out of sandwiches, if you get a stand with the right aspect; dead in the line of workers.'

Denney put both elbows on the table and sipped her own tea. Jack Smith said nothing.

'That's good,' Denney said of the tea. 'I've been waiting for that a long time. Why didn't you come earlier?'

'Waiting to see who you brought back from the market Waiting to see if you brought the dicks back.'

Denney put down her cup in genuine indignation.

'Waiting to see if I brought the dicks back?' she said with angry grievance. 'You've been waiting to see if I'd give you away? I like that! Look, Jack Smith, you just wake up. If I'd been telling dicks about you I wouldn't be here. They'd be here. You just think that one out for yourself. I wouldn't be here squinting down the barrel of that gun just to show the dicks the way to my homestead. They know the way, if they want to find it. They don't. They think you're pinching cars out York way. Or was it Mundijong last time?'

'Merredin,' he said. 'On the way to Kalgoorlie and the border. Say, you ever heard of a place called Merredin? I never did.' He was easier in his manner now, and he was blowing on his tea and drinking it. 'Don't you listen to the radio, or read the papers or somethin'?'

'Haven't had time,' said Denney. Those papers! She'd carried them round all day and not read them. They were lying, still bundled, where she'd thrown the cigarettes when she'd first come in.

'What did the radio or the papers say?' she asked.

'You ain't heard? Didn't no one down there at the market tell you?'

'I didn't have time to talk. Listen, selling stuff at the market is hard business. You got to choose your moment for auctioning. Prices go up and down. You got to watch what's going on. And you got to drive your stuff in, and unload it. Then get it on the floor. Then offer it when you want to sell. You don't have time to talk.'

'You do all that?' he asked.

'Of course I do it,' said Denney, lying with aplomb. That's a lie she'd tell any one . . . except the Market Galahads and Ben. A matter of personal prestige, of course.

'How come you can't lift that dresser then?'

'Where's your brains?' said Denney. 'A dresser isn't a case of fruit. It's heavier to begin with. And it's long upwards. Like up the wall. A case of fruit is long wideways. Like this.' She spread her hands as if demonstrating the length of a flat case of fruit. 'You hold them different . . .' There she was talking in his half-illiterate lingo. How catching can it be?

'Okay, okay! You were too busy lifting stuff to find out I'm heading for the South Australian border.'

'That's what your radio told you?'

Jack Smith patted the pocket where he kept the transistor. 'That's what she told me. How about putting that chop on? I'm bloody empty.'

The fire was cracking hot now and Denney got up. She put pepper and salt on the chop and a sliver of butter on the stove top. Then she put the chop on the sizzling patch.

'What else did your radio tell you?' she asked.

'Don't you know nothing?'

'I just know I got to sell my stuff. I got to go to the Library and find out about passionfruit. I got to buy those cigarettes. And I got to get home and feed and water . . .' Talking the way he talked . . . how crazy was she, anyway?

'I know. I know. I saw you. I get sick a' watchin' you race round like you got ants eatin' you someplace. I get sick a' watchin' you through that door eatin' your dinner, and sittin' on the doorstep smokin' cigarettes.'

'Then why didn't you come in?'

'Like I said. I was watchin' to see if you brought dicks. I saw that other fellow come. Who's he?'

'The local grocer,' said Denney, turning over the chop but not turning round herself. 'Brought some cool drinks.' She had nearly said beer, but an extra sense of caution stopped her. He might be the kind of person who couldn't take beer: who went berserk when he had alcohol in him. 'There's ginger ale in the dresser cupboard, if you want some,' said Denney.

'Ginger ale!' he said with bitter sarcasm. Yes, she was glad she hadn't mentioned the beer.

'So what about him?' said Jack Smith, meaning the local grocer. 'What did you tell him?'

Denney turned the chop again, this time viciously.

'What do you think I told him? Do you think I want to be in the *can*? You've been in the can. You know what it's like. What do you think I want to get there for?'

'Why? What you been doin'?'

'Looking after you. Do you know what? I could get twenty years for that.'

She retrieved the hot plate with the vegetables from the oven, skewered the chop on to it and brought it to the table. She took it right round the table to Jack Smith and put it in front of him. He was looking up at her.

'Twenty years? How you know?'

Denney shrugged.

'I read it somewhere. Somebody did it once. They got twenty years.'

As she went back to her place she believed it herself.

Jack tore his knife and fork into his meal. He ate furiously for a few minutes.

He pushed his third mouthful into his cheek.

'Twenty years!' he said. 'What do you know? Ain't they bastards? What they gave you for stealing a car over here?'

'You ought to know. You stole one in Kalamunda and one in York and now one in Merredin.'

She started to laugh. How crazy could she be? She'd said something funny, and she could laugh. Yes, Ben was right. She was a zany. Now . . . now at long last she knew what he meant. She just didn't know the difference between something funny, and a moment when death itself stood poised on her doorstep.

Jack Smith didn't laugh but his manner was easier. The agate hardness had gone out of his eyes, the tenseness out of the way he held himself. He no longer kept one eye on the gun.

'Tell me some about this chap came up here tonight. The one what brought the ginger ale. When I saw him coming, I wasn't sure you hadn't ratted. Then I saw you walkin' down to the gate with him. An' I reckoned he went away in a huff. You'd put a flea in his car.'

'You bet I did,' said Denney. She lifted the teapot and poured more tea into her cup. 'Double charged me for a tin of peas on last month's order. He got what's what.'

She believed that too. If she went to Heaven when all this was over she would make a special supplication for Albert

Barnes because of what she told Jack Smith about him. Not that she believed in supplication, or even Heaven, but it was something to say to herself to cheer herself up.

'You oughta told me. I'd a put a shot a pellets in his backside. The dirty robber.'

'You save your pellets for the rabbits. You got to do some rabbit shooting round here before you're much older.'

Denney looked at Jack Smith over the rim of her cup.

'What you mean? Rabbit shootin?' he said with his mouth full.

'They're beginning to come in over the hills. You got to help me get rid of them. They eat out the grazing worse than the kangaroos. Last March we had a cyclone brought ten inches of rain out there on the sandplain, the other side of the range. All the winter the grass was shooting like nobody's business. Rabbits sprang up there by the million.'

'How come I'm goin' to shoot rabbits? I might be someplace else.'

Denney shrugged.

'That's okay by me,' she said. Then she paused. Very slowly she added, 'You can stay here, Jack. I need help. You'll be all right with me and I can do with someone for those rabbits. To put in the passion vines too.'

Now she was indeed an accessory after the fact. She wasn't doing this for Jack Smith only. She was doing it for all the people he might yet kill. She was giving them a chance the same as she had given Albert Barnes the chance to die in good company. She owed it to them to give them a sporting opportunity to escape their fate. It had all been her fault because, last night, when he had lain there on the floor she could have taken that gun and escaped. This morning at nine fifteen ack emma she could have stopped at Albert Barnes's store and got him to phone the police. She could have told Inspector Riley the truth at roughly ten fifty-five, nearly an hour and three-quarters later. It would have given those 'dicks' a chance to catch Jack Smith. She hadn't done any of those things, and now she was stuck with Jack Smith. She had swallowed poison, and now she had it.

Jack Smith, chewing noisily, watched her. Tonight he wore his larrikin manners. Denney had found herself, without volition, speaking in the same staccato semi-grammatical way that he had been speaking.

'What about this chap what brings the groceries? What about this other feller lives here? The one whose boots I got on?'

'I just got to tell them I hired you. From down south, or somewhere. I got to get you some decent work clothes, and some dye on your hair.'

'Yeah, that's a good idea. I always wanted to have black hair, like a fella I knew could knock anyone down with one hand. All comers. Black hair, he had. An' shoulders no bigger'n mine. I never could find out how he did it . . . *What was that?*'

Jack grabbed the gun and stood up, knocking over the chair behind him. He stared at the wall against which the dresser stood.

'That,' said Denney without moving, 'is the timber in the house contracting. In the daytime it expands in the heat. Night-time it cracks away from the joists when it contracts. Sometimes it causes a leak in the roof.'

'You sure?' said Jack, staring at her, face white, eyes as black as any of the Market Galahads.

'Sure,' said Denney, nodding her head calmly. 'Sit down, and I'll put some more hot water in the tea. You can do another cup. You heard it. It came from the wall.' She got up and went to the stove to make some fresh tea. 'Down in the bush the nuts fall and the branches crack when the temperature changes. You got to get used to those noises, Jack. It's the weather. Some time when the east wind rises you'll hear the windmill start up with a clank. That's how I always know the east wind is coming. First it comes in the tops of the trees, and high up, so the windmill vanes catch it. Then by and by the curtains in the windows begin to move. It comes in full force then and it's down at ground level. Not just high up where the trees and the windmill catch it . . .'

Jack Smith was sitting down again, uneasily, on the edge of the chair. He nursed the gun across his knees.

'You're a one for talkin',' he said. 'Don't you ever stop?'

'Well, *you* talk,' said Denney. 'You tell me what you've been doing all day.'

She brought the pot of fresh tea to the table, collected the used cups and saucers and carried them to the sink. She took clean ones from the dresser.

Jack Smith was watching her.

'Don't you ever do nothing else night time but drink tea?' he asked, heavily sarcastic.

'You tell me what else there is to do. Drink tea, smoke cigarettes and *talk*.'

'Okay, okay. Might as well,' he said. This time he was placating Denney.

'Well, you talk. You tell me what you were doing today.'

'Sleepin'. I always sleep when I get sick and faint.' He watched Denney, craftily, as he said this. 'I faint when I don't get enough food in my insides. Like I did last night.' He paused. 'I fainted, didn't I?' he asked defensively.

Denney nodded.

'I guess you were hungry,' she said. 'You had a lot of food into a stomach that had been empty too long. It had shrunk up. That's what happens to stomachs when they're empty a long time.'

He nodded, then stirred the sugar into his tea.

'Yeah. That happens sometimes,' he agreed. There was a small silence, then he added, 'I did that once when they got me in the delinquent jug, an' you know what? When they got me in the Court . . . yeah, the Kids' Court . . . the officer, he said, "Yer Worship," 'e said. "this feller has fits. Epilepsy fits".'

Jack Smith slewed his eyes quickly round to Denney.

'What you think of that?' he asked. He was vigilant, suspicious.

Denney pursed her lips thoughtfully.

'I'll tell you what I think,' she said judicially. 'This officer in the Court, maybe he was the one they appoint to put up a case for you. In a Court there has to be someone to speak for a person as well as against him. This officer might have been a cunning sort. He might have thought this idea of fits might get you off. It could make you out a sick person, you see. Then they wouldn't send you to prison. The delinquent jug, as you call it.'

Jack Smith nodded.

'Yeah,' he said bitterly. 'It sent me to a hospital all right. One of them places where the psychos go. Asking questions all the time. What's yer father like? What's yer mother like? What you like to do? How'd you get those bumps on the back of your head? An' that scar on yer chin . . .?'

Denney nearly slopped her tea.

Funny, but she'd forgotten all about that scar. Jack Smith

held that small receding chin of his down all the time. She mustn't look up now. She mustn't let him see she was looking for it. Later . . .

Jack Smith drank a mouthful of tea greedily and reached for the packet of cigarettes. They were sharing one packet again. Denny intuitively knew this was not the right minute to get up and fetch another from the carton which was still out on the back verandah.

He lit a cigarette and slid the packet down the table to her. He went on:

' "And about this twin brother of yours. What about this twin brother? What's he look like. Where's he?" '

Denney's heart dropped. She almost heard it clatter in the cavity of her chest.

The twin brother! Had there or had there not been a sudden guarded look in Inspector Riley's eyes when she had said something about a twin brother. Had she said something? What had she said?

Well, whatever she had said might have been all right because they might have mentioned the twin brother over the air or in the papers. Dear God, why hadn't she read those blasted newspapers!

Denney began to get muddled in what Jack Smith was saying about the sort of questions they'd asked him in that 'hospital'. She was listening, but while she listened she tried frantically to go over in her mind that conversation with Inspector Riley this morning. The subject of twin brothers had come up, she was sure. Or wasn't she so sure? Was it just on her mind? What had been said over that tea this morning?

'In the end I told them all the things my twin brother done. An' I told them the snazzy things he could do too. Like shoot a gun from behind his back, an' climb a two-hundred-foot tree – you know, them mountain ashes in Victoria – with only an axe an' spikes on his shoes. An' he could sail a yacht in the Hobart race too. All the same he was a bad 'un. I told them that too. But I didn't know where he was. I couldn't tell 'em that one. Anyhow I was always covering for him. I was always taking the rap for him. I told them that plenty. I told them he done most of the things they got me for. But I wasn't going to tell them where he was. No, siree! Not me.'

A wooden beam in the roof cracked again, but this time Jack Smith did not start. He had fallen silent, ruminating sadly on the history of his twin brother.

'Funny, when it's quiet, you say everything's dead still,' said Denney softly. 'All the time it's not still. The timber up there is quietly . . . quietly expanding or contracting. Then it goes off with a crack like that . . .'

'Yeah,' said Jack Smith, also quiet now. Talking about his twin brother's prowess in adventures and his sins against society had somehow given him release. The gun was back across the corner of the table now and Jack Smith leaned his elbows on the table, his chest against it, his head a little bowed as if, soon, he might go to sleep.

'Nothin's ever quiet,' he said. 'Down there in the bush where I was laying today, there's things moving under the leaves an' in and out the bark of the logs all the time. An' there's little things flying in the air. You can't hardly see them, but they're there, flyin' all the time . . .'

'Down by the creek is the best place,' Denney said. The mood in the room was one of quiet solace. 'I don't get time now, but when I was a little girl we used to come up here. Me, and my four sisters. And we used to go down to the creek to the pools above the waterfalls to catch gilgies.'

'Gilgies? What's gilgies?'

'Little freshwater crayfish. We used to catch them and put them in a tin to take home. The one that got the most was the best fisher, but sometimes one would knock over someone else's tin right there on the edge of the pool. And there'd be a howling match.'

'What did you do with them? Eat them?'

'No. We just used to take them home and put the tins on the tankstand, and maybe we'd forget all about them and then someone would find them days later, and they'd all be dead. I hate myself now when I think of what we did to the gilgies when we were kids. We just hunted them to see who could get the most. We didn't really want them. And we took them home, and they died. I don't know. Kids are awfully cruel.'

Jack Smith nodded his head.

'It's all right if you eat them.'

'Well, there's a purpose to it in that. The other way . . . just gloating because you got the most. Then letting them die. It was like picking the wildflowers.'

'You pick wildflowers up here too?'

'Not now,' said Denney, vigorously shaking her head. 'For one thing, it's against the law now. But I wouldn't anyway. I like to let things live. But when we were kids we used to walk for miles to find wildflowers. We went all over the bush. Down in the gullies, and along the old zig-zag. We got wonderful orchids down there in the water traps by the points of the old zig-zag. We used to scream out every time we'd got a special one . . . or something better than the others. I always wanted to get the biggest bunch . . .'

'Did you?'

'Sometimes. We used to go down to school on the plain in that old zig-zag train. And when it stopped at one point for the engine to shunt off to the other end of the train we used to jump out and pick a bunch of wildflowers and run down the points to pick up the train again at the bottom of the hill.'

Denney stopped.

'Golly, it was fun,' she said. She reached for the packet of cigarettes. She slid it down the table and Jack Smith stubbed out one cigarette and took another.

'Once a girl on the train who used to do that with us fell and broke her arm. After that we weren't allowed out of the train. The guard used to come along and threaten to take our names and addresses for breaking the Law.'

'The bloody Law,' Jack Smith said, dragging heavily on his cigarette.

'All the same, if you wanted to hear things, when the bush was quiet it was best to go down by the creek,' said Denney. 'You could lie down in the fern there and just listen. First it was the water creeping and falling over the stones : just eddying round the old fallen log and under the bushes. Then there were the leaves that fell into the water, and the lizards rustling. Then you'd hear the tiny beetles, and a dragonfly alight on a leaf.'

'I bet you never heard a dragonfly get on a leaf. They don't make no noise at all.'

'I did. I swear I did,' said Denney. 'You had to listen very hard. You had to watch it and then, just as it came down on the leaf . . .'

'*What was that?*' Jack Smith straighened with a jerk.

Denney laughed.

'That,' she said, 'was one of the fowls falling off its roost.'

'I don't like those things that make a noise out there.'

'It's only because it's so quiet. Wait till the wind rises. It could come any minute now. Then you don't notice the ordinary noises, because the world isn't quiet any more . . . everything's moving.'

Jack was sitting up stiffly, his head cocked. He had slowly and carefully taken the gun back on his knee, his eyes were on the open door and the patch of yellow lights shafting out across the verandah.

'I can hear something,' he said.

Denney listened.

'Maybe that's the east wind coming,' she said at last. 'Things seem to stir a little first. There's a sort of change in the air. You know what, Jack? It's like as if the bush is getting ready for the wind. Pulling in her petticoats, you might say.'

'What we leave that bloody door open for?'

Denney shrugged.

'I forgot it. You forgot it. What's it matter, Jack? No one will come. Not at this hour.'

He turned his head and his eyes met hers.

'You swear you don't tell anyone I'm up here when you go down to that market?'

Denney looked at him down the table with clear eyes.

'Yes, I swear, Jack. I didn't tell anyone. I never will tell anyone. You've got to believe that. This time you've got to believe someone. I'm in this too. You figure it out for yourself, Jack.'

'Twenty years in the can, huh?'

'I guess it would be twenty years.'

The windmill clanged. The vanes spun round in the wind and the bore shaft squeaked as it brought water to the surface.

Denney relaxed and smiled.

'There you are,' she said. 'It was the east wind coming. Listen to the water coming up. That's life's blood to my farm. Come on, Jack. Come on out and you can practise turning it off and on. Anyhow, I'm never quite tall enough to turn on the cog from the big tank to the house tank. You can climb up and do it for me.'

She went to the door and on to the verandah. He came too, but he carried that gun.

Would he never have enough faith to put it down, and leave it down? she wondered.

The moon was up and the farmyard was flooded with white

179

light. The shadows of the trees lay sprawled across the ground like black etchings, the leaves caught the moonshine in slivers of silver. The sheds stood dark in haunted shadows, and below the garden, beyond the rails of the horse paddock, the bush trees could each be seen white trunked by moonlight and only dark where the silver light could not penetrate.

Denney stood at the top of the verandah steps.

'There you are,' she said. 'It's beautiful, isn't it? What were we sitting in the stuffy house for?'

Jack, at first warily, had followed her. Now he stood beside her.

'Go on,' Denney said with a challenge. 'Turn off the windmill. I showed you how last night. Bet you've forgotten . . .'

'Not me,' said Jack Smith. He walked down the three steps to the ground. He looked around, holding the gun like a soldier about to advance into the unknown evening of the jungle.

'Well, you'll have to put that thing down to turn off the windmill,' said Denney, determined to win her point that Jack Smith would have to learn to live without a gun frozen to his right hand.

'I'll put it down when I'm good and ready,' said Jack. 'Not before.'

He advanced over the gravel square, looking cautiously from left to right. Each way he turned his head Denney could see the pale, almost ghostly white of his face.

'You got to learn to do it some time, Jack,' Denney said. 'You got to learn to walk at night without a gun. And live in the daytime outside the bush . . .'

The words froze in her mouth.

All around there were shadows moving. Not tree shadows, not shed shadows. Not the shadow of a night owl flying noiselessly from branch to branch. Not the moving of the east wind in the sapling trees.

The shadows came out of the trees and out of the sheds, but they weren't tree shadows nor shed shadows, for they moved out into the gravel yard.

They were noiseless, like the night owl flying from branch to branch.

Jack Smith was walking more easily now towards the windmill. He was walking quicker, looking up at the mill, the vanes stirring lazily around. He did not see the moving shadows; and Denney's tongue was stiff in her mouth.

Out of a nightmare she suddenly found release.

'Jack . . . Jack!' she cried. '*Jack!*'

He spun round.

The shadows moved in concert, and there was a voice. It was the loud authoritative voice of the Law.

'Drop that gun and put your hands up, Jack Smith. You're surrounded.'

He was frozen a moment, then he spun round to Denney. He lifted the gun.

'You bitch!' he screamed. 'You bleeding bitch!'

His gun shot fire, and guns all around him shot fire. First one, then all of them, but mostly Jack Smith's gun shot at Denney. She felt a bee-sting on her right ear and a needle in her arm.

She threw out both her arms.

'Jack,' she cried. 'Jack, I didn't bring them. I didn't bring them. I didn't, I didn't . . . I swear I didn't.'

She ran forward, but a shadow materializing from the side of the house reached her and spun her round.

'That's all right, Missis. Take it easy.'

He looked and felt and smelt like a policeman. Big, strong, and redolent of coal tar soap.

Denney struggled.

'Let me alone. I want to go to him . . .'

'Just stay steady, Misses. They've got him all right. He's down on the ground . . .'

Suddenly she stopped struggling and stood stiff in the policeman's arms.

'He shot me,' she said aghast. 'He shot me.'

'You still got plenty of kick in you. I don't think he shot you dead. Here, sit down on this step and we'll see if there's any damage.'

Denney was propelled towards the step on which she had been standing less than three minutes earlier. With his hands on her shoulders the policeman pushed her down so that she found herself sitting, the hard wooden plank of the step under her. She was facing the yard again now, and there were arc lights everywhere. The place was flooded with light and it wasn't moonlight. Cars were moving in on her backyard, their spotlights showing a figure prone on the ground, arms outstretched, a gun a yard away and three figures standing over him, and one kneeling beside.

Car doors were slamming and noisy boots were crunching over the gravel. Voices were addressing one another in loud tones.

Denney put her elbows on her knees and buried her face in her hands.

'It was so quiet,' she said. 'So quiet. We talked about it. About the things in the bush that can be heard if you listen hard. Like a dragonfly dropping on a leaf. And all the time you were all there . . .'

There was another man beside the first policeman now. They were circling her and touching her. First her right arm, then her ear. They were asking her questions but she didn't listen to them and wasn't answering them.

'He shot me,' she said incredulously. 'After all I did for him, he shot me.'

She shivered.

The policemen were speaking to one another.

'Looks like she's got lead in her right forearm and one's nicked her ear. Elsewhere she's about all right.'

'Probably suffering from shock. We ought to have brought the doctor out with us.'

'You can't do that sort of thing when you got guns. The first thing the judge asks did you go out with intent to kill. If not, why take a doctor.'

'Howzit with him?' The speaker nodded his head in the direction of the dark slim figure lying inert on the ground.

'You go and see. I'll stay with the lady.'

Denney dropped her arms and looked up.

'Tell him I didn't bring them,' she pleaded. 'Promise me you'll tell him I didn't bring them . . .'

Across the gravel square, walking away from that prostrate figure, was another figure she knew better.

Her heart lurched.

'Ben!' she said. 'Ben!'

He came towards her. He bent down and looked into her face.

'You all right, Denney?' he asked quietly.

She couldn't answer him.

'A coupla pellets, but harmless I think,' the policeman said.

'Okay,' said Ben. 'I'll look after her.'

'Howzit with him?'

'He's dead,' Ben said simply, his voice without expression.

'Cripes. Quite a battlefield.'

'Oh no!' said Denney. 'Oh *no*!'

The policeman walked away and Ben sat down on the step beside Denney. He took out his handkerchief and wiped away a trickle of blood from her cheek and her ear. He did the same to her right arm.

'We can pick that out with a pair of forceps,' he said of the lead pellet.

'He wouldn't have known I didn't bring them,' Denney said desperately. 'Why did they have to kill him?'

'Look, Denney,' said Ben, his voice measured and quiet. 'He shot you. You said it yourself. That about adds it up. You or him.'

'He never had a chance,' said Denney. 'You were all around . . .'

'Neither did you, standing on the step. You had the lighted kitchen behind you. Just a bottle on a fence, Denney.'

'So was he.'

'Okay, you both were. So it had to be you or him.'

Denney was silent, watching that group on the other side of the yard. Presently one of the men went into her shed and flashed his torch around. He came out with a piece of tarpaulin. He carried it across the yard and they covered the figure.

The men began to scatter now, but two remained by Jack Smith where he lay on the ground. Several went to the spotlighted cars and one was examining Jack Smith's gun in the spotlight of another car.

'I think you'd better come inside, Denney,' Ben said.

She shivered.

'No,' she said. 'I want to stay here.'

Inside would be the plates they had not washed up. The teacups would be on the table and the dead cigarette butts in the saucers they had used for ashtrays. The coals would be dying out in the fire.

'We talked about catching gilgies and picking wildflowers . . .'

A tall lean figure left the group of men by one of the cars and came across the gravel to the step.

'We'd better go inside, Denney, so we can look at those wounds. Constable Woods tells me he thinks there are only two . . . and they're slight.'

It was Detective-Inspector Riley.

Denney looked a long way up to him.

'No,' she said. And her teeth chattered. 'I want to stay here.'

'Okay,' Inspector Riley said. 'You've always got to have your own way, haven't you, Denney? Ben, go in and see if you can rustle up a rug to put round her shoulders. Might have a look-see if there's any sedative about the place. Second best, make it a whisky or brandy.'

'I don't take sleeping tablets,' said Denney with asperity.

This was not strictly the truth, as she occasionally did take a phenobarbital and there was a bottle with two or three tablets in it on the bathroom cabinet. But she wasn't going to have Inspector Riley pry into her private life. Next thing he would be arraining her before Court on a dope charge.

'There's a beer in the fridge, but it would make me sick. There's some cooking brandy in the dresser cupboard,' she added dully.

'Make it the brandy then, Ben,' said Inspector Riley. 'You'd better give yourself a stiff one too. We'll leave the beer for the men when we move on.'

'Whose beer are you talking about?' asked Denney, dazed and angry.

Ben had risen from the step and Inspector Riley took his place. He sat so close to Denney his shoulder touched her shoulder, just above where the pellet was beginning to make itself felt.

'It's your beer, Denney,' Inspector Riley said wearily as he took out a packet of cigarettes. He offered her one. First Denney shook her head and then suddenly changed her mind. She put out her hand, but it shook so much that Inspector Riley put the cigarette in her mouth and lit it for her.

'Must be getting cold,' Denney said.

'That rug, when Ben brings it, will help. It's not cold, Denney. You're suffering from shock. We'll get the doctor to give you the once over when he gets here.'

'Why does he have to come? Jack Smith's dead, isn't he?'

'Very dead.'

'Why did you have to do it?'

'I didn't do it. Not that I wouldn't have shot him if I'd been quick enough on the trigger. It needed someone a lot faster than me to save your life, young woman.'

'Pooh! It was only a shotgun.'

'A shotgun can kill if you get the full blast in the face. Or in a vital spot. It has been known to do just that.'

Denney was silenced. She drew on the cigarette and Inspector Riley remained silent beside her. A few minutes later Ben came out with a glass of brandy and water and he handed it to the detective.

'Drink this, Denney.'

Again she was going to say no, but changed her mind. Something was very queer in her head now, because she couldn't feel anything. Not even fear; or doubt, or guilt. Her mind was a blank. Maybe the brandy would help her. It would warm her anyway, and she was cold. She wondered why she could see beads of perspiration on the detective's face.

Ben had put the rug round her shoulders and she huddled it round her, careful not to spill the brandy. Its gentle fire warmed and soothed her. She wondered vaguely why Inspector Riley, sitting there in his shirt sleeves, no coat on, was not cold. The windmill was clanging wildly and the east wind had come in firm and strong.

'I sent him to turn it off,' Denney said bitterly. 'If only I'd gone myself . . .'

Ben had gone inside the house again and there were several others in there too. She could hear them. They must have gone in the front way. Were policemen allowed to break into other people's front doors? And how'd they look if she asked for their search warrant?

Inspector Riley began to speak very slowly, very patiently.

'Denney, when you came down to Perth this morning, why didn't you tell us Jack Smith was here?'

'Because I promised him I wouldn't.'

'Ah.'

There was a silence.

'What did you come down for? You don't usually go to market on Wednesdays, do you?'

'Cigarettes.'

'Why didn't you get them at the local store?'

'Because I said I was going to market. He believed me. I had to tell the truth, didn't I?'

'Do you always tell the truth?'

'Of course,' said Denney scornfully. She took another sip of the brandy. She was beginning to feel better, warmer inside, and clearer in the head. It was a very strong brandy.

'But you told me you were going to the Library to look up passionfruit. You didn't look up passionfruit. Why was that?'

Denney was suddenly wary.

'Because I forgot, because I looked up something else. How did you know I didn't look up passionfruit?'

'Because I followed you into the Library.'

'Why did you do that?' asked Denney indignantly. She took another swig of the strong brandy and a long puff of the cigarette. The rug fell off her shoulders during these operations and Inspector Riley placed it on again.

'Because we were talking about Jack Smith . . . idly. You remember? Everyone was talking about Jack Smith and there wasn't anything very odd about that until . . .'

'Yes? Until?'

'Until you mentioned Jack Smith's twin brother.'

'Ah. So he did have a twin brother.'

'No, he didn't. What he had was an imaginary counterpart, sometimes heroic, sometimes villainous. His twin brother was his only real companion because the twin brother was the only person he could manipulate himself. He could make him into a hero, or the opposite. He could hide himself behind that fantasy. Jack Smith was a pathological type, bordering on schizophrenia. Do you know what that is, Denney? Commonly called a split personality. He lived sometimes in the real world and sometimes in a fantasy world. He could consciously use the fantasy world to excuse, or even manipulate the real world. His case was complicated by epilepsy . . .'

'How do you know all this?'

'Listen, Denney, the police aren't fools. Jack Smith has got a case history as long as your arm in the Eastern States. It didn't take us four hours of telephoning to pick that up. It was all in this morning's paper. Didn't you read it?'

Denney remembered the bundle of papers she had carried round all day. They were still lying on the verandah, somewhere behind where she sat now.

'If you had,' said Inspector Riley dryly, 'you wouldn't have entertained him to dinner in your house, nor would you have invited him to do your chores for you . . . such as turning off the windmill.'

Denney spoke very slowly, and a little thickly.

'You are trying to tell me he was mad.'

'I'm afraid so. Mad, and very dangerous.'

She felt sick in the pit of her stomach. She drank the last drop of the brandy. Her hand was shaking again.

'Don't tell me any more, please,' she said. 'I was sorry for him. He'd had a rotten deal. The cards were all stacked against him . . .'

There was a silence and when Inspector Riley spoke again his voice was kinder.

'Don't be sorry, Denney. You did a kindly humane thing. Fortunately nobody else but Jack Smith suffered. And if you look at it rightly . . . the only lucky thing that ever happened to him was when he went down on the ground there tonight, and out like a light.'

'A kindly humane thing?' said Denney, turning and looking at the Inspector. 'Aren't you going to hang me for being an accessory after the fact?'

'Accessories don't usually get hanged, though I admit I was trying to frighten you with that one.' He shook his head. 'It doesn't do the police any good to bring a charge they can't prove, you know.'

'Why can't you prove it? There's all those tea-things inside. And cigarette butts in the saucers, and fingerprints everywhere.'

'Look, you've got a sister who's a lawyer, haven't you? Do you know what she'd do? She'd put you in the dock and make you, and incidentally his Honour, or any jury, see that an oath was a sacred thing. She'd make them see that the oath you had to take in Court to tell the truth and nothing but the truth . . . so help me God . . . meant something to them as well as you. Then she'd make 'em look silly if they accepted that one and didn't accept the promise you gave Jack Smith this morning. There's plenty of reasons for your conduct, Denney. A promise, intimidation by a gun, confusion over the twin issue. Why, even I could be called as a witness for the defence on that one.'

Inspector Riley shook his head.

'I could charge you, Denney, and you deserve it. But I'd never make it stick.' He put his arm along her shoulder. 'But don't do it again,' he said. 'The price was too high.'

'What do you mean, high? You get all your salaries whether you're hunting murderers or playing poker back of the Police

Court, don't you?'

'I wasn't thinking of the costs to us. I was thinking of Ben.'

'*Ben?*'

Inspector Riley stood up. He looked down at Denney.

'Only one bullet killed Jack Smith tonight, Denney. It was the fastest marksman who saved your life. You know who that is.'

He turned away to go back to the group that had converged again on the covered body of Jack Smith.

'Think it over,' Inspector Riley said, and he walked away. Ben?

Denney got up from the step and walked unsteadily across her back verandah to the kitchen door. Ben was pouring boiling water from the kettle into a large teapot.

'Ben . . .' said Denney, leaning against the door jamb, her legs barely holding her up. 'Ben . . . don't make any tea. I couldn't bear to drink tea ever again . . .'

'It's not for you, it's for the police. They'll be held up here for hours.' He looked at her over the kettle. 'I'm taking you home. We'll have coffee. Coffee was always my drink anyway, you know that.'

'Ben, I've had too much killing, and too much brandy, so excuse me if I'm silly. I always was silly, anyway. Zany is the word, isn't it?'

He stood, tall and brown and not unkind, looking at her.

'But wouldn't going home with you . . .' said Denney, 'at this hour . . . to drink coffee . . . be compromising me?'

'It would,' said Ben, putting down the kettle. 'But you're coming all the same.'

He came round the table to where she stood, leaning in the doorway.

'Excuse me continuing to be silly,' said Denney, 'but I don't follow your argument. You see, there's my farm. And the feeding . . .'

'I'll send a man out from Kalamunda on our way through.'

'I don't ever leave my farm, Ben.' This with slightly inebriated dignity.

Ben folded his arms and stood, legs slightly apart, and looked at her.

'You're going to leave it now, Denney. For keeps.'

Denney waved an irresolute hand in the air and succeeded finally in pointing outside to the yard.

'Ben, Inspector Riley told me that it was . . . that . . . I mean . . .'

He nodded.

'My bullet. I didn't mean to kill him, Denney, only wing him. But he moved. I don't like killing things, much less people, but I know that one has got to live with what one can't alter. I can't undo it now. Maybe I might even do it over again. I don't know. But I've got to live with what I've done. So have you.'

He paused.

'You're a little drunk, Denney, but I think you can catch on to a good logical argument. Someone owes me a life for the life I took when I shot Jack Smith. I think it's you, Denney. Also I think you're thoroughly irresponsible and I can't afford to leave you where I can't look after you.' There was a kindness in his eyes, but Denney declined to see it.

'You mean I'm coming home with you?'

'That's what I mean.'

'Thank you, Ben, for being so clear,' said Denney politely, then she swayed away from the door jamb. Ben caught her and put her upright in a chair by the table.

Inspector Riley came back through the yard up on to the verandah and into the kitchen. He looked at Denney, now leaning forward across the table, her head in her arms.

'We'd better get the doctor to look her over,' he said to Ben.

'After that I'm taking her home,' Ben concluded.

Inspector Riley lifted the lid of the teapot and looked in.

'I didn't ask you how you managed to get here in time.'

'I was burning grass off down at the bottom of my place. Thought I'd fix it up before the weekend and the fire bans were on. One of Denney's sisters sleuthed me out. She said there was pandemonium in the dovecote because something was wrong with Denney. I came up through the back way, up the old gully route, when I struck your patrol.'

Inspector Riley nodded his head in Denney's direction.

'You going to take her home to your place or down to her sisters?'

'My place,' said Ben shortly. 'With or without permission.'

Inspector Riley grinned.

'I never wanted to buy into a domestic argument,' he said.

It was half an hour before the doctor, who had been brought

out from Kalamunda, had looked Denney over, removed two lead pellets from the fleshy part of her forearm, and given her a sedative.

With the rug round her shoulders Inspector Riley helped her into the seat beside Ben in Ben's car.

They had said good-bye and Ben had started up the engine when Denney seemed to come out of her torpor again.

'Excuse me please, Ben, I wish to speak to Inspector Riley in private.' She was aware she was being excessively polite. Strange what strong drink will do to some people. 'A few words, if you will excuse me . . .' she repeated slowly.

'All right, I'm not listening,' said Ben.

The detective put his head in the car window.

'What's it, this time?' he asked.

'What do they do,' Denney asked in a strained whisper, 'with Jack Smith? I mean where . . . how does he get buried? If there aren't any parents . . . there isn't anyone to care . . .'

'A Government grave, I guess.'

'You mean a pauper's grave?'

'Well, that's an old-fashioned way of putting it.'

'Then please,' said Denney slowly, her speech a little thick. It was the brandy again. She had had a second glass. 'If you please, will you kindly arrange that Jack Smith has a private burial, with a clergyman, and a prayer book and all. And a good coffin. And Inspector Riley – ' She tried desperately to say the right thing, but as always she only succeeded in putting it the wrong way. 'God,' Inspector Riley thought, 'would forgive her, for she had had a long day, been shot at, had witnessed a killing and was now full of brandy and barbiturates.' 'And Inspector Riley,' Denney said slowly, 'charge it to my account.'

He dropped his foot from the running-board. Then collected himself.

'Certainly, Denney,' he said gravely. He turned and walked away.

Denney knew she'd said it the wrong way. *Charge it to my account*. Dear God! Why had she put it that way?

'Ben,' she said, the tears packing up behind her eyes. 'You know what I mean, don't you? I couldn't bear it if there wasn't anyone to care, not even at the end. When he's dead . . .'

Ben put his hand on her hand. For the first time in a long while he smiled.

'Zany one,' he said, but Denney knew he meant it kindly. In death Jack Smith would receive something from someone. He would not go alone, unsung and unhallowed to his grave.

Tomorrow she would find time to think.

At least she had Ben. And Ben, God help him, poor soul, had her.

Lucy Walker

Love, misunderstanding, heartbreak, tenderness . . . in the unfamiliar, exciting setting of Australia's vast Outback country.

THE OTHER GIRL. Three very different girls find themselves drawn to one man—and each is sure she'll lose him to one of the others.

HEAVEN IS HERE. Every girl within hundreds of miles was chasing Hugh Wilstack, and Jeannie vowed not to join the crowd. But her heart betrayed her. . . .

THE DISTANT HILLS. Angela was forced into a "marriage of convenience" through a cruel misunderstanding—could love grow from such a disastrous start?

SWEET AND FARAWAY. Lesley came out from England for her cousin's wedding—and found herself a virtual prisoner in the hands of the master of a vast Outback estate.

THE CALL OF THE PINES. Cherry came out to Yulinga as a governess, but a strange twist of fate threw her into a struggle for survival—and for the man she loved.

COME HOME, DEAR. Penny's love for John Dean had always seemed the most real thing in her life—then Ross Bennett came home. . . .

LOVE IN A CLOUD. Sonia loved John for his gentleness, Nick for his virile handsomeness—how could she decide?

FOLLOW YOUR STAR. Like many another girl, Kylie discovered the man she loved was an enigma—but she had to follow her star, wherever it might lead. . . .

HOME AT SUNDOWN. Two girls—and ten men—on a dangerous expedition, with feminine rivalry not the least of their perils.

REACHING FOR THE STARS. Ann came to Australia as an honored guest—and then found it had been a terrible mistake. . . .

A MAN CALLED MASTERS. It was Penny's chance for independence—but was she a match for the silent man who needed her?

THE STRANGER FROM THE NORTH. She had to do a man's job—and was doing it well . . . until the stranger rode in and took over.